THE ORIGINS OF

CHRISTIAN E. BARTH

iUniverse, Inc.
New York   Bloomington

The Origins of Infamy

iUniverse books may be ordered through booksellers or by contacting:

iUniverse
1663 Liberty Drive
Bloomington, IN 47403
www.iuniverse.com
1-800-Authors (1-800-288-4677)

Because of the dynamic nature of the Internet, any Web addresses or links contained in this book may have changed since publication and may no longer be valid. The views expressed in this work are solely those of the author and do not necessarily reflect the views of the publisher, and the publisher hereby disclaims any responsibility for them.

ISBN: 978-1-4401-3893-5 (pbk)
ISBN: 978-1-4401-3894-2 (ebk)

Printed in the United States of America

iUniverse rev. date: 5/15/09

ACKNOWLEDGEMENTS

Among the myriad sources I consulted in writing this book
are the *Philadelphia Inquirer,* the *Philadelphia Bulletin, Atlantic City Press, Ocean City* (N.J.) *Gazette,* City of Philadelphia
Historical Commission, Ocean City Public Library Archives,
Temple University Urban Archives, *Courier Post* (N.J.), *Philadelphia Daily News, Ocean City Sentinel Ledger,* Ocean City
(N.J.) Historical Museum, the *Temple News,* the *Oregonian,*
The Stranger Beside Me by Anne Rule, *The Deliberate Stranger* by
Richard Larsen, *Blind Fury* by Anna Flowers, *Ghost Towns and
Other Quirky Places in the New Jersey Pine Barrens* by Barbara
Solemn-Stull, *No One Here Gets Out Alive* by Jerry Hopkins
and Danny Sugarman, Ocean City Chamber of Commerce,
University of Washington Library, *Inside the Criminal Mind*
by Stanton Samenow, the *Seattle Press, National Geographic
Magazine, The Pine Barrens* by John McPhee, *The Lords and
the New Creatures* by Jim Morrison, Burlington, Vermont Office of Public Records, *Among the Lowest of the Dead* by David

von Drehle, *Psychopathology of Everyday Life* and *The Interpretation of Dreams*, by Sigmund Freud (translated by A.A Brill), *Social Theory and Social Structure*, by W.K. Merton, *Defending the Devil* by Polly Nelson, *Sleazoid Express* by Bill Landis and Michelle Clifford, *On the Origins of Species* by Charles Darwin, *Tales of Times Square* by Josh Alan Friedman, "The Kiss of the Sun" by Dorothy Gurney.

THE ORIGINS OF

INFAMY

PROLOGUE

Late in the afternoon on the eve of my execution, my biographer posed a question: "If given the choice between shark attack, or being drowned by an alligator, which way would you prefer to die?"

"Well, that all depends," I said to Dick Larsen, seated opposite me in a folding metal chair, "on the size and species of the fish. A shark attack would be over quicker if you were taken by a Great White. Its teeth would penetrate your abdomen and your lungs would fill with blood before you knew what hit you, or puncture the femoral artery if it bit off your leg. You'd be comatose with shock and not actually feel what it's like to drown because you'd have passed out from loss of blood by then. A smaller predator, say, a five-foot long Hammerhead mistaking you for a fish, would prolong the agony by nipping at you a few times and leaving you to bleed to death slowly-that is, if the other sharks, scenting you, don't finish the job first."

"I agree. For posterity, too, it would seem more heroic to perish at sea," Dick reasoned.

He was writing notes in preparation for an afterword to his latest edition of my biography, *The Deliberate Stranger,* first published in 1980. We had known each other since the early 70's, when I was working for the re-election campaign of Washington State Governor Dan Evans and Dick was a political reporter for the *Seattle Times.* In the last few days he'd done his best to keep the conversation light, hoisting my spirits with tales of last-minute rescues from *Ol' Sparky,* the ghoulish nickname given to the oaken throne upon which I was to be electrocuted bright and early the following morning. Dressed in jeans and an unironed button-down shirt, he was sincere and unpretentious, with congenial mannerisms that eased somewhat the instinctive mistrust I'd reserved for the countless self-serving evangelists that arrived at my cell that week with tape recorders in hand. Unlike other visitors with hidden agendas, he seemed to recognize the uselessness of referencing meaningless Scripture, reciting the Lord's Prayer, or prying a confession from my lips on the day before my death.

"Although," it occurred to me, "dying in the jaws of an alligator does have the lure of the exotic."

"Exotic? Hardly," he said, returning my mischievous smile. "An alligator would tease you for a while before it killed you, maybe let you swim up to the surface before pulling you under. Sort of the way a cat swats at a dazed mouse before killing it. Not to mention, your bloated corpse, half-chewed by fish, would wash up on the bank a few days later, and you would have to be identified. Not too glamorous a way to be remembered."

I saw right through this morbid discussion as Dick's method of desensitizing the impact of my looming execution. His face, wearied by the sorrow of hopelessness, was etched with deeply creviced seams, the kind drawn on the expressions of the longshoremen debarking the ships moored alongside the bulkheads of Tacoma, Washington, my hometown. When he asked if I had any lingering thoughts I might wish to share with him, here on the eve of my passing, a great silence filled the cell as I thought of what to say.

"Take your time," he said, leaning both elbows on his knees and peering into my eyes, as though silently and with clairvoyant exactness he was preparing to shepherd me across the deep and treacherous rivers of the afterlife. Although he never gave me any reason to disbelieve him, the way rheumatics can feel a front of inclement weather aching their bones, I sensed he was narrowing in on an incriminating matter he wanted to discuss. With the jovial façade of our trivial conversation behind us, the room grew maddeningly silent. The solace of knowing that the misery of my anticipation would be over soon, and that I would probably be dead by this time tomorrow, offered little relief for my anguish. "What I mean, Ted, is that we're coming to the end of the road here, and what with about seventeen hours left, give or take, now might be as good a time as ever to get whatever it is you need to off your mind." He spoke evasively, covering the scent of his tracks as he did whenever stealing down the passages of my blood-soaked memories. "You know, cleanse your soul, so to speak, before tomorrow."

Despite his vow of confidentiality, during the few afternoons we had met I never told him or anyone else about all the killings. Neither did I recount the details of every murder I committed. What incentive was there for me to repent now? I held out little hope for clemency or a last minute pardon. My appeals had been exhausted, and Governor Martinez had already signed my death warrant. The authorities would never find where I scattered the remaining bodies. I made certain of that. Until now, I figured that the satisfaction of taking a few secrets with me to the chair was a small measure of revenge, a keepsake from this life I'd take with me to the other side. Savvy of prison rules of barter and exchange, I bargained for one last walk outside in the fresh air while I considered whether to answer him.

"Let me ask Leverette," Dick said.

With a weightlifter's physique and sinuses that whistled like a pug dog, Leverette would often saunter confidently down the hall, slashing his baton through the air in mock swipes as though practicing for when he'd be able to rein blows upon the skull of one of the derelicts under his charge. "If I were warden," he boasted one unusually chilly March afternoon two years earlier, "there'd be no special wing for you. I'd take ya'll out back and shoot each of you between the eyes, just like I'd put down a rabid coon rootin' through my garbage cans." He would often poke his nose teasingly into the cells of the black inmates, asking them in a calm, instigating tone sounding somewhere between Klansman and confidante, "Bet you'd like to have a crack at me boy, wouldn't you?"

He handled me gentler than usual on this afternoon, however, consolingly patting the back of my hands after cuffing me, then gesturing to Wendell, the other guard assigned to death watch. A kind though superstitious black man, Wendell avoided looking me in the eyes and maintained a safe distance, as though to utter words to a man so near death would forever curse him under some inexorciseable voodoo spell. He whistled down the hall after Leverette finished shackling my ankles. A buzzer sounded, sliding open the cell door. Drawn like swamp mosquitoes to campfire light, the prisoners gripped the poles of their cages, peering at me as I was escorted down the hallway by the two guards. A sickening cry leaped from the cell next to mine.

"Listen, Dick, don't waste your time with that crazy Bundy motherfucker, I've got a story for you!!" hollered Gerald Eugene Stano, a serial killer sentenced to die for the mutilation of a dozen hookers he first raped, then stabbed to death and dumped in the moss-slickened culverts along Florida's southern highways. Compactly built, he wore crooked eyeglasses bordered with thick black rims that magnified a set of black, jittery eyes. His demons led him to scream horrifically each night after lights out, as though he was purging a tormenting swarm of nesting bats from his brain. He kept pace alongside us, pressing his cheeks through the bars.

"Get the fuck back in your cage!" Leverette shouted, unclasping his nightstick. Like a beaten hound, Jerry scurried back into the shadows. We went past a security checkpoint staffed by a drowsy guard who nodded to Wendell, then mumbled incoherently under his breath something about vindication as he pushed a red button. A click sounded and a thick metal door opened into a steamy vestibule, then through another door leading out to the warm Florida sunshine.

A flutter of crows swished above the doorway, startling me as I squinted into the January sun. It was somewhere between three and four in the afternoon, I determined, gauging the length of my shadow on the ground as a humid trade wind gusted in from the Gulf of Mexico. I heard a murmurous chatter, low and faint, like the dull roar from a distant football game. Out beyond the exercise yard, beneath the arched limestone pillars of the prison entranceway, a fervent crowd of onlookers celebrating my demise had gathered behind a barbwire fence. From a distance they resembled a slide of squirming paramecia. Bloodthirsty revellers cried for my death in lustful chants, jabbing toward the heavens giant hand-painted signs proclaiming such slogans as *Fry-Day*, and *Burn Bundy Burn!* A pickup truck festooned with yellow lights flashed a sign that read *Burn In Hell*. An accompaniment of crying gulls swooped in languid circles atop the gathering, dive-bombing an onlooker pitching them scraps of food. Apart from the mob, near a line of slowly moving traffic, what appeared to be a small girl was skipping along the roadside, a sparkler dangling from each hand. A shower of phosphorescent light dripped behind her as she looped about the crabgrass, daintily flicking her wrists about in orchestral symmetry near an enclosure of nuns bowing in candlelit vigil.

Dick pulled a cigarette from a crumpled pack of Marlboros bulging from his shirt pocket. With his palms cupped above his chin to block the wind, he lit me a cigarette, and then his own. He gestured to the guards to keep their distance and had me follow him a few steps away. We faced the deep mangrove forest outside the gleaming loops of ribbon wire connecting the gun towers. "Ted, I'll get right to it," he said, drawing closer to me. His urgent tone took on the contagion of hysteria encircling us. "You made some conflicting remarks about those two co-eds who were killed near Ocean City, New Jersey in 1969. You were speaking in the third person and told one of your psychologists here something about seeing two women on the beach, and it being your 'first time.' Murdering, I presume? Then, earlier today, you told one of the other psychologists that you wanted to clarify what you had said earlier, that you'd been on the boardwalk in Ocean City that spring but hadn't killed those girls. What's most confusing to the FBI and the state authorities is your peculiar degree of interest in the investigation, because for years now you've been having newspaper clippings about these murders sent to you here. They think you know something, Ted, that you're not sharing. Obviously I'm under no authority to guarantee you that what you say will buy you any more time. What I *have* been assured is that whatever information about these killings you want to pass along, specifically, your involvement in them, if any, will be taken under serious consideration in deciding what happens tomorrow morning. Now I'm sure you're sick of answering questions and doing interviews, but this may be your last chance, and we're almost out of time. Not to mention, I'd like to set the record straight, you know, for the book." His next question was buoyant yet full of pretense, like a buddy calling to discuss the matter of a long overdue wager. "Did you hear what I asked, Ted?"

"Yes," I responded, half-listening, distracted by the loudening throng amassed like medieval villagers eager to witness a beheading. The descending Florida sun, the gulls, the fireworks, the opalescent sheen cast from the electric signs, all these images coalesced to form a surreal mosaic, evoking a hazy recollection of boardwalk rides and Ferris wheel lights from that Memorial Day weekend at the Jersey Shore, twenty years earlier.

"Yes, meaning yes you heard me, or yes, you killed those two girls?"

"I heard what you said," I answered, suppressing a burst of mischievous laughter. The irony of the moment was not lost on me, for the closer I neared the end, the quicker I found myself circling back to the point in my life when things went horribly wrong. Although I would tell Dick all about my fateful visit to Ocean City in due time, I thought a more apt beginning to the story of my unravelling was several months before my journey to the New Jersey beaches, when I was living in Seattle, succumbing to a debilitating infatuation for a young woman named Caroline Ramming.

PART I

SEATTLE

ONE

I met Caroline on the first day of the 1968 fall quarter, my first year at the University of Washington. I was seated in the back row of Guthrie Hall that September morning, waiting for my Introduction to Psychology class to begin. She walked in late, flipping her blond, rain-darkened hair out from under the collar of a fringed poncho before occupying an empty seat two down from me. I leaned back in my chair, staring at her each time she leaned over to whisper to a friend. Her tanned, well-lotioned face contrasted strikingly against her deeply set eyes, a distinctive light shade of green that reminded me of the boiling waters of a Yosemite Valley mineral pool. Though she wore her hair styled long and parted down the middle, with her high cheekbones and aquiline nose, she had the type of perfectly proportioned Anglican features that would have allowed her to wear it any length. Instead of paying attention to the professor's introductory lecture, I dreamed up witty icebreakers, resolving to acquaint myself with her after class ended.

I hid in the shadows of a cherry tree along one of the Quad pathways. Carolyn came bounding down the steps, cradling her books to her chest. I followed her, lagging behind a safe distance as she crossed the newly mown lawns, trying not to lose her in the sun glare breaking through the rain clouds. I tracked her every movement down the promenade, pausing when she did, ducking behind a bush as she stopped to talk to a friend. After they waved goodbye, she made her way downhill to Drumheller Fountain. Facing south, she crossed her legs upon a cement bench circling the turquoise water and began drawing, periodically gazing up at Mt. Ranier, visible in the distance. Two Greeks were winging a Frisbee back and forth across opposite ends of the rippling gleam behind her. I grabbed the disc midair as it veered off course, expertly returning it with an underhanded flick of my wrist. My feat, I was delighted to see, hadn't gone unnoticed.

"Nice grab, showoff," she teased. "Weren't you just in my psych class?" She cocked her head, squinting up at me as I walked over to acknowledge her compliment.

"I sure was," I said, smiling broadly. "I'm Ted Bundy."

"Caroline Ramming." She placed her sketchpad beside a packet of colored pencils and offered her hand. "Our professor seems real uptight, don't you think? I hope he doesn't hurt any mice or anything like that."

"I hope so too, though I doubt it, because it's just an intro course with no lab. I worked at an animal shelter in the summer between my sophomore and junior years in high school," I lied. "I came away profoundly discouraged by the way people treat animals. Mahatma Gandhi once said, 'The greatness of a people can be measured by how well it treats its animals.' Wouldn't you agree?"

"Absolutely. That's kind of you to say." A sophomore from Mercer Island, she was taking the class to fulfill a core requirement of the Liberal Studies Program. She really wanted to be an artist, she confessed, though her father was urging her to choose a more practical profession, like nursing, or teaching school. As I glimpsed the worn neckline of her t-shirt, the torn knees of her jeans sewn with quilted patches, I saw a rich girl caught between conformity and rebelliousness. Though only twenty-one years old myself, I offered career advice as though I had attained a great deal of wisdom it was my duty to share with her.

"It's your life, and if you want to be a painter, why don't you do what'll make you happy and be a painter? Obviously your parents want what's best for you, but at the end of the day what satisfaction will you ever get out of life doing what somebody else wants you to do? Look at it this way: Do you, or did you, have a summer job?"

She nodded. "Waitressing."

"Did you like it?"

"Sometimes. Sometimes not. Depended on the day of the week, really. Friday night, people were nasty, still irritable from work. Saturdays they were nicer and tipped better."

I sat down next to her. "Bet you didn't like it when rude customers hollered at you to fetch more bread or refill their water glasses. And didn't you hate it when they left no tip because they were pissed off that you didn't bring their burgers fast enough, and then griped because they were too well done?"

"Or when they drink coffee and sit there for an hour, and don't get the hint you want them to get moving till you take away their saltshaker and ketchup bottles?" She laughed, slapping her knee.

"We've all had jobs we hated, Caroline. Do you think there's any real difference between waiting tables and running around all day taking orders from doctors, other than you can't quit when September rolls around? How do you know you can't make a living doing what you love to do unless you try?"

"You know something, you're right, so right," she said, smiling to herself, as though charmed by the wonderment of this discovery.

"May I see?" I asked, glancing down at her work.

"Don't make fun of me," she teasingly pleaded, handing me the pad. She had drawn a close-up of the mountain peaks, enameling them with a float of clouds that licked against the lush green valleys below the snowline. In the foreground a hawk circled a distant treetop nest.

"You're talented," I said, holding the drawing up close. "Very talented. I couldn't draw a straight line if my life depended on it. I guess that's why I plan to become a lawyer."

"You're certainly persuasive enough."

I casually asked for her number so we might exchange notes if one of us missed an assignment. As she tore out a sheet of paper and handed it to me, I simultaneously placed down my notebook, purposely leaving it there beside her after we said our goodbyes.

She phoned later that evening. I acted befuddled when she said I'd left my notebook behind at the fountain, and expressed sincere gratitude that she'd extended me the courtesy of a call. She saw that I was from Tacoma, for I'd pasted a return address on the inside cover. The girls at the University of Puget Sound, where I spent my freshman year, would often pinch their noses at the "Tacoma aroma" drifting through the classrooms on damp mornings when the sour yellow haze drifted in off Commencement Bay. Or they'd shirk fearfully from the paper mill workers who catcalled them from under the clock tower, those saddened lifers conscripted to a life of smoldering toil on the Port of Tacoma barges. When I confessed to Caroline that I was from these working bluffs north of downtown, I didn't know what to expect. Certainly she'd be polite, but would she consider dating me? She said she was unimpressed by Mercer Island boys who came to pick her up for dates driving expensive roadsters bought by their fathers. She wasn't resentful, nor did she remark regretfully on any past mates. "A lot of you boys need to step out of your fathers' shadows," she said with a chuckle, like a sister offering advice to her younger brother. Although I never knew my father, I perceived her generalization as a compliment, for she was viewing me in the same light as one of those affluent boys riding their parents' coattails.

***

Because I fell for Caroline so quickly and she came from Mercer Island, I was patient with her where otherwise I wouldn't have been. I took my time in the ensuing weeks, never pressuring her during our dates, biding my time until she felt comfortable enough to sleep with me. But as much as I enjoyed her company, I never completely understood where I stood with her. At times she could be aloof, never looking at me in class, or quickly sneaking out the door after we were dismissed. I'd never been in a committed relationship, and as such couldn't say for certain whether her behavior was part of some elaborate mating ritual, or even whether we were dating exclusively. I lost sleep thinking about her, and when I did eventually nod off I would fall away into a dreamless hibernation. Alarm clocks and police sirens were useless in stirring me. I once slept through an entire day, and on the following afternoon went to class in a narcoleptic haze. Consumed with her whereabouts, instead of studying or going to my other classes, I frittered away endless hours staring out my window down at the Lake Washington shorelines, wondering what she was doing at that moment, at what hour she turned in at night. Worrying who she was with. Fathoming the destinations of the seaplanes and cruise ships leaving harbor, I often fantasized we were a married couple aboard them, first-class passengers embarking on a vacation toward some distant port like Hong Kong or the Fiji Islands.

She appeared unannounced at my door on the Tuesday before Halloween seeking approval of her costume, an alluring rendition of Raggedy Ann she wore hidden under her coat. Playfully adjusting her wig, she spoke in the clipped tone of a naughty brat. "If you're not there when I call, Mr. Bundy," she audaciously reprimanded, rolling down her red and white-striped knee-high stockings, then seating herself on the edge of my bed, "or if you unhook the line to nap, I can always go out and find another boyfriend more attentive to my needs."

Even with the sight of her tilted hips presented for my taking, I suddenly lost my concentration as I climbed on her and opened her legs. With that one word-*boyfriend*- she had authenticated our relationship, leaving little doubt or mystery as to its interpretation. Having waited nearly two months to hear this spoken, I recited the word endlessly in my mind as I kissed her bare stomach, like the refrain from a favorite song you hear on the radio first thing in the morning and hum to yourself all day. But I was too swept up by my affections toward her to allow them to complement my arousal. When she noticed I was having difficulty, she lowered her hand and began softly rubbing outside my jeans. As she went to take down my pants to move things along, I stopped her, unable to bear the humiliation of seeing her beating futilely away at my limp pecker in broad daylight.

"What's the matter?" she asked.

"Nothing," I said calmly, a sweat breaking across my back. I hurriedly lifted her dress and forcefully ground my hips into hers, sensing my first warm stirrings coincide with the urgency of my movements. At first she responded friskily as I pressed my fingers between her legs and held her tightly against me, but when I snatched the hem of her underwear too roughly and tried flipping her over, she interrupted our momentum.

"Ted, Ted, listen," she whispered reassuringly, holding my chin. "Take your time, there's no hurry."

I came inside her after finding my rhythm, as she did not whisper curt instructions to withdraw. She lay motionless on her back as I caught my breath, her eyes fixed on the ceiling. As I was already made self-conscious by my weak performance, I immediately attributed her silence to my inadequacy. Or was she struggling with regret, embarrassment, or some form of feminine post-coital guilt? I reached my arms behind her waist and tried cuddling with her, but she resisted. I couldn't understand why she stood and dressed with her back turned to me, or why she looked away from me, planting an awkward peck on my cheek before rising to leave.

Several days later I should have been cramming for my midterms. Instead I sat anxiously at my desk waiting for a return call from Caroline. We had briefly spoken earlier in the day, our first conversation since our afternoon together. She rushed to get off the phone, saying she was late for class, had something important to tell me, and would call later this afternoon. Four unending hours had passed since her last class ended. It was nearly five o'clock and I hadn't heard from her. While in the short time I had known Caroline she was prone to fits of spontaneity, her punctuality was an ingrained discipline from which she seldom wavered. Although we had made no definitive plans to meet until the following afternoon, when her sorority was to host a costume party after the football game against UCLA, my instincts were tweaked by her uncharacteristic tardiness. A sense of suspicion, though as yet unfounded, riled inside me like a doused campfire ember fanned back to life by a sudden wind.

A stack of papers was strewn across my desk, besides a jaggedly arranged scattering of unopened books, *The Basic Writings of Sigmund Freud,* Robert Merton's *Social Theory and Structure,* and *What Jung Really Said.* The sheer girth of the texts made the notion of reviewing their contents seem futile, for my exams were only a week away. The clean new pages stuck together as I peeled them open, sounding like a pair of socks crackling with static electricity. I glazed over the passages, rereading sentences three and four times. I tried processing the language, but my eyes kept drifting away from the page. It wasn't that the subjects didn't interest me. On the contrary, they were utterly compelling, making my inability to study them now all the more vexing. Although I declared psychology as my major at the start of the semester and had begun entertaining notions of one day going to law school, the ambition necessary to sustain any interest toward my future was absorbed by distractions like these where I could do little but stare out the window, fixate over Caroline, or wonder how others not in my life spent theirs.

My attention was drawn to a letter that had arrived with the day's mail. Poking out from under a pile of bills and returned checks lying on the corner of the desk, it was sent by the Dean of Student Academic Services. I couldn't bear to reach over and reread it. If I accumulated any more unexcused absences, he cautioned, I risked flunking my courses altogether. The prospect of expulsion from classes, of being reported by the University to the draft board, was a fear so real, so apocalyptic, it consumed the nagging qualms I felt toward Caroline, making my worrisome obsession over her whereabouts miniscule by comparison. And if my death was not fated within the napalm-burned Mekong Delta, it would surely catch up with me upon my return stateside-not heroically, as a soldier in a body bag, but worse, as a quadriplegic or some listless shell-shocked zombie wetting himself at the first pop of a summer evening firecracker. I couldn't understand what caused these preoccupying diversions, but sensed they were symptoms of a worsening condition.

With time on my hands while waiting for phone to ring, I chose an alternate tack, studying with an eye on self-diagnosing my illness. I opened W.K. Merton's book, scanning its table of contents. I hesitated when I saw a chapter titled "The Self Fulfilling Prophecy" and went to it, for in passing conversations I had heard reference made to this strangely contagious disorder: "The self-fulfilling prophecy is, in the beginning, a false definition of the situation evoking a new behavior which makes the originally false conception come true. The specious validity of the self-fulfilling prophecy perpetuates a reign of error. For the prophet will cite the actual course of events as proof that he was right from the very beginning. ..Men respond not only to the objective features of a situation, but also, and at times primarily, to the meaning this situation has for them. And once they have assigned some meaning to the situation, their consequent behavior and some of the consequences of that behavior are determined by the ascribed meaning." I pondered Merton's reasoning. Fearing academic failure, would I will myself to flunk out of school? Caroline hadn't returned my calls, yet she needed to speak with me. By the same reasoning, would she be calling for any other reason than to break up with me?

Intrigued by the eerily accurate application of this logic to my situation, I continued, skimming through Freud's text, *Psychopathology of Everyday Life*. I hesitated when I saw a chapter titled "Childhood and Concealing Memories," and read on: "I believe we accept too indifferently the fact of infantile amnesia-that is, the failure of memory for the first years of our lives-and fail to find in it a strange riddle. We forget of what great intellectual accomplishments and of what complicated emotions a child of four is capable. We really ought to wonder why the memory of later years has, as a rule, retained so little of these psychic processes, especially as we have every reason for assuming that these same forgotten childhood activities have not glided off without leaving a trace in the development of the person, but that they have left a definite influence for all future time. .. It is quite possible that the forgetting of childhood may give us the key to the understanding of those amnesias which, according to our newer studies, lie at the basis of the formation of all neurotic symptoms." *Neurotic symptoms.* The phrase stuck with me. My interest grew sharper the more I read, for come to think of it, I couldn't remember the first four years of my life. Could the events from that period have influenced the strange direction my life was heading, and provide answers as to why I found myself mired in this apathetic stew that held me captive in my quarters, unable to focus on anything but Caroline? Was my withdrawal into solitude symptomatic of a darker sickness lying in wait?

I was preparing to delve deeper into the murk of my psyche when the back door closed loudly downstairs, shimmying the panes. I stepped furtively toward my window, watching my landlady tramp down the backyard steps leading down into her garden.

Vernetta Rome was a slender, lanky-boned widow whose husband had been a logging company inspector. He fell to his death a year earlier when a harness leashed to his waist suddenly gave way. I'd been staying in one of the upstairs rooms in her Queen Anne Hill home since the end of August, having answered an ad posted in a University Avenue bookstore. She believed me when I told her I had signed up to take the law boards and needed a quiet place away from campus to prepare for them. After she helped me carry up two trash bags full of clothes, a backpack, and a pair of skis, I promised I would have September's rent for her in a few weeks. When I was late with October's payment also, I wrongly assumed she would pity me and readily grant an extension past the due date. I found her out back, uprighting a birdfeeder pole tilted by the night winds, on the day I came to her with the news. Her mimicking outburst in response to my question was unexpectedly severe and reprimanding.

"I may be a day or two late with the rent, is that OK?" she mocked. "I don't know how I should answer such an idiotic question, Ted, do you?" Her forehead was pinched in a disbelieving scowl. "First it's September, now October? What about November, should we try for three straight?" Her thin, painted eyebrows arched sharply upward. She held her expression, as if knowing that her emasculating ridicule might penetrate deeper if it basted for a moment in the airy silence. Letting go the pole, she whisked away to a rickety trellis dividing her property from the neighbor below us.

As I hadn't been given an answer to my question, I warily followed her.

"Your story is starting to sound familiar, but I suppose I don't have much choice, do I?" she asked, tearing off another strip of tape from a roll. She had a way of making me feel grossly irresponsible, like I had let her down by betraying her trust. "There's a five-dollar late fee each day that goes by and you don't pay me. Do you think you can remember *that*?" Her disapproving tone, suddenly shriller, had ratcheted up a notch. My head clouded with a sickly warm rage requiring every shred of self-restraint to suppress. I suppose it was fortunate we remained several feet apart, for had her neck been within reach, I might have succumbed to my anger, perhaps crushed her slender throat with my thumbs, or brained her against the tree. I remember looking off to the neighboring homes, scanning among the sea of rooftops and lush backyards to see if anybody had witnessed this humiliating spectacle unfold. But the homes stood quietly, the dampened air soundless but for a vesper sparrow caroling atop a distant weathercock.

Vernetta switched on a floodlight, disappearing behind an old spruce near where she had scolded me that day. She retreated from its shadows seconds later clenching a hefty pail filled with pulled roots. The bowing handles chinked faintly, bumping up against the side of her legs. She placed the pail down by her side and kicked off her clogs. Her raven-black hair, which normally fell down her shoulders in a disheveled tangle, was tightly braided, the wispy edges crimped together with leather ponytail holders. She hitched her skirt where it had caught under her knee and folded up the unraveled hem, knotting the loose fabric so it rested like a downed quail upon the center of her thigh. Thrusting her rump limberly into the air, she crawled down the rows, cropping the withering bulbs and yanking at the lifeless roots, which she dropped in her bucket. Although I'd never been remotely attracted to Vernetta, a swarming lightheadedness passed over me. The sight of her dirty knees and blackened feet triggered a sensuality I never thought capable of feeling toward a woman for whom lately I'd harbored nothing but unfettered contempt. I hadn't glimpsed any of Vernetta's uncovered regions before now, as she always wore her long skirts down past her knees when gardening, or slacks when journeying to the mountains. I couldn't seem to reconcile these sudden stirrings of arousal with the caginess I had been witness to on the day I was late with the rent. And then it occurred to me, perhaps Vernetta *did* see me, and was displaying herself for our amusement, a challenge to see where such voyeuristic playfulness might lead.

Putting down the bucket beside her again, she placed her hands on her hips and gazed toward the Cascades. I thought I had seen the white of her eyes. Had she caught me spying, or was she merely surveying the clouds pillowed over the mountains in expectation of rain? The gamesmanship awakened a bawdy, exhibitionist streak in me. I unzipped my trousers and stepped out of my underwear, edging leftward across the floor, slowing as I came to the window. I stood barefoot in front of my mirror, allowing her a side view of my hips as I went through all the routines of primping-running a hand through my hair, scanning my eyelids for unsightly crusts, inspecting my nostrils for errant nose hairs. The late afternoon air sensuously chilled my bare thighs, like an exhalation of cool breath. I removed a pair of tweezers from the top dresser drawer and began unsteadily plucking at my eyebrows, maintaining an attitude of preoccupation. Aroused, and nervously anticipating her discovery of me, I cautiously snuck another peek to see if she was looking. She was still faced downward, refilling the upturned soil where she'd planted, tamping it with her fingers. As she reached beside her for a handful of seeds, I returned my attention to the mirror, but not before she glanced my way. She quickly looked down at the bucket as our eyes met, and for an instant before she recommenced working, her face held a bewildered expression, as though she was second-guessing herself. My eyes darted back to the mirror, where I caught myself smirking at my reflection, barely able to suppress my glee.

A loud rippling clang vibrated the drawer pressed up against my thighs. Startled by the disruption, I dashed for the receiver, knocking over a can of pencils I'd sharpened in preparation to study.

"Hey there, Ted," Caroline said.

"Hey sweetie, where have you been? I was starting to think you didn't love me any more," I said, relieved to hear her voice.

"Just busy getting the house ready for tomorrow. Sorry I haven't called."

That evening, she and her sisters had been putting up decorations for their haunted house and applying the finishing touches to the homecoming mural. Although I expected a certain amount of bitchiness and frustration from her, as their project was behind schedule, I heard in her voice an emotionless detachment chilly as the wet shade under a pier. I intuited something was bothering her, but what exactly? "Not a problem," I said, offhandedly accepting her apology. She continued to address me formally, as though we had just met.

"Listen, meet me by the attraction water tomorrow," she said, referring to the effervescing sluiceway cutting through the fish ladder, a labyrinthine cement stockade structured along the far banks of the Ballard Locks. "Nine o'clock. On the opposite side," she added, causing me to ponder as I drew on my pants why she thought it necessary to pinpoint the coordinates to a location we both knew well. Stranger yet, Caroline and I were late risers, preferring to sleep in on chilly weekend mornings. As such, the early hour she had chosen to rendezvous was even more unusual than her terse responses. I tried oaring the conversation to charted waters, allowing some room for elaboration while I deciphered her objective.

"Did you paint outside today?" I asked. Sometimes her professor would hold class outdoors on the flagstone veranda between the Art and Music buildings when the view to Mt. Ranier was pristine, as it had been today.

"He cancelled class because of homecoming this weekend and all." Girlish voices filled the room, followed by the crackling noise of paper. Their sorority's housemother, Beatrice Taylor, was primly offering instructions on how to best scissor construction paper from a loom when the muffled thud of a doorknocker echoed in the foyer. Men filed noisily into the vestibule, their booming voices echoing rich greetings through the hallway. "Hold on a second, Ted," she said, muffling the receiver. I heard a garbled sound, like an underwater conversation. Her hand slipped while she was talking, leaving a part of the mouthpiece uncovered. Instinctively certain my suspicions were not founded upon the obscure logic of paranoia, I listened closely for insightful whisperings within the room, now suffused with festive chatter. A deep voice, distinctive from the others, struck with brute stabbing anger. I recognized it as belonging to Kevin Fontaine, a reserve wide receiver on the football team. Caroline had mentioned him from time to time, always careful to distinguish their friendship as platonic. Because they grew up near one another and had attended the same prep school, she reassured me their relationship was more like brother and sister. Although he was polite toward me whenever we met, I didn't care for the way he would look at Caroline, and suspected he had his sights set on her.

"Just tell him we're going to the bonfire instead," he whispered.

...to the bonfire instead... What did he mean by this? Instead of what? Instead of where?

"So I'll see you tomorrow morning?" Caroline asked me, her tone lacquered with false cheeriness.

"What are your plans for tonight?" I asked.

"I don't know yet."

"Have you decided on a costume?"

"Not yet," she said.

"No more Raggedy Ann? I think she suited you perfectly. I was hoping to see more of her. Or less." I gave her a few seconds, but her end was silent.

"We'll see," she said.

"Okay, I guess I'll look for you by the fish ladder tomorrow." After hanging up, I considered the most logical scenario, that I was being diverted to the bonfire so I wouldn't run into Caroline. Would she be there with Kevin? Knowing I wouldn't be able to sleep that evening until I knew for certain if she was lying to me, I dressed quickly, then got in my car to hunt her down.

Due to its advantageous placement between campus and the I-5 overpass, the Blue Moon Tavern, a renovated mechanic's garage on the border separating the University District from Wallingford, drew an eclectic assortment of regulars to its taps. Jack Kerouac had swilled there, it was rumored. So had beat poet Allen Ginsburg, etching his initials with a penknife into one of the wooden, draught-soaked booths. The renowned establishment also drew Caroline and her circle of friends, who would meet there religiously on Friday evenings for amateur night when the bar hosted open-mike poetry readings and live acoustical performances. She had never invited me to join her, assuring me it was her custom to unwind at the bar, a hangout where she and her sisters could be themselves and not subject to the righteous gaze of their housemother, or the watchful eyes of competing sororities on the lookout for indiscretions. I had always believed her, and never took my banishment personally, until now.

After parking on Forty-fifth Street, I reached for a fifth of Jack Daniels kept sleeved in an old tube sock tucked under my front passenger seat. I chugged heartily as I went forth into the shivery nighttime dampness, crossing over the pedestrian walkway of the I-5 overpass. The warm rye bit harshly as it gurgled down my pipes, drifting swiftly into my empty stomach as fast as I could guzzle. As the violent highway rush rumbled underfoot, I searched my memory for troubling signs I might have missed. Other than Kevin, no lurking suitors came to mind. Halloween was tomorrow. Would that mark some sort of anniversary between us, a celebration she had been secretively planning for? Across the way, the Blue Moon's risqué door sign grew clearer through the mist.

Brassy chords of house music stirred through the entrance alcove. The dimly-lit interior, toasty with body warmth and radiator steam, gave the appearance of a roadhouse on the outskirts of a mill town. Every inch of free wall space not festooned with Halloween trimmings was pasted with local announcements advertising clubs and VFW halls where local bands were scheduled to play. A boisterous assembly of drinking patrons, cramped in the three nicked wooden booths lining the walls to my left, ricocheted flights of beery conversation above the break of cracking billiards. Each seat at the bar was occupied by bespectacled graduate students and rougher locals. Caroline, I disappointedly noted, was not among them. Seeking to blend in, I maneuvered self-consciously toward the bar, keeping an eye out for familiar faces to approach so I would have an aura of purpose and not feel so all alone. I held up my chin and smiled broadly as I went past tables, pretending I saw somebody I knew and was moving toward them. Although several people I vaguely recognized returned my nod as I passed by, their gestures as our eyes met were not welcoming enough for me to join them. I longed to share in their merriment and watched enviously as they tipped back mugs of beer. Keenly aware I'd need to continue drinking, especially if I were to appear at ease when I ran into Caroline, I aimed thirstily for the shiny brass taps looming straight ahead.

I squeezed in against the bar. My image, captured in the grainy haze of the mirror behind the liquor bottles, reflected the front door behind me. Although my position offered an optimum vantage point by which to monitor the foot traffic coming and going through the door, the view's drawback was obvious, as it allowed for the possibility of Caroline noticing me before I saw her. I sensed a purer response to my questions would issue if my approach was sudden and preemptive, not allowing her time to improvise excuses. After eagerly chasing back a whiskey with a cold beer, I eyed a darker, unoccupied area of wall space next to the jukebox. I grabbed my change from the bar and wandered in that direction, stationing myself so I could spot Caroline when she came in.

Meanwhile, on a handcrafted stage behind the pool tables, an Irish folkie decked in a green velvet cap and long embroidered skirt stepped out from behind a makeshift curtain. As the house lights dimmed, she broke into an Irish slip jig, crooning verses from "The Battle of Otterburn." Soon the crowd warmed, clapping in tune with the fair maiden's step, giving the scene the air of a hokey Renaissance festival. From somewhere in the room I heard a familiar peep of childish female laughter. *That laugh. I know that laugh,* I thought. My first guess was that it came from near the bar-or was it the tables? I looked out over the crowd, but the glare from the stage light blinded my view of individual faces. Determined to match a face with the voice, I was walking past where I had earlier sat when a hand reached out from a barstool, nabbing my wrist. Startled, I turned to face Kailani Anouke, Caroline's Kappa Alpha Theta little sister.

"Hello, Ted Bundy," she said, giggling as she let go of me.

Because I recalled hearing her distinctive bubbly laughter not only seconds ago, but also in the background during my earlier conversation with Caroline, I suspected she was part of the afternoon conspiracy to divert me. Polynesian-complected, Kailani had almond-shaped eyes composed of a darker nectar of her skin. Her hair was swept upward to her crown, where it fell straight down her back, ending at the belt loop of her Levi's. She'd met Caroline when she was the sophomore resident advisor at McMahon Hall, and Kailani was a freshman. Her parents, Caroline had mentioned, owned a vast sugar plantation along Kauai's lava shoreline and would have fresh persimmons delivered weekly to their sorority. I kissed her and asked if I could buy her another martini.

She placed the skewered olives to her mouth, sexily pulling all three of them off the toothpick in one hungry lick. She hadn't had a morsel to eat since breakfast, she confessed, blushing as she chewed. She'd had a rough day, she said, and was on her way back from the store to get some last minute party favors for tomorrow night, when she decided to stop in for a beer. Her story made little sense, for unless they were on dates, the Theta sisters never traveled unescorted to bars. I wondered what she was doing here, drinking by herself on a Friday evening. If she was a participant in the scheme to divert me from Caroline tonight, wouldn't she have been sent to the bonfire instead, to make certain I was there?

"So where's Caroline?" she asked. I was surprised by the directness of her question, that it was she who had asked this of me first. Was she trying to find out what I knew? Her eyes twinkled expectantly as I went to answer. She fidgeted, stroking the sides of her glass.

"That's a good question," I said. "She called me from your house this afternoon, all upset by how I hadn't called her in a couple of days, that I didn't take our relationship as seriously as she did." I took the lie a step farther, cloaking it in truth. "So are you and your sisters ready for the party? How are the decorations coming along? Sounds like you guys were working on them when I talked to Caroline earlier. You were there, weren't you? I thought I heard you laughing in the background. Or maybe I'm crazy, who knows." I wanted to let on that I'd been aware of Kailani's presence in the room earlier and wasn't holding back any secrets from her now. Perhaps in the wake of these revelations she would feel compelled to disclose the truth and tell me all she knew.

"Yeah, we're completely behind schedule," she said, looking away for a moment, waving to a friend.

Seeking to further disengage her, I digressed, urging her to tell me about the farm where she'd grown up. She was delighted by my interest, saying that most mainlanders never asked her any questions of substance beyond luaus, leis, and outrigger canoes riding the breakers off Waikiki Beach. I kept the conversation light, sensing it would be foolish to press her for answers to questions we weren't drunk enough yet to talk about.

I ordered her another martini, and then another. For the next hour she rambled in long-winded circles. I kept looking for Caroline among the thinning crowd, and my impatience began stirring. Kailani bummed a cigarette from the man sitting next to her, coughing harshly as she blew out the smoke. The nicotine rush knocked her off balance, and she had to grab onto the barstool to keep from falling. She signaled to the bartender and asked for the check.

"Listen, Ted, I would love to stay and chat, but I have to get back to the house. So I guess you'll be there at our party tomorrow night?" Her face was frozen in attention while she waited for me to respond, as though in a moment of forced sobriety she was allowing herself one last chance to bring back what information she'd been sent to find.

"I should be. I have a few other parties off-campus I need to hit first." I added, "Oh shit, I almost forgot. I was supposed to call Caroline. Where is she, anyway?" By the hesitation that followed, I sensed I had crossed a line and couldn't go back.

"Ted…"

"Hmmm?"

"It's nothing. Just forget it."

"Come on, there's something you're not telling me," I anxiously insisted, careful not to sound accusatory. "You can't just lay your cards out like that and then take them back. Where is she?" Though fearing her answer, I was desperate for the payoff.

"I told you before, Ted, I don't know," she pleaded. "Look, I'm gonna split. I have some more errands to run. And besides, if we sit here too long, people might get the wrong idea," she added.

"Such as?"

"I don't know, like we're fucking or something," she said, laughing bawdily at her crude choice of words. Her flirtation was unexpected, though not unwelcome. The thought of cheating on Caroline, especially with one of her close friends, held an erotic allure of revenge. In the meantime, my curiosity got the better of me.

"I know all about Kevin, if that's what you were getting ready to say," I blurted.

"Look Ted, I don't know what you're talking about," she said defensively. Satisfying a curious need to gain some derivative payback on my disloyal girlfriend, I placed a hand under the bar, slipping my fingers between Kailani's legs. I moved slowly up the seam. She let me get as far as the middle of her thigh, to the space friction makes warm, before lifting my hand out by its thumb and playfully throwing it back at me.

"I can't, Ted," she said, blushing.

"Sure you can."

"No, I won't," she said firmly, sliding a glance at the bill.

"Why?"

"Why? For starters, you have a girlfriend."

"An apparently unfaithful one, from what you're telling me." I gave her a second to rebut me, but she didn't. While I normally wouldn't allow a woman to pick up the tab, I relished watching Kailani reach in her purse. She took her time in removing her money, as if giving me ample time to offer my share. I simply sat in my stool for a moment, challenging her to request my contribution, before stalking angrily into the night.

Two

As much as I wanted to drive over to Caroline's sorority house and wake her, by the time I left the bar it was past her midnight curfew. I slept fitfully, thrashing and tossing under the sheets as though sweating out a malarial chill. My mind kept replaying endless fantasies of treachery and deceit in prurient detail. With perverse glee I pictured Caroline nude, being taken by Kevin, heard their slapping hips, the guttural, breathy grunts of their lovemaking.

Weirdly, despite such a lack of meaningful rest, I didn't wake in the same ill-tempered and vengeful mood as when I had turned in. Although I was still heartsick, the bitterness I took to bed with me vanquished somewhere in the black areas between dreams. I seemed unable to maintain the energy needed for such rampant speculation. Prepared to accept my relationship's fate, I found comfort knowing I could soon put behind me whatever grim news my soon-to-be ex-girlfriend was to share, which would allow me to prepare for my exams no longer tormented by her absence.

I rushed to get ready in the morning coldness, throwing on a pair of jeans, a brown corduroy blazer, and a black turtleneck which I spiffed to make certain its folds lay just so. I struck one last pose in front of the sink mirror before leaving, gazing admirably at my clothes, proud of the ensemble in light of how hastily I had pieced it together.

Although I was sure that reconciliation was a hopeless wish, I nevertheless took a detour on my drive to the seaside village of Ballard, stopping in downtown Seattle to buy a bouquet of flowers from a stall vendor at Pike Street. Along the waterfront the morning sun fanned through the clouds in luminous cylinders, spearing the ferry line shuttling passengers out across Elliot Bay to Vashon Island. It could have been the caffeine, or maybe it was the sunshine breaking over Mt. Olympus, but for a moment, whatever vestiges of resentment were leftover from the night before momentarily evaporated. The drive at sea level, the sun spotlighting down on Puget Sound, it all was strangely therapeutic, displacing the incessant gloom I blamed on my prolonged confinement indoors. I pledged not to form any more baseless conclusions about my girlfriend or concoct assumptions about our relationship until we stood face to face and she vouched for their authenticity. Instead of moping over my plight, I suddenly looked forward with grand expectations to a weekend filled with wistful celebration and extravaganzas, and pondered what costume I might wear to the Theta party as I rode into Ballard.

The Hiram H. Chittenden Locks are situated on the northern banks of the ship canal connecting Lake Washington and Puget Sound. Caroline and I would often take drives there on days when the sky cleared and the steelhead were running, or if she wanted to set her easel to face the afternoon sun. I walked excitedly onto the picturesque grounds, past the visitor center and the exotic plants arrayed alongside the twisting botanical garden paths shadowing its entrance. Droves of curious onlookers were gathered to observe the salmon migration firsthand. Children clustered by the safety railings, tossing dollops of meat gristle and stale bread pieces into the water. The dam spillway roared into Salmon Bay underneath me as I crossed over the locks. I felt my palms grow sticky, matting the tissue paper bounding the prickly rose stems. Drawing closer to the far canal wall, I anxiously glanced through a misty rainbow toward the rolling grass hill where Caroline often painted, but she wasn't there.

I followed the footway down to the fish ladder. Spectators mingled quietly, canted over the guardrail by the observation deck, mesmerized by the salmon hopping through the percolating vat. I quickly scanned their faces as I drew closer, giving them a once-over a second time to check if what I was seeing was something real or a mirage created by the distorting reflections glazing off the vaporous wisps. I looked disbelievingly yet a third time as I walked through another veil of spray. The frustrating sense of defeat was like losing something, and in desperation and denial searching a third and fourth time under pillows and desk drawers and closets, places you already hunted more than once before. I turned to look where I'd been, re-checking the locks, the control tower, underneath the shadows of the gardens and trees. Not factoring in the possibility that she would stand me up, I was driven out of my mind about what to do next. I gripped the chill metal rails overlooking the water, hissing like a hot springs pool. For several moments I went nowhere, staring idly into the foaming surface while I regained my wits. I was terribly self-conscious, embarrassed to face the retired couples, tourists, and love-struck young couples jostling alongside me. I feared they could read what I was thinking, had intimate knowledge of my humiliation.

Devitalized, I tramped back over the dam footway and angrily heaved the bouquet over the rails. I broke into a full sprint, like a fireman summoned from the dead of night. People walking back to the parking lot sensed me yards before I reached them, jumping fearfully out of my way with wide-eyed, stricken expressions. Blowing past an old man stooping to admire a plaque in front of a tree, I had half a mind to barrel into him with the full force of my hurtling frame, but satisfied myself instead by screaming toward the sky at the capacity of my lungs. I hollered nothing in particular, emitting a violent war cry like a Seminole warrior exhorting his tribe with a bloody white man's scalp in hand. By the time I reached my car I was panting. I leaned against the door, my thoughts speeding alongside heaving breaths as I debated what to do next. I kept wondering why she was doing this to me. Did she want me to chase her, or was this just her way of getting my attention? My mode of revenge then came to fruition, a deviant scheme that had lain dormant in my mind, waiting patiently for just the right circumstances to set it in motion.

On my way home I stopped off at a Queen Anne Hill Safeway store to buy a Halloween mask. The manager, a haggard bald man with drinking circles under his eyes, gestured toward the aisle where the costumes were kept. Hyper, and in nasty mood, I thought it might be a tantalizing challenge to finagle something from right under the old bugger's nose, for I suspected that his lungs could not withstand the exertion of trying to stop me if he decided to give chase.

I plucked a shopping basket by the checkout counter and proceeded toward the costume aisle. The shelves and bins were practically bare, heaped with small piles of latex masks turned inside out. Most of what remained were caricatures of the presidential candidates or superhero costume boxes that had already been picked over. I checked both ways down the aisle as the snapping noise from the manager's label gun abruptly stopped. The sound of his footsteps grew fainter. A door, perhaps a utility closet, clicked open from somewhere inside the store. *He's reloading his stamps,* I thought, or making a drop in the cashbox. Now was my chance. I thrust a handful of the masks into each jacket pocket without seeing which I had chosen. Looking up again, I was stunned to see an old woman glaring puzzlingly at my pockets. She was clutching a bag of cotton balls into one liver-spotted fist. In the other were several coupons. Holding her stance, she seemed plagued by indecision. I smiled cordially, probing the masks as though checking vegetables for firmness, quite certain I'd appear guilty if I didn't give the impression it was my intent to buy the items the whole time. Although she continued about her business, I wasn't confident she had ascribed the scene to a dementia-induced trick of the flickering brain or a slip of her failing eyes. I feared she might snitch to the manager, perhaps dutifully seek him out and urge him to notify the police. Exhilarated by these dangers, my heart beat quickly, stabbing joyously into my ribcage. I heard the door shut again, and in a few seconds the clicking from the label-gun recommenced. With the old woman no longer in sight, I made my escape, stalking quickly down the aisle and toward the exit doors. I waved an unrepentant goodbye to the manager, thanking him for all his help and wishing him a pleasant holiday. I whisked rapidly toward my car, listening for the sound of his footsteps, a desperate shout for me to stop. The pleasurably frantic excitement provided a quick spark of adrenaline, returning the self-esteem I had feared was irreplaceably lost.

THREE

At twilight I sat parked outside the Kappa Alpha Theta house, waiting for the right moment to sneak in on the coattails of the arriving guests. A shutterless, whitewashed two-story colonial, the third in on Greek Row, Caroline's sorority resembled a posh seaside inn that at one time might have housed a decorated Confederate general resting from his wounds. The front was lavishly decorated for the Halloween party, with rubber tarantulas caught in cottony strands of imitation spider webs stretched across the portico below the second-story windows. A styrofoam headstone was perched slantwise in the ivy bed so those coming up the flight of steps could read its epitaph. On Memorial Way, students that had been to the football game returned with their dates. Along with the trick-or-treaters, they waited for the light to change at the intersection of Forty-fifth Street and Seventeenth Avenue. A dozen or so costumed partyers pointed and laughed at the gravestones as they headed up the steps leading into the house. Now or never, I thought, inspecting my dopey red eyes in the rear view mirror. After squirting them with Visine, I gulped from a bottle of vodka, took a deep breath, and threw on my Richard Nixon mask. Locking my car door, I stepped quickly across the street, falling in behind the group.

The party was in full swing. Though claustrophobic, I immersed myself within the jam of people greeting one another in the entrance foyer. The sounds of The Classics IV singing "Spooky" spilled out of the sitting room to the right, where black lights fluoresced the bed sheets draped over those dressed in togas and as ghosts. Keeping in character with the future President-elect, I hunched over, zealously protecting my anonymity as I sneaked off into one of the packed rooms. I spotted Caroline and Kevin from a distance. They were in the kitchen, seated together at a dinner table draped in black and orange crepe streamers. I stopped short, shaking with anger. Leaning in toward one another, they were sharing an intimate moment of laughter above the glow of a candlelit jack o' lantern centerpiece. Kevin, dressed as a surgeon, wore aqua-blue surgical scrubs and a head reflector. His white lab coat was splotched with fake blood, and a stethoscope hung from his neck. Caroline was his nurse in white uniform. Despite the inordinate amount of time I had spent anticipating this moment, words escaped me. I never considered what I would say to Caroline when I saw her, or how I would say it. Reassessing, I walked out back to the patio and drew a beer from a keg. I slugged it down, draining two more in succession before handing the pouring hose to a mummy. Needing another, I stood waiting till he took his turn.

"Lean your head over, man," he said.

I looked toward the sky. He flicked the lever open, letting the cold beer stream down into my throat. My feat drew a small round of applause from two pledges dressed as a pixie and a leprechaun. When I went back inside after bowing to acknowledge their adulation, I noticed that the crowds near the entranceway hall had all but vanished, having crammed into the other rooms. I slinked up the stairs, fully expecting to be stopped cold. I had never been upstairs, as men were strictly forbidden, even if you were signed in as a guest. I knew Caroline's room was the first after the landing, for she had often complained of hearing the noises that echoed from downstairs during parties. Her door was open. I locked myself in after slipping inside unseen. I can't say what I was looking for exactly, or what I expected to find. I didn't turn on the lights, and figured if I heard the keyhole jiggling I could leap out her window onto the roof and dart out the back alleyway. The front yard gaslamp threw a dim shine upon a homespun afghan folded neatly upon her bed. Guided by weakened night shadows cast through the windowpanes, I went over to her desk in search of a diary, but found it was too dark to read what she kept in her drawers. Her trashcan, standing next to a milk crate filled with records, was filled to the brim with balls of crumpled paper. I stooped down and went through them, sniffing a ball of toilet paper unusual in that its inner layers were heavy and damp, with a strong odor like pool chlorine.

Blindsided, I dropped the sticky clump of tissue when I saw what was inside, as though it were a snake curling around to bite me. A warm sting flooded my chest, my face. I sat perplexedly on the floor for a moment, staring blankly at the condom, haunted by an image that would never lose its clarity in the years that followed, much as I'm certain a husband never forgets the sight of walking into his bedroom and finding his wife under another man. As my dizziness receded, Caroline's anguishing betrayal slowly gave way to boiling anger, a dire yearning to inflict a level of emotional pain that would scar her soul for life, words so full of hate they would be painful for her to recollect in her old age. Infused suddenly with the thrill of ambushing her and forcing her to confront her own deceit, I hastily rewrapped the condom in the toilet paper, clenching it in my fist as I stormed downstairs into the kitchen.

Caroline and Kevin smiled inquisitively at me as I stood before them. Her eyes froze wide open when I peeled off the mask. "Peek-a-boo!!" I said. "Hey sweetie! Hi there, Kevin!" I leaned down and gave her a long kiss, aggressively pushing my tongue between her lips. She smiled insincerely as I drew away from her, as though needing to be seen as a good sport. Lipstick stained her teeth.

"Listen, I'm so sorry I didn't make it this morning," I said. "I was out late last night and met up with some friends afterward. You aren't mad at me, are you?"

"I didn't make it either," she answered hesitantly.

"I think I'll let you two have a moment," Kevin said, smiling reassuringly at Caroline. An expression of quiet relief spread over her face, as though the two of them understood he would be waiting in the wings to intervene on her behalf if her plan did not run smoothly.

"Listen, Ted…" she said, gazing into my eyes. "I'm glad you came, because there's something we need to talk about."

"What is it? What's wrong?" I asked, smiling obliviously, continuing with the charade as if I hadn't a clue what was coming next.

"I don't know how to say this, but…"

"But what?"

"It's not that I don't like you, Ted, I think you're a swell guy and all, but…I don't know, I just don't think this is going to work out." Her words came a little too easily, I thought, despite her initial loss for them. It was as though the hard part was behind her, and she was coasting in on the ease of her relief.

"Are you seeing somebody else?" I asked, bracing for the agonizing confession of her infidelities.

"No, of course not."

"Then what is it?" I asked, having fun with her. "Was it something I did to you?"

"No."

"Something I said?"

"Not really." She looked away for a moment, as though the words she had chosen to explain herself troubled her as greatly as her own indecisiveness.

"Well, what is it? Was it something else?"

"Sort of."

"Such as?"

"I don't know." She took a deep breath, uneasily scrutinizing me. "The day we messed around, it just seemed like you weren't making love to me. It was like you were angry at someone or something, and were taking it out on me. It's hard to describe. You were very-how do I put this...*aggressive* toward me. I don't know if that's the right word, but that's what it felt like. I think maybe we should've waited longer, I don't know. I never felt scared with a man before, and I... can't feel that way again." She looked up at me again. "I'm sorry, Ted, I can't be your girlfriend. I'm just not ready to take it to the next level."

"*Aggressive?*" I hissed. "You were the one who came knocking, as I recall."

"Ted, this really isn't the place for this discussion," she said quietly.

"Hey, that's not a problem," I said. "It's not a problem whatsoever. You know something, Caroline, I should have gotten you pregnant when I had the chance."

"What do you mean by that?" Scowling, she drew back, as though whiffing the smoke of a slaughterhouse incinerator.

"Instead of answering that question, let me ask you this: Do you think you're ready to take it to the next level with your new boyfriend, Kevin?"

"We're just friends, Ted."

"Just friends?" I mocked, furrowing my brow. "Or friends who fuck?" I flung the pulpy lump of tissue at her chest. She stared at the ground, expressionless.

Bitterly sarcastic, I said, "Listen, Caroline, do me a favor, okay?" When she didn't answer me, I asked her again. When she still wouldn't respond, I asked her the very same words. I waited until she looked at me. "Three things: first, shame on you, you spoiled cunt; second, I want you to know that I fucked Kailani, and we enjoyed ourselves immensely; third, may your first baby with Kevin be stillborn. Better yet, may it be born as the Devil."

FOUR

With each passing moment our separation grew more difficult to bear. I had hoped my anger would lessen as the days wore on, but it only grew worse, hardening into resentment. Despite the conviction with which I had spoken my last words to Caroline, I was desperate to have her back. I repeatedly called her sorority house. The first few times her sisters lied for her, saying she wasn't around. They grew nastier toward me as the calls continued, icily ordering that I stop pestering their friend and move on with my life. Soon nobody picked up the receiver, or angrily slammed it down when they learned who was on the other end. I drove by their house nightly, slowing to peek at Caroline's window, searching for the movement of her shadow behind the drawn curtain.

My behavior hadn't gone unnoticed. Unbeknownst to me, the Theta housemother had been keeping a scrupulous log of my actions and called the campus police. They in turn notified the Dean of Men, who called me into his office exactly one week after the party. Rather than expel me from school immediately, he offered the choice of withdrawing instead. He assured me that I would receive a grade of incomplete in each class and be eligible to reapply for admission next fall, but only if I stayed out of trouble. I drove in a daze after my meeting with the dean, losing all sense of direction. Circling aimlessly under the monorail's concrete piers, I desperately racked my brain, contemplating what few options remained. I thought of phoning my mother and explaining to her all that had happened, but didn't want to unnecessarily upset her, not yet.

Vernetta's car wasn't in the driveway when I arrived home. I walked dejectedly upstairs, only to find that an eviction notice, ordering me to vacate the apartment immediately for failure to pay rent due and owing, had been taped to my door. As I shakily put the key in the lock, I saw my name handwritten on an envelope at the bottom of the door. I tore open its glued seams:

> *November 6, 1968*
>
> *Ted:*
>
> *I am truly sorry things did not work out as I had hoped they might. I would have given you some more time to get your things in order, but I have a new tenant who is anxious to move her things in. As you can see, the complaint has no docket number, as I haven't filed it with the court yet. I am giving you the weekend to move out your belongings. If you are not out of my*

*house by this Sunday, not only shall I file the
Complaint for Eviction, I will also swear out a
criminal complaint for that little flashing episode by the window. I was tempted to call the
police and have you thrown out then and there,
but since I know you really don't have anywhere
else to go, I figured I would be nice and give you
until the end of this weekend to make alternate
living arrangements. Consider this a warning,
however, and don't come to court with the back
rent, or I shall be forced to go on record before
the judge and tell him all that has happened.*

Vernetta Rome

I crumpled her letter in a ball and threw it down the stairs, then stormed into my room and began packing my belongings. As things stood, I could think of no other options except returning home. I could enroll in community college in Tacoma, but that would mean living at home and bearing the risk of running into my former classmates at Puget Sound, who would certainly view me as a failure. I thought of what relatives I could stay with in Washington while living out my suspension. I extrapolated the possibilities to other regions of the country, including Philadelphia, where my maternal grandparents still resided. After packing up the last of my clothes, I scribbled out a longhand response to Vernetta's note and nailed it to her door:

Dear Vernetta:

*I am in receipt of your letter to me dated No-
vember 6, 1968. Kindly accept this letter as a
response to your baseless allegations. It goes with
out saying, I was COMPLETELY taken aback
by your false accusations. How could you have
hallucinated such bizarre BULLSHIT? You are
a dried up OLD WOMAN. To think I would
somehow derive sexual pleasure from exhibiting
my naked balls to you is BEYOND ALL COM-
PREHENSION. So, by all means, report me to
the police. Nevertheless, despite your inane, de-
famatory accusations, I shall grant your wishes
and have my things out by this Sunday. Don't
be there. SHAME on you, you old buzzard.
May you rot in hell. SLOWLY.*

Warmest regards,

Theodore Robert Bundy

FIVE

I moved back to Tacoma, where I spent most of the Christmas holidays hurriedly filling out college applications. I sent one to Temple University in Philadelphia, and by way of some strings pulled by my grandfather, Samuel Cowell, I was accepted for the 1969 spring semester.

The prospect of traveling so far from home seemed enticing at first. I would distance myself from the harrowing sorrows of my recent past, avoid the draft, and be able to test Freud's theories on infantile amnesia. Although I looked forward to my explorations, I recalled the wickedness of my grandfather's antics, grim stories that had trickled back to me over the years through correspondence I kept with distant cousins back East. I'd heard that he once took a belt to an employee, brutally beating the old migrant worker in broad daylight for accepting a tip from a customer. In defending his actions to the Plymouth Township Police Department, he explained that he'd caught the worker ogling a customer's wife through a kitchen window, and the matter quietly went away. Another tale had him dousing his truck with gasoline when it wouldn't start, and in a spiteful rage popping the hood and setting fire to the engine block. There was the story about his pet boa constrictor, named Bacchus. He had allowed his neighbors' children to hold and pet the snake until it bit one of them near the eye. Enraged, my grandfather was said to have grabbed the serpent by the neck and clipped it in two with a pair of garden shears, tossing the pieces on the grass, where the forked tongue continued to dart in and out its head, as though guillotined. Afterward, based upon what they had seen, children ran past the house as though it were haunted, or ding-donged the front doorbell and fled.

Since I had no firsthand knowledge of Sam's temperament, I resisted the urge to pass judgment on him just yet. When I asked my mother to confirm or deny these tales, she would only say that my grandfather loved me like a son and that I had idolized him when I was a boy, often following him around in his yard, reciting the definitions to dictionary words he quizzed me on while at work in his greenhouse. He was still vigorous at seventy-one years old, and though downscaling his workload in recent years, he maintained a profitable landscaping business and was considered an expert in the field of shrubbery maintenance. A member of the Philadelphia Horticultural Society and the Roxborough Flower Club, he often won First in Show ribbons at the Philadelphia Flower Show held annually at the city's Convention Center.

According to what I was told, Samuel had called in a favor

owed to him by a client on the admissions board at the University's College of Liberal Studies. A deal had been struck: I would move back East for the spring semester and live with him and Dolores, my grandmother, at their home in the Philadelphia suburbs. In consideration for my lodging and meals, I would work for Sam, helping him with the spring planting and lawn cuttings when the weather grew warm. My plan was to stay through the summer, then re-enroll at the University of Washington the following autumn once my apprenticeship was completed.

One day I rummaged through our Tacoma house when my mother and stepfather weren't home, searching for family pictures taken between 1946 and 1950, the years we lived in Philadelphia. I was able to locate just one photo of Sam, a blurry black and white snapshot of me posing on his lap in our den, taken at a time he must have been visiting from Philadelphia. He was thin, handsome, with narrowly set blue eyes and a full head of wavy black hair anchored by a sturdy widow's peak. I could see how my family said I looked just like him. The faded date scribbled on the back of the picture, which I peeled out of an old photo album, showed that it was taken on Christmas morning in 1951, when I was five-years-old. I was wearing a Western shirt and a Hopalong Cassidy toy cap gun and holster set, along with a matching pair of cowboy boots Santa had also left under the tree. I studied the photo that night until I grew drowsy to the clang of tugboats dropping anchor in the Tacoma Narrows, hoping the fresh images thumping under my eyelids would transport me farther back in time to when I was teething a rattler in my crib in Philadelphia.

That night I dreamt I was in first grade. My teacher, Mrs. Daley, was dressed in a bright red skirt and had a stethoscope dangling from her neck. I was always frightened of her. She was alternately passive and volatile, once dumping the contents of my desk onto the floor when it was messy, and on another occasion angrily lifting me by my hair and throwing me into the closet for eating a crayon. In my dream she was seated behind her desk, smiling at me. I was wearing shorts, saddle shoes, and navy knee socks. She called me up to the front of the class and had me sponge down the chalkboard as the other students watched. She smiled at me from her chair while I worked, combing out her long red hair with an ivory-handled brush. When I finished my task she told me to come to her. Removing a heeled shoe, she started slowly massaging my groin with her stockinged foot. Then she turned me by my shoulders to face my classmates, who were now laughing hysterically, pointing to my erection. I began to cry, tears clouding my vision. The next thing I knew I stood facing an old sea captain. We were on the deck of a battered sailboat upon a calm, nameless sea. He was wearing a floppy leather hat and had no eyes, just caves of pinkish wet meat in his sockets. Shirtless underneath his grimy overalls, he shoved me off the deck into the cold water. I sliced my hands on the razor-sharp barnacles as I tried climbing the keel. The cuts stung in the salt water, as though held over an open flame. I kicked frantically until I lost the strength to tread water, then gave up and slipped under the surface. The last thing I saw was the wobbly image of his smiling wooden teeth as he pulled a finger across his throat, rearing back his head in laughter, an image fading as the depths suffocated me in red blackness, with no rescuer to throw me a line as I went under.

I awoke clawing at the bed sheets, damp with a mix of drool, perspiration, and semen dribble. I perused *The Interpretation of Dreams,* in which Freud associated the dreams of adulthood with early childhood incidents latent in our repressed memories. "Dreams are the royal road the unconscious," he wrote. "A large number of dreams, often full of fear, which are concerned with passing through narrow spaces or with staying in the water, are based upon fancies about the embryonic life, about the act of birth." Though I sensed I was heading in the right direction by returning to Philadelphia, I feared the validity of Robert Merton's theory. If my disturbing pattern of behavior had led to my dismissal from school and the near-eviction from my apartment, what order of calamity would follow sequentially? I should've known that the more I fiddled with the past, the greater the chances I would tweak some resilient memory with a timer all its own. I should've known that my brief flirtation with good fortune-being accepted into school, the chance to discover what ailed me-was no more than a delusion that would soon burn itself out, like a self-immolating star crumpling of its own force.

PART II

PHILADELPHIA

Six

I searched nervously among the expectant faces waiting at the end of the jetway at Philadelphia International Airport. Certain I had given my grandparents the correct flight information, I looked for directions to the main concourse, speculating that there had been some miscommunication. Were they waiting for me by the baggage carousels? I was relieved to see a short, heavy middle-aged woman in a raincoat and red plastic scarf standing by a television monitor listing the flight schedules. She seemed lost also, worriedly looking both ways down the dankly lit terminal walkway and at the passengers picking up their boarding passes at the check-in lines. It was reassuring to know I wasn't the only wayward soul lost in a city of strangers. Perhaps Dolores and Sam had been delayed and dispatched this kindly neighbor to fetch me, rather than have me wait all alone by the gate. As our eyes locked I approached her.

"Ted?" she sheepishly asked in a squeaky, adolescent voice. "Do you remember me?"

It didn't immediately resonate that this chunky woman was my grandmother. I was too young when I had last seen her to recognize her now. She had brown-dyed hair coiffed into hair dryer curls bobby-pinned back from her forehead. The rain beads on her scarf reflected the fluorescent colors transmitted by the arrivals screen behind her. She touched my cheek, holding me out in front of her while she studied my face. In obsessing over Samuel I had completely forgotten about Dolores or speculated how she might appear, for no physical description of her or picture had been given to me in preparation for this moment. Because a certain informality regarding surnames had always been practiced within our family, I didn't even know how to properly address her. Smelling of mentholated ointment, she had a nervous jollity and shifty eyes that wouldn't stay focused on me. Her mouth upturned and flattened, twitching the wrinkle lines forming vertically across the ridges of her lips.

"Shall we go get your things?" she asked, rather than how my flight was. *Where is my grandfather,* I thought, *and why hadn't he come along with her?*

On the ride to my grandparents' home in Roxborough, on the city outskirts, Dolores behaved like a shy hostess anxiously trying to please houseguests she is unaccustomed to entertaining. She asked for my mother and wanted to know how my stepfather was doing, whether he was still cooking at the Army Medical Center at Fort Lewis. I was politely responsive, assuring her all was well in Tacoma and that little had changed. I was still overwhelmed to be in a strange land I didn't yet recognize, a place where I would be spending the next several months of my life seeking clues from my boyhood. Nervously anticipating my introduction to Sam, and groggy with jetlag, I wasn't in much of a mood for conversation.

"Is everything OK? When you got off the plane, you looked like you'd seen a ghost," she said.

"Everything's fine. I just feel a little guilty, like I'm inconveniencing you and Sam," I said. "I really appreciate you taking me in on such short notice."

"Oh, sweetheart, what in heaven's name ever gave you that idea? You're our grandchild, you're welcome anytime, you know that. And as far as what happened back in Seattle, I wouldn't worry too much, if I were you," she said. "People make mistakes, Ted, but the most important thing you need to understand is that you have family you can lean on."

Though her compulsion to patch the quiet lulls with conversation was well meant, I didn't want our discussion, congenial as it had been progressing, to meander toward the topic of my dismissal. A recapitulation now would be unsettling and serve to taint this otherwise pleasant reunion. I pretended to be interested, whistling faintly in awestruck admiration as she gestured toward the bronze-lit columns of the Museum of Art, rising like the Parthenon out of the snowy rains lashing the wooded hillsides along the Schuykill River. She asked if Boathouse Row, framed in white holiday lights speckling the churning night current, drew memories. Then she touched upon more specific anecdotes, jogging me from my travel-weary daze.

"Samuel took you there once, hoisting you on his shoulders to see the Dad Vail Regatta. Do you remember that?"

"I can't say I do."

As we passed by the Fairmount Park exit, she said that he had taken me to see the Elephant House at the Philadelphia Zoo when I was three. Did that ring a bell? I was encouraged by her questions, curious to see where they might lead.

"Don't remember that either," I said. "Speaking of which, where is Sam?"

"He has a snow removal business that keeps him busy when it storms like this."

I didn't ask when I'd meet him, and suppressed what I really wanted to say, that I thought it was strange he hadn't traveled to greet a grandson he had not seen in almost twenty years.

We exited the expressway at Green Lane in Manayunk, chugging up the narrow turns banked with stone retaining walls. The road crested at the hilltop intersection with Ridge Avenue, where we turned left. The wind was blowing harder, batting the traffic light. The rain had changed over to snow, powdering the cars parked along the street, gusting across the verandas of the downtown row houses. I guessed down which of these roads she might turn, in which of these Protestant churches I was baptized. When she slowed to a light at the 7100 block, her eyes cast toward a vacant lot on the northwest corner of Domino Lane, which she said separated Lower from Upper Roxborough.

"That's where we used to live," she said quietly, as though

she had difficulty believing it was true, but had a moral obligation to inform me anyhow. I was flabbergasted. Why hadn't I been told beforehand that my grandparents had moved from my childhood home, the place I expected to be staying?

"Isn't that where I was born?" I asked, even more curious why Dolores had neglected to inquire whether I recalled this place, as she had the other sights on our drive over here. Presently, all that remained on the scoured tract were a sign directing drivers down the street toward a new cocktail lounge, and a notice that the land was available for sale or lease. Marked off by flagged boundary stakes, the lot had been razed, with sparse wisps of dead grass fluttering atop the bulldozed foundation. A crumbling fireplace chimney was all that once stood of it.

"That's true," she said.

"When did you move?"

"Oh, that's been a while, ten years at least. Sam sold it to our family doctor, and for a while we rented it back from her until we moved. Last week the mayor told Sam they're going to build a pizza restaurant there. Won't that be nice?"

"I didn't know you'd moved," I said, trying to mask my disappointment. I felt like a boy who feels for the first time what it is like to be cheated out of something rightfully his. I had presumed this was where I would be staying, the mysterious home whose walls would solve the riddle of my boyhood. Dolores didn't bother to slow down when I turned my neck to gaze as she drove past the property.

"The house was falling apart, and we couldn't afford the upkeep. It was just too big for Sam and me, so we moved to our new house," she said, adding, as though not wanting to disappoint me, "which is where we're going now!" She spoke anxiously and with a tone of false enthusiasm, a zip in her voice like she was antsy to change the subject. "Are you looking forward to starting classes tomorrow?"

"Most definitely," I answered, though confused and wondering what to think.

My grandparents had moved to Lafayette Hill, the next town over from Roxborough. Theirs was a plain two story brick home set back on a small tree-lined hill on Columbus Road. By the fresh tread marks and footprints tracked in the wet driveway snow, I could see that we had just missed Sam. I followed Dolores's lead up the front steps with my suitcase and backpack in hand. The snow, mixed with frozen rain, fell hard from the pink sky, fizzing as it sifted through the branches of the naked front yard elms. I whisked the melting flakes from my shoulders and wiped my soles on their welcome mat.

Painted avocado green, the modestly furnished living room was trapped with the odors of an old person trying to keep up with the daily maintenance required of housework, but failing at it. Though spotless, the olive wall-to-wall carpeting was worn thin at spots from foot traffic. Dust breaded the mint dishes and Hummel figurines decorated the higher shelves of the credenzas that could no longer be reached. Space was cramped, and I was careful not to bump into the dining room table, adorned with a bowl of wax fruit. I followed Dolores into a small kitchen. She offered to heat up some Spaghetti-O's, but I declined, as I was exhausted from the flight and by the three hours time-zone change. Although it was just ten o'clock at night, it felt like three in the morning. She showed me upstairs to the guestroom, where I climbed into bed without undressing. Wondering, as I fell asleep, when I would finally encounter my grandfather.

I was startled awake by the shudder of an icicle breaking off a gutter. The noise traveled the length of the roof, sounding like the crack of ice on a thawing pond. I sat up and gazed wearily through the window into a large backyard I hadn't seen the night before. The snow had fallen heavily overnight, glowing with a violet incandescence in the faint morning light. I saw a weatherboard barn a short distance from the house. Windowless and decrepit, its wobbly joists bowed and the roof sagged inward under the weight of a drift. Drawn by a rasping sound, I shuffled to the other window facing the street, where neighbors were shoveling their driveways and scraping ice off their windshields. A door creaked open in the hallway. I turned halfway around, hearing a distinctive clank of porcelain, the droplets from a tapering stream trickle feebly into a toilet. Several seconds passed, followed by a series of effortful spatters, as if somebody was ringing the last drops from a towel. Squinting, I stood facing Sam, who had opened the door without knocking, rousing me from my early morning daze.

"Morning. Thought I might get you to help me shovel a little snow, handsome," he said in a low raspy voice, clearing his throat of a gob of spittle. His small wiry outline was backlit by the bright hallway light. He leaned against the doorway, scrutinizing me. I examined the shadowed half of his face once my vision focused, amazed by how much older he looked compared to the old Christmastime photograph. Though his hair remained thick and full, deeply scalloped blabs dotted with skin tags hung sadly underneath his eyes. He spoke in a redneckish accent steeped in origins hard to place, drawing out the O in snow, but with a peculiar twang. A Philadelphia accent, I would later learn, woodsy, woven with a trace of the pines. His voice was strangely familiar, lingering, like we had picked up where we had left off, returning to an earlier conversation I couldn't recall but felt certain had taken place.

"Good morning," I said awkwardly. The hallway light shimmered off the bristles growing from the indents on his cheek where his razor had missed. There was a glint of cockiness in his expression, as if he took joy in baptizing me into the rigors of working before sunup. Saying nothing more, he tossed a set of work clothes on the window seat, leaving the door open as he walked out.

I met him outside. He was lowering a large gas-powered snow blower down off his truck, an old Ford F-1 pickup with the words *Cowell Landscaping and Tree Services* painted in white lettering on the door. Without breaking to acknowledge me, he gave the ignition chord a crank and began blowing. To display a little initiative, I followed behind him with a snow shovel, hoisting out the heavy wet clumps spit from the chute as I cleared a path down the driveway. Though a certain amount of satisfaction was inherent with this early morning exercise, I felt the first stirrings of homesickness, for the stink of exhaust puffing out the carburetor reminded me of the smell of air caught in the gondola sheds at Snoqualmie Mountain Range. I gazed wistfully down at last year's lift ticket, still paper-clipped onto my parka zipper. I enjoyed a fleeting recollection of standing in the lift line, the glacial sun warming my cheeks after a brisk run down the mogul trails.

After showering and dressing, I stood at the top of the stairs for a moment, listening to my grandparents' over the faucet splash and whistle of a teakettle.

"I can't believe you had that boy out there shoveling first thing in the morning, Samuel Cowell, what in heaven's name is the matter with you?

"He came out himself. I didn't ask him."

"Well, I wouldn't expect anything less from him. He's a good boy. So he gets fresh with one broad. It's not like he knocked her up or anything."

"Fresh? That's putting it lightly. Sick is more like it," he said.

"Well, hopefully the change will do him good. It's far too soon to pass judgment on him, don't you think?"

"No. Born sick. Sick boy. Grew up to be a sick young man. Don't you remember what he did to Olivia Farnsworth?"

"He was, what, four years old, Sam?"

"It's a pattern of behavior I'm talking about. Even giving him the benefit of the doubt, I still say he's a draft dodger, Dolores. He should be in basic training, as far as I'm concerned. He's damn lucky I have connections. If my Legion buddies got word of this or found out what he did to that rich skirt in

Seattle, they'd treat me like I was harboring a criminal. But he is my flesh and blood, even if he is a weird apple, so against my better judgment I will allow him to stay in my home. But if he screws up on my watch, so help me God, Dolores, he'll be out the door with my foot broken off in his ass."

His threat didn't scare me. He was old, and I knew I could stand my own if we came to blows. More disheartening was his harshly opinionated language, not the heartfelt longing you would expect from a grandfather toward kin. And who was Olivia Farnsworth? As a child, what awful thing could I have done to her to engender this man's grudge? I tramped noisily down the stairs to alert them of my presence, making a show of yawning and stretching as I entered the kitchen. I pretended to be oblivious to the suddenly hushed tone of their conversation. Sam, flushed with outdoor redness, was reading the morning paper at the kitchen table. Dolores was seated across from him, smoking a cigarette.

"Good morning, sweetheart. Did you sleep well? I understand your grandfather had you out doing a little shoveling," she said through a blue pillar of cigarette smoke drifting toward the ceiling light.

Sam barely lifted his head from his paper. I sat down uneasily between them, where a placemat was set. As he read about Nixon's inauguration yesterday, I devoured the fried eggs and scrapple Dolores forked onto my plate. He quietly chuckled to himself, all the while pouring teaspoonful after teaspoonful of sugar into his coffee cup, swirling it around, then gulping it back in three swift swallows. I wondered about his politics, if he had an opinion one way or the other. Would it be imprudent to reveal my Republican leanings? Because he worked with his hands, I figured him a Democrat, a man of the people, a person to whom some polite anti-war commentary might earn favor. But he was also a veteran, and appeared to have a fair amount of self-earned dough that he certainly wouldn't want taxed to death by the liberals in Congress.

"These fucking protesters, throwing rocks and firecrackers at dignitaries," he said to himself, reaching into an open box of donuts.

"Samuel, your language," Dolores protested, albeit with a faint smile, as though she was amused by his tirade but too proper to admit it.

"They used to block traffic in Seattle," I interjected, pleased to let him know that I, too, was sickened by the disrespect shown by the protesters who had marched on the Capitol yesterday. My statement elicited no reaction from him as he reached for a pad of paper. He mapped out the bus routes to Philadelphia. The simplest way, he suggested, was to go straight down Germantown Pike until it ran into North Broad Street.

"Watch out when you get into Mt. Airy, south of Germantown Avenue," he said, winking. "Gets black as midnight, if you know what I mean, especially in East Mt. Airy. If you get off at the wrong stop, whatever you do, don't ask a spoda for directions."

"A spoda?" I had a feeling he was referring to a black person, and played along for his amusement.

"You know, a nigger, when he says, 'I spoda do this, spoda do that." He burst into a Tommy-gun laugh. I forced a laugh in response.

"Let's see what's on the television tonight, shall we?" Dolores broke in with a tense smile, separating the television schedule from the circulars. "Let's see now, at seven-thirty we can watch *The Avengers*. This looks like a great episode: 'A number of secret contacts are systematically eliminated after several key agents return from their mysterious holidays.'"

While the thought of watching television shows with my grandparents was not part of the exciting new beginning I had envisioned for myself, I knew I'd have to be patient with them, earn their trust before I could find out more about Olivia Farnsworth, why they spoke so secretively about her, and how she was connected to my past.

SEVEN

In the succeeding months I fell into the monotonous routine of taking the SEPTA bus to school each morning and coming home right after school ended, walking home from the Germantown Pike stop. I was receptive to the idea of meeting new people, but as was my experience at Puget Sound and the University of Washington, I quickly realized that being a new student required an outgoingness I'd never been able to put forth when around new faces, a skill I would need to sharpen if I were to assimilate. My classes proved unchallenging, and I soon grew bored with their repetitiveness. Sadly, I didn't make any new friends, for I learned not long after matriculating that Temple was a commuter school, with most of the students abandoning campus after classes ended. The snow didn't fall again that winter, so there was no work for Sam to give me. And because it was too bitter cold to spend any time touring Center City Philadelphia, I withdrew, retreating to the silence of my lonely quarters. I took note of my grandparents' humdrum routine, vowing to never be as they were now. The dismal simplicity of their unvarying rituals was depressing to come home to, with one day indistinguishable from the next. Contented with their obsolescence, they had no visitors or friends, with the local evening news telecast on Channel 10, anchored by John Facenda, being the center of their social activity.

Then a spate of warm February winds washed away the last of the snow that had fallen in the January storm. I saw the sun for the first time in a month. I knew that outdoor work loomed near and Sam would be seeking a return on his investment. Though the air was still cold enough that I needed to wear gloves, on the last night of the month I wasn't surprised to hear him grumble over dinner that there was no reason we couldn't get a jump on spring cleanups the next morning. I looked forward to getting outside and was raring to dispel his initial assessment of me as a draft dodger. I was even more determined to prove that my disastrous autumn was a fluke, a blemish on my record I made it my foremost mission to decontaminate. By proving my ability to endure the grueling manual labor we were about to undertake, I hoped to earn enough trust and respect so that Sam would confide what he knew, and maybe even reveal the true reason he was not sharing whatever information he might be keeping from me.

The following morning, the first of March, we set out on our first landscaping project of the season at Leverington Cemetery, a few miles down Ridge Avenue. It was my first time in Sam's truck. The compartment was messy and smelled like peat moss, with a snuff-spattered white coffee cup balanced under the gear shaft and the windshield arced with snow deicing chemicals. He didn't speak a word as we drove down Ridge Avenue, but as we stopped at the intersection where the old house once stood, I caught him peeking knowingly at what remained of it with the same lost and staring expression my grandmother had shown. As the light turned, it took a honking semi behind us to jolt the old man from his daze.

"Ever hear of Kelpius the Mystic?" he suddenly asked.

"Who?"

"He was a seventeenth-century conjurer who lived as a hermit in an earthen cave in the woods behind Ridge Avenue," he began, speaking with the condescending magnetism a kindergarten teacher might in retelling Aesop's fable about the scorpion and the frog. "The cave is still there. Locals sought his supernatural powers to remove stubbornly entrenched demons Episcopalian deacons couldn't exorcise," he said, "and to poultice fatal wounds doctors couldn't heal with conventional medicines."

"Back where we just passed, isn't that where your old house was?" I asked, anxious to hear how his version of its history compared to what my grandmother had recalled. As though he hadn't heard me, he further digressed, expanding on the local history. He spoke of Edgar Allen Poe's recollection of a journey he had taken in a skiff down the Wissahickon Creek in 1844, retelling it in a theatrical baritone as he imagined the poet's voice might have sounded: "The Wissahickon is of so remarkable a loveliness, that, were it flowing in England, it would be the theme of every bard, and the common topic of every tongue, if, indeed, its banks were not parcelled off in lots, at an exorbitant price, as building-sites for the villas of the opulent…"

He told these stories so convincingly that I couldn't discern when the truth ended and the bullshit began. I pretended as though they were true, however, coyly asking follow-up questions designed to bring Sam back to 1950: Where exactly was the cave? Will you take me to the creek sometime and show me the turns he paddled? Did we take walks there when I was a boy? He shrugged off my questions and wouldn't give me a direct answer, then gruffly announced it was time to get to work as we pulled up to the graveyard fields.

The cemetery occupied the blocks between Conarroe Street and Martin Street. The fields were fenced off from the parking lot to Roxborough Baptist Church, where Sam was a parishioner. He seemed impervious to the cold, needing only a thermal undershirt and a red-checked flannel work shirt layered over it to keep him warm. He backed the truck through the parking lot, then gave me a key to open the back fence gates. I released the truck gate and hopped up into the bed, stepping over a folded tarp and a bucket of steaming water. The six trees, baby dogwoods wrapped in burlap root-balls, held cement-like clods of compacted earth. Sam warned me to be careful as I handed them down, saying he had once hired a worker who allowed the metal wire handles encasing the burlap to slip off the truck with his fingers still in them. The man severed a nerve when his shoulder was torn out of its socket, and had to wear his arm in a cloth sling for the rest of his life. Sam pointed to the wheelbarrow. "Follow me," he said over his shoulder.

I leaned my shoulders down into my stance, carefully steering the heavy wheelbarrow around the granite monuments, cutting treads through the wet frost, flattening the onion shoots sprouting up through the winterkilled sod. Sam kept far ahead, pacing off yards in the distance as though he were a gold prospector warm on a clue. I hurried to keep up with him but he strode briskly for an old man. I took note of the fading Dutch and German surnames inscripted into the wind-eroded markers, some of them dating back to the 1700's. Were my forebears interred aside these family plots? Because I didn't want him to think of me as a slacker, instead of asking him all about the Cowell ghosts I pushed onward through the graveyard, propelled by a continuing desire to please him.

"Here's where it is, I think," he said, reaching a clear patch of yellow grass about twenty feet beyond a sunken tomb. He pulled a crumpled sheet of yellow legal paper from his pocket and studied it intently. Confidently, he shoved it back into his pocket and waited till I caught up to him. "Now, here's what you're gonna do: Dig a hole to the level of the root ball. Make it wide, about three times the size of the ball. Don't go any deeper than that. These roots will grow out of the sides of the burlap, and you can easily smother them if you don't give 'em enough breathing room.

"Before you stand the root in the hole," he said, "sprinkle

a little fertilizer into the backsoil-that's the soil you already dug out, then fill up the hole halfway with the dirt. Then, when it's halfway filled, what you want to do is pour a little water over the dirt to settle out the air pockets. Then fill the rest of it in. Each of these trees needs to be about ten feet apart. Think you can handle that?"

"No problem," I said, hoping to place him at ease by leaving me to do this job unsupervised. There were so many things to remember, but I was too prideful to admit that I had forgotten my orders in all the excitement. Instead of asking him to clarify, or scribble down the instructions, I nodded.

"Are you sure?" he asked.

"I got it."

"That's what I like to hear. I'll be back in about an hour to get you. You should be done by then." And with that he was off, muttering something about buying fertilizer.

I remembered the trees were to be ten feet apart, but in which direction were the rows to extend? The soil was hard with clay, and made digging difficult. I jumped on the spade, practically splintering my heel bones as I tried to loosen it. It took me a half-hour to dig the hole, and in that time I chafed open a blister between my thumb and forefinger.

Sam returned in an hour, as he said he would. He wiggled each tree, jerking the trunks to check their sturdiness. He stepped back, squinting at the row as though he were a surveyor marking boundary lines, or a golfer plumb-bobbing a putt. I waited for the adulation I sensed was forthcoming.

"Come here," he said flatly. A peculiar note sullened his tone.

I did as instructed, and he made me stand where he had.

"Do they look even to you?"

"Does what look even?"

"The trunks. Clean the shit out of your ears," he barked.

The abruptness of his scolding stung me. I squatted down to his eye level to survey my work again. True, some of the trunks were tilted askance, but only slightly, and certainly not enough of a deviation to call for the anger in his tone.

"Do it over," he said testily, grimacing.

"Excuse me?" I asked, forming the most demonstrably arrogant expression I could muster.

"Don't make me repeat myself," he said, standing and pointing a finger at me.

I stood my ground. "You said dig the hole three times as big as the ball."

"I also said not to dig the hole deeper than the height of the ball. Do it over right this time, and pay attention, for Christ's sake," he said, stomping to his truck.

I did as I was told, angrily replanting pursuant to his instructions. A fiery ache grinded at my lower back, and we weren't even halfway into the day yet. *Keep it up, old man. Just keep it up,* I thought.

But when he came back fifteen minutes later, he was all smiles and praises before he even had a chance to inspect my work. "I'm sorry if I sounded like an asshole earlier, Ted, but if any of these trees die, it's my balls they break," he said with self-reproach as we walked back to his truck. I could see I had struck a raw nerve. I let him continue, for I was elated by his approval, and sought to align myself against whomever it was that he was ranting, for it would shift the blame from me. "These fucking pastors and their little old lady bookkeepers are constantly breaking my balls," he said, gesturing toward the stained glass rectory windows. "They're probably looking out the window at us right now." He acted their part, in a fit of mimicry lifting his nose, adjusting his starchy collar. "Once, back when Dolores and I were first married, or maybe it was right after your mother was born and I was just getting the business underway, your grandmother used to get me to do a lot of free work for our old church, the First Baptist Church of Manayunk, down on Green Lane. You know, cut the yard, edge the beds, spring cleanups, whatever it took to drum up business through the congregation. Those were the days when we still used the roller mowers with no engines. And so I did it, thinking that all the freebies would pay off when it came time to do the big job. One day the pastor asked me if I would re-sod their yard, a big expensive job. I figured I had earned the chance to impress him by doing all this shit until that time for free. I had to lay out all this money for the grass seed, had to drive to a sod farm all the way near the Jersey Shore, and when I gave the pastor my bill, he looked at me, and do you know what he said to me, Ted? Do you want to know what he said?"

"Of course," I answered as he stared directly at me.

"He said, 'If I knew you were going to bill us, Sam, I

would have hired a professional landscaper.' I remember, it was August, and it had been so unbelievably fucking hot that day I had to pour my jug of water down my boots to cool off my feet. That's the thanks I get. That's the one thing you have to realize if you're going to run your own business, Ted. If you do work for less than people should pay you, they will offer less than you're worth, and take advantage of your kindness every time," he said, hoisting the wheelbarrow back onto the bed and shutting the latch.

I enjoyed the wisdom he imparted, forgave his feisty combativeness. He was a perfectionist, he said, and that was why he had more work than he could handle. I appreciated how he cut right through the bullshit, the hypocrisy of religion, and saw through to the business hustle in every transaction. There was bitterness in his spirit, but with a purposeful logic essential to it. By confiding in me, was he thinking of grooming a protégé? My need to impress the man was overtaken by a desire to have him like me. But how would I get this grizzled codger to respect a young draft evader that until this morning he seemed to detest? The only time I recalled seeing him smile was when he cracked the joke about the blacks that lived in Mt. Airy, and those remarks had stemmed from his disgusted take on the protests on Capitol Hill. So to bond with him I made the mistake of sharing anecdotes from the bizarre exhibition of insolent mockery toward authority I saw on campus the day the Temple administration voted to cancel classes.

EIGHT

Like the University of Washington, Temple was mired in the throes of a fervent antiwar movement. Bowing to pressures from student group leaders and faculty members upset with school policies, the administration cancelled classes one Friday in late March in observation of a "Day of Conscience." The daylong festivities called for a number of speeches on campus and meetings between student leaders and administrators to quell the disturbances before they turned violent. The rumor was that keynote speaker Jerry Rubin, outspoken leader of the Yippies, was to be arrested by the federal authorities for his conspiracy in inciting a riot at the Democratic National Convention in July.

But on the day Rubin spoke there were no police or national guardsmen present among the small crowd congregating on the campus walkway behind Barton Hall. I thought this was strange, considering the notoriety of the speaker at the podium. Rubin was short with black frizzy hair that poked haphazardly into the air. He wore a red and yellow Viet Cong flag cloaked around his shoulders and was surrounded by four angry-looking black henchmen, each with Black Power fist hair picks stuck through their Afros. They intently surveyed the audience beneath the podium and the grounds in front of Paley Library with the humorless and self-important expressions of secret service agents trained to sight assassins.

"Trying to stop college demonstrations is impossible because they are popular demonstrations. Unless you napalm campus demonstrations, what are you gonna do?" Rubin asked over the squealing amplifier feedback echoing harshly across the mall. He timed several seconds, allowing for the raucous applause that followed. "It's almost as impossible as stopping the Vietnam War!"

A student next to me handed over a white plastic bucket of loose bills and pennies. The words "Jerry Rubin Defense Fund" were scribbled on the side. I passed it along quickly without dropping in a dime. To me, what was most disingenuous about grandstanding hippies like Jerry Rubin and Abbie Hoffman was the undeniable spirit of capitalism that flourished beneath the camouflage of communist views these men preached. Here Rubin was, selfishly accepting handouts, when I knew his legal defense costs would be underwritten by some leftist, pro-bono legal organization like the ACLU. If Sam were here he would plunge a bayonet into Jerry's liver, I thought, a tinge proudly, as Rubin continued to rant, raising his voice to the crowd and flapping the flag like a bullfighter's cape.

"They really ought to indict the airlines. Let's face it, it's the fuckin' airlines who made Chicago possible. Chicago wouldn't have been possible without Youth Fare," he exhorted, pathetically needing to refer back to the convention to win applause the way a once-famous rock and roll band now playing the club circuit will inevitably encore their most popular top-forty hit. I looked around for any girls that might be approachable, but the few in attendance were devotees of Jerry's, riveted to his every last word. "America is on a suicide trip," he continued. "They're fighting losing wars, they're putting up with men like Johnson and Nixon. Did you ever meet a kid who said he wanted to grow up to be like Richard Nixon? All they've got left is Nixon and weapons. Schools are scared of ideas. What does that building say to you?" he asked, pointing to Barton Hall behind him. "It says do not fantasize, do not take off your clothes, do not say fuck, get good grades in class. The whole thing is a conspiracy to arrest the spirit."

I never conceived that I might be enlisted to partake in these rebellious activities, and that my participation would be an integral component of my grade. I didn't realize my mistake until after I had enrolled, when I read the course description for Field Session in Human Services: "Detailed examination of a Community Action Program and government anti-poverty operations, including programs on housing, health, crime, and employment. Directed student involvement through interviews, an internship and volunteer service is stressed." The description seemed vague and I had no idea what to expect from the course. I figured it would get me out of the classroom and into an internship at City Hall, or at worst, some other government office building of lesser prestige downtown.

We met once a week for three hours in the faculty offices on the second floor of Curtis Hall. The professor, Judah Cohn, a young Swarthmore-educated liberal, wore a yarmulke pinned to his wiry blonde earlocks and rimless spectacles he was constantly adjusting. He wore a "Free Huey" button on the lapel of the same leather fringe jacket he wore every day. He doled out assignments at the end of each class, which met once a week. Sitting cross-legged on his desk, he espoused radical views, urging us to take on the school administration and the government by submitting editorials to the *Temple News,* and articles to more extremist publications such as the *Liberation News Service.* He served as the unofficial faculty advisor to such student groups as the Resistance and Young Socialists Alliance, Young Americans for Freedom, and the more radical Temple chapter of Students for a Democratic Society. He even advised the Black Panther Party, helping them set up a local headquarters on Columbia Avenue in North Philadelphia. He hadn't taken attendance after the first day of class, and though there were only six of us, he never asked my opinion on the leftist ideologies he espoused. I wasn't disappointed by his lack of interest in me, for I was unmotivated to succeed when I saw that the only out-of-class internships offered, like volunteering for the United Communities of Southeast Philadelphia, or the Philadelphia Tutorial Project, were for assisting the inner city poor and offered little hope for advancement. Unprepared, I had hoped to slide through class unnoticed. But Professor

Cohn caught me off-guard, calling on me the Monday following Jerry Rubin's speech.

"Mr. Bundy, do you care to comment on the ineffectiveness-and I know I'm being overly euphemistic-of the Johnson administration's policies toward Vietnam. What with Nixon being sworn in last week and pledging to remove our troops from southeast Asia, what are your thoughts concerning the war? Do you believe in the sincerity of our newly elected President when he pledges to remove our boys from the jungle? And furthermore, Mr. Bundy, here on campus, regarding the five demands presented by the Steering Committee for Black Students to President Anderson-don't you feel President Anderson owes it to the black students to start a Black Studies program? And of course, Jerry Rubin's speech-what conclusions did you draw?" His tone had a confident liberal sneer, and he seemed enthralled by the fanciful grandiosity of his delivery.

All eyes were on me. I was excited, for it was not often lately that I found myself at the center of attention. Though I didn't want to alienate these mostly liberal students, my principles did not allow any leeway for intellectual dishonesty. "I will say this," I offered, further culling my mind for the most articulate yet neutral response I could muster. "Insofar as President Nixon is concerned, irrespective of one's political underpinnings, he deserves the benefit of the doubt. It's far too early for any of us to cast aspersions, and it remains to be seen whether he makes good on his promises. With respect to the second part of your question, as a white man I do not believe

I'm in a position to offer an opinion on what might benefit the Afro-Americans as might an Afro-American."

"What about Johnson and the Civil Rights Act? He was white."

"Was he not the one who took us into Vietnam?" I asked.

"Actually our involvement started with Kennedy."

"A Democrat also," I said.

"And Mr. Rubin's speech on Friday?"

"Funny you should mention that. I noted an editorial in the latest edition of the *Temple News* discussing that very topic. The author noted how ironic it was that Jerry, wearing that flag, so righteously endorses the cause of the North Vietnamese, yet does he know that the University of Hanoi dress code specifies that hair must be worn at a short length? There are also dress restrictions, and every student has to haul dirt two Sundays a month. Oh, and only children of Party members are eligible for scholarships."

"Interesting observation, Mr. Bundy. Your point is well taken. You always struck me as a Republican. I was right." But as we walked out after class, the professor said, "Mr. Bundy, I'll need to see you a minute."

I was flush with fear, suddenly regretting I had contradicted him, and that I came off as a smart ass. I cautiously approached his desk. He was neatening a stack of papers to put in his leather satchel. He looked up at me quickly, then back down, shuffling the sides and neatly patting the edges into place.

"I don't necessarily agree with your politics, Mr. Bundy, but I appreciate what you bring to the classroom. You're quite argumentative, and that's terrific," he said, placing the stack into a scratchy leather briefcase. "Have you ever given any thought of applying to law school, or maybe getting involved with the campus Young Republicans?"

"I've thought about it, but I own a landscaping business, and on top of that I have a two-year-old I have to feed. I just don't have the time," I said.

He smiled. "I think I have a solution to your conundrum. Now, how do I say this? I'll just say it: I wouldn't have any problem with you not showing up anymore. This is really a class for people that want to make a change on campus. With your politics, I just don't think you make a good fit with what we're trying to accomplish here. It's a pass-fail class. I'll pass you, if that's what you're worried about," he said. He gathered a clipboard naming a list of students taking a bus ride to the GI-Civilian Coalition rally to be held that weekend in Central Park, put the list in his briefcase, and condescendingly patted my shoulder. "Give it some thought," he said on his way out the door.

I was demoralized, had failed again, victimized by my own stupidity. The piercing sense of exclusion was not made any better knowing I would pass his course, just as the dean's promise to readmit me to the University of Washington if I kept my nose clean hadn't moderated my disappointment any. Instead, the professor's words kindled a deeper species of rage that had been mounting since I moved in with my grandparents. It wasn't the type of volatile emotion that required an immediate outlet that petty thievery, marijuana, or drinking binges would temporarily quell. Rather, it was an anger accumulating layers with each unfortunate episode, allowing itself room to expand, functioning on its own, growing stronger each time I tried to push it down and extinguish it. Alone in the battle to exorcise my festering demons, I foolishly sought an ally in my grandfather.

Like a child anxious to show his parents a good report card, when I saw Sam that evening in the kitchen I told him of the unpatriotic half-truths Rubin had spouted. He was unimpressed, acknowledging my recollection with shrug of indifference as he crushed a saltine cracker over his chicken-noodle soup. "So let me get this straight," he said, aggravatingly clicking the metal of the spoon again his front teeth as he slurped. "A liberal Hasidic Jew professor asks you a question, and instead of telling him what he wants to hear, you smart-off to him, and he tells you he doesn't want you back in his class."

"He gave me his word he would pass me."

"You're gonna take the word of a kike you wise-assed?" he asked with a mouthful of noodles, his mandible bones popping as he chewed. "Christ, you really know how to make friends, Ted Bundy, you really know how to make friends," he laughed to himself as he placed the dishes in the sink.

With that statement I gave up any hope of the man ever believing in me. There was simply no pleasing or predicting him. I couldn't help but wonder if he actually wanted me to dislike him, to resent him enough so I would maintain my distance and not muster up the confidence to ask any more questions about the family. Perhaps he sensed there was information I wanted to know, and was testing to see what lengths I would go find it. I refused to be discouraged, realizing the only thing that had earned me a glimpse of his admiration, albeit oddly displayed, was when I had replanted the dogwood trees to his satisfaction. To prove him wrong, to weaken his stubborn resistance, it became my mission to outlast him by exceeding his unrealistic expectations and outworking him at his own occupation.

Sam didn't warm to me by the time the weather grew hotter. He was intensely critical of my work, always pointing out what areas of the yard I had neglected in my haste to finish our spring cleanups in Chestnut Hill, where most of his clients lived. I had either torn the pachysandra vines while raking the leaves, or had forgotten to sweep the brick apron of somebody's back patio. Oftentimes he took my rake from me and stared pensively at it, yanking off the dead vines with the inspective glare of a tennis player picking at his strings to psyche out an opponent awaiting serve. Or he would dream up some last minute task for me to do while he talked to a customer, like spraying tar on a tree wound, or crawling under its branches to retrieve a stray leaf. When I saw it was his mission to take full advantage of my obvious desire for his acceptance, I switched tacks, aiming to outfinesse him with my resiliency, revealing to him the weakness of his old age by finishing before he did. He was usually working out back in his barn when I left for school, and when I came home he would pass sulkily by. He spent a lot of time in his barn. I'd watch him through the kitchen window each evening before he came in for dinner, padlocking the door, looking both ways, tugging at its hasp. Though intrigued to know what kept him cooped up out there, I dared not venture forth to visit him, as I was unable yet to accurately gauge his temperament or understand his remoteness.

Dolores was equally inaccessible. Judging by her candidness the night she drove me home from the airport, I figured as time went on she might share more stories with me of when I was a boy, or at least offer a fresh perspective on the father I never knew. But she did not, and was mostly uncommunicative. Except for the night when she picked me up from the airport, she never once left the house, and stayed sequestered in her bedroom during every spare hour she wasn't preparing meals. After scouring the dishes she would retreat upstairs and close the door, not to be seen again until the next morning. She gloomily shuffled down the halls in her slippers, wearing the same ratty bathrobe while clutching her hankie, stinking more every day like a stew of feminine perspiration, rubbing alcohol, and Vick's VapoRub. She became noticeably thinner as the weeks went by, constantly tightening her bathrobe belt around her narrowing waist. Widening circles of gray skin colored her eyes, and her skin dropped into a jowl that trembled with regret whenever she spoke. I knew that she didn't have a fever or was otherwise contagious with disease, for she didn't shirk or draw back from me when I went to kiss her goodbye in the morning. Whenever I sought a moment alone to ask what was ailing her, Sam always seemed to appear, his presence silencing her. When he walked out of their bedroom, he would allow himself the smallest area to exit, squeezing out the door and closing it quickly behind him. As for photographs, I saw none about the shelves, and even if there were any albums I dared not snoop to uncover them, fearfully remembering Sam's legendary uprisings. Each time I said to myself there was no way I'd last the semester, the fear of war crept upon me.

Despite his merciless criticisms, Sam didn't think my ineptitude was so severe as to end our arrangement, and took full advantage of his new field hand. And that's exactly what I felt like on many an afternoon, an indentured servant fresh off the boat from England, forced to till his master's soil. Get in, get out, became my mantra. I approached each day of work like a man sent upriver to do his time as painlessly as possible so he can return to his life as it was before his troubles began. This was the only attitude that would allow me the fortitude to persevere through this atmosphere of bleak desolation. Oftentimes I looked within myself to see what lessons there were to be learned from the monotonous constancy of my toilsome work. The only things I knew with certainty were that this wasn't what God had in plan for me, and that I had learned nothing more about my childhood in the months since I'd arrived here. Dolores gave me a Two Guys department store calendar she won for opening an account, but I stopped tallying the remaining days until the semester ended, for marking them off made time move slower.

NINE

Sam and I arrived at a client's home in Chestnut Hill on the Sunday before the last full week of May. A stately eighteenth-century colonial painted in white trim, it may very well have been the most magnificent house I had ever seen. The lavender azaleas under the first story windows were in full blaze, and a weave of ivy wormed up the brick façade, reaching past the second floor. Before we stepped out of the truck, Sam whispered, "Jack Dwyer, this Mick is something else. God Almighty, does he ever want to be a Main Line WASP. Look at the pants on this clown, will you?"

The man Sam spoke of was walking in front of his detached garage. He smiled at Sam, who hopped out of his truck to greet him. He was bald, about fifty, and wore leather boating shoes and seersucker pants with red ship anchor prints woven into them. Sam met him underneath the portico sheltering the front door. He followed him around the side of the house, listening and nodding as Mr. Dwyer gesticulated his landscaping design.

I had just finished emptying the grass catcher when a tall young blonde stepped out the front door. She was clad in a pair of crushed velvet flares and a sleeveless white shirt tied in a knot at her midriff. She walked toward the driveway apron and removed the cover off an Aston-Martin convertible, shaking out the pollen dust. I began thatching up a spot of dead grass near where she stood

"I hear you're visiting from Oregon or somewhere," she said.

I looked up, flattered that my name had been spoken in my absence, among these lush gardens and trickling lawn fountains. I was shy and at a loss for words in the presence of such a beautiful young woman. My isolated tenure under Samuel's domain had severely warped my acumen for charming ladies, I sadly noted, grappling for words that once would have flowed effortlessly.

"Sam told my dad," she said.

"I'm spending the summer here," I said. "My grandfather asked me to help him out. I'm pre-law at the University of Washington. I'm sorry, my name's Ted, by the way."

Her name was Avery. Stunning to behold, she had bewitching green eyes the shade of lake water shadowed by elms, and pouty lips I longed to reach over and kiss. Her white-rimmed sunglasses, designed as cat-eyes, were balanced on top of her forehead. She went to Rosemont College, a Catholic women's college near Villanova, and had just returned home from a semester abroad in Paris. Impeccably well-mannered, she seemed interested in what I had to say and listened compassionately when I confided that I was being treated like a galley slave.

"I never would've signed on for such torture had I an inkling that my summer would be anything like this," I said, leaning my weight on the rake. "It fucking sucks." I quickly apologized for my language.

"Oh, I'm sorry to hear that," she said, cocking her head to the side as if feeding sugar drops to a sick bird. "Well, a bunch of us are going to a midterm mixer at Drexel tonight. It starts at nine. It's only like a dollar or something to get in, if you'd like to join us."

Before I had a chance to ask directions or solidify plans, Sam reemerged from the backyard, stalking toward me. Avery whispered quickly, "Listen, if you can't make it tonight, my family has a place in Ocean City. If you can get down there, I usually go with my friends to the Ninth Street Beach. Look me up."

Here I was, a lowly landscaper's apprentice being invited to the beach! I recalled seeing advertisements for available summer rentals in Ocean City and Wildwood thumbtacked to the corkboard kiosks behind Sullivan Hall at Temple and on the notice boards outside the classrooms. Aware of his propensity for eruptions, I anticipated Sam and cast a backward glance toward Avery, who gave a quick wave, then threw on her sunglasses and started her car. Sam said loudly in her presence, "Let's go Romeo, we have work to do."

Steaming, I reached the truck before he did, even though we weren't in a rush to be anyplace.

"I saw you talking to Avery over there," he teased as we got back in the cab and drove off. Staring straight ahead, I sensed the weight of his eyes on me. He seemed eager to know what we'd spoken about.

"Yes, you most certainly did," I said irately. "You were standing right there."

"Somebody sounds a little pissed," he taunted.

"Did you really need to say that in front of her?"

"What did I say?" A wise-ass grin plastered his face.

"Call me 'Romeo' like that? Are you in some kind of rush, Sam? I thought this was our last job for the day."

"Look, I'm just trying to save you the time," he said. "Her fiancé goes to Wharton or something like that."

I didn't recall seeing Avery wear a diamond, for that had been one of the things I first looked for. And she mentioned nothing about a boyfriend, as women are quick to announce when they sense they are being prowled.

Calmly, Sam said, "Ted, let's play a little game here. For the next five minutes, I want you to look at the cars as we drive past them. Not the shit cars, which you won't find around here in any event. No, take a close look at the Caddies, the Mercedes Benzs, the Aston-Martins. Now with each car we pass that's driven by a female, I want you to tell me what each of these broads has in common."

I played along, looking over at the women strolling by the stores on the Germantown Avenue sidewalk. Two gorgeous tanned ladies with cable sweaters tied over their shoulders laughed as they slipped into McNally's Tavern. A woman in a red Mercedes convertible pulled alongside us. She had beautiful smooth skin, perfectly applied hot pink lipstick, and wore a madras headband. Grinning to herself, she was either too deep in thought to detect my scrutiny or doing her best to ignore me. I saw his point, but refused to indulge his satisfaction and acted the dumb, slow-witted grandson. They were strikingly beautiful, most of them.

"I give up," I said.

"Tell me, do you see any beasts driving these cars? Of course not. You know why? Because the husbands that own the cars have money, and as much as you hear lately all about this women's liberation shit, find a woman a rich man that can buy her a nice home in Chestnut Hill, and she'll forget all about her need to be liberated. It's just like my grandfather told me, Ted: Every woman is a whore, the only difference is their price."

"Looks like I'll just have to earn enough money to buy one of them," I said as our pickup truck rattled uphill past the Merion Cricket Club in Haverford. I gazed longingly at the canopied clubhouse terrace, arrayed in front with dozens of grass courts filled with thin, long-legged women in tennis whites, gracefully volleying.

"And people in hell want ice water," he retorted. "You're missing the point. You see, the shitty thing is, guys like you and me would never stand a chance with a gal like Avery. Haven't you ever read *On the Origins of Species*, by Charles Darwin?

The process of natural selection applies to humankind as well, my friend. The pretty ones get chosen by the rich men and breed with them. Ugly women don't get chosen, and are virtually extinct in towns like Chestnut Hill. Beautiful women from good homes understand this. It's bred into them. Even if you did all the things you were supposed to in order to get this Avery broad, to her you're still a boy from a working class family from Tacoma, Washington, and her old man belongs to the Union League in Philadelphia and has a house on the bay in Ocean City, and you don't. These are things you just can't change, Ted, no matter how hard you try."

"Maybe I do come from money. From what my mother tells me, my father was from old money. Which makes me, as his son, old money, right?"

For the first time I caught him at a loss for words. I sat quietly for a moment, offering him the chance to refute me. He gave me a darting glance as I awaited his reply, but said nothing more. He quickly jumped out of the truck when we got home. I decided I would pin him down with more direct questions after dinner, when he was more susceptible, watching television in a post-digestive narcosis.

As I was changing out of my work clothes, I heard something crash inside my grandparents' bedroom. I hurried down the hall and pressed my ear to their door. "Dolores, what's going on in there? Are you okay?" I opened the door when she didn't reply. The shades were drawn tightly so that no sunlight peeked through. My grandmother was slowly writhing on her bed, moaning. A broken lamp, its demolished bulb shattered, was scattered in pieces on the carpet. The smell of urine was overwhelming. She had torn the coverlet off and her shit was smeared on the bed sheets. Her nightgown, pulled halfway up her legs, revealed ankles stained with tiny red sores that looked like bug bites scratched raw. The skin on either side of her temple was irritated, as if surgical tape had been ripped from it. As her eyes shot toward me in a jittery stare of vulnerability and childlike wonder, dementia was the first malady that came to mind, either that or an epileptic convulsion.

"Sam, is that you?" she asked. "I'm sorry. How long were you standing there?" Glassy-eyed, she lifted her head and slowly pulled the coverlet to her chest, revealing a thick, shining blade scar where her left breast should have been.

"Just a few seconds," I said, contemplating how to maneuver through her delirium. "Are you okay?"

"I think so, just...trying to figure ...I forget things... where's Ted?" She gazed about the room, the ceiling, then down at her hands, orienting herself.

I listened for my grandfather. He was out back, hosing down the mowers. "He's out back, hosing down the mowers," I said, remaining to her side and out of her line of vision, aware she might snap out of her spell at any moment. I kneeled to the carpet and made as if I was picking up the pieces of the lamp. "Listen, Dolores, while we have a second, we need to talk about something," I said. "Ted's starting to ask a lot of questions about what happened to Olivia Farnsworth."

She reached for her night table and held her hand on the edge, as if grounding herself against a dizzying swoon. It was heaped with ooze-crusted cotton balls and gauze pads blotched with ointment stains. "What did you tell him?" she asked, still too infirm to twist her head in my direction.

"I told him I couldn't remember that far back. Can you?"

"Oh, Sam, I try not to," she said. "Did he mention anything about Cecelia?"

I paused, fumbling at the mention of this strange new name. I heard the *squeak squeak* of the backyard spigot turn, the pipes shudder as Sam shut off the water. When I looked directly at my grandmother again, she had sat up and was gazing at me. A twinkle of recognition passed across her cloudy stare. "Ted?" she asked. "How long have you been standing there?"

"Not long, really, I just wanted to make sure you were alright. You were talking to yourself."

"What was I saying?"

"You were whispering something about Olivia, or maybe her name was Cecelia. You kept saying, 'we need to tell our grandson, we need to tell our grandson.'"

She sighed and turned to her side, sobbing into her pillow.

"I'll go get Sam," I said, scooting out the room before she fully came to.

I found Sam squatting beside a mower turned on its side, dripping water. He was holding it in place while sharpening a mower blade with his free hand.

"Let me give you a hand," I said, propping the mower as he refitted the blade onto the screw mount. "Dolores thinks

I'm you. She kept babbling something about somebody named Olivia. Who's Olivia?" I casually asked.

"Dolores has her spells now and then," he said, drawing his fingernail perpendicular across the blade, testing it for sharpness. "I wouldn't worry about it if I were you." He quickly stood. His knee popped, and he winced and shook his leg "Go put this back in the truck," he growled, handing me the file before he went into the house, "and stop sticking your nose where it doesn't belong."

The next day my grandmother was nowhere to be seen. She didn't tell me that she was leaving, or where she had gone. A note placed on the kitchen table that morning left instructions to Sam for reheating a tuna casserole for dinner, and a pot roast for Monday. I asked Sam where he had taken her, for her car was still in the driveway. He glumly replied that we would talk about it that night after dinner, and we went to work.

He came into my room later the same evening. I was propped up in bed, memorizing lines from *A Long Day's Journey Into Night* for a scene in my Introduction to Theatre final on Monday. As if overcome by one of his abrupt mood shifts, he gleefully informed me there'd been monster-sized striped bass swimming in the Great Egg Harbor Bay, and suggested we try to fish some of them out of the tributaries the next morning.

"And afterwards I thought we might take a trip to the shore," he said. "One of my clients has a place in Ocean City. He's thinking of selling me his boat, and I want to take a look at it, maybe make him an offer. What do you say? Want to come along, take a day off from cutting?"

"Definitely," I said, enticed by the idea of a Saturday not spent mowing lawns. Even more exciting was the prospect of finally visiting the Jersey Shore, this place I had read of at school, heard about from Avery, and would finally get to see. Would we be visiting the Dwyers' at their beach house? Because I still had my suspicions of Sam's motives, I withheld my jubilation.

"Maybe afterwards we'll stop off and have a few beers. Make sense to you?"

"Makes sense to me."

"Okeydoke then. I'll get you up around six. I just need you to give me a hand with a certain secret project before we go there." He winked clandestinely. "It won't take long, but I'll need your help."

I agreed, of course, curious as to what this "secret project" entailed.

TEN

The following morning Sam filled a thermos of coffee for our road trip, and I grabbed two six packs of beer from the refrigerator. We hadn't made it to the end of Columbus Road before he had me hold the wheel as he poured whiskey from a flask into the thermos. Belching after a slug, he said we needed to make a stop in Chestnut Hill.

We pulled up to a large fieldstone home. The streets were quiet but for the soft tapping of sprinkler nozzles and the hiss of their rain wetting the grass. Sam reached toward the back seat, removing a crumbled lunch bag from under a pair of jumper tongs. He unrolled the opening, handing me four long nails and a hammer.

"Mr. Judson Trowbridge Webster," he said, parodying the regal-sounding name with haughty affectation, "has taken it upon himself to use the services of another landscaper this season, somebody local. Robertson's I think. You should've heard him on the phone yesterday, telling me my prices are

too high. I wanted to tell him to suck my dick, but he probably would've taken me up on the offer. Some of these Chestnut Hill trust-funders are cheaper than Jews, Ted. We'll just
have to teach Mr. Webster a little lesson now, won't we? Now,
these are copper nails," he said, holding one up for me to see.
"They're like poison to the trees. Rots them from the inside
out, worse than a fungus or Japanese beetle. By July these
leaves will have fallen off, and by August the trunk will start
leaning toward his house. By the time autumn rolls around,
Mr. Judson Trowbridge Webster will be calling Samuel Cowell
to the rescue. You'll see."

He handed me the nails and a hammer.

"Go ahead, he's not home," he coaxed through the window. "I'll keep the engine running."

The idea of trespassing didn't sit well with me. While I had
no specific knowledge what local or state laws I was violating, I
knew I had to stay out of trouble if I was to stay in good graces
with the dean. A stunt like this would surely get me kicked
out of Temple if they were to find out. I got out of the truck,
fearing repercussions if I didn't follow the old man's orders.
After all, the lines between when my workday ended and lei-
sure time began were never clearly drawn. A giant sugar maple
spanned partway over the street, its roots so old they cracked
open the sidewalk. I went to my knees and banged a nail into
the trunk, wrapping the hammer in a chamois cloth to muffle
the sound it made striking the nail head. Chips of bark flew
off and sap squirted onto my knuckles. I maintained a steady

clip so as not to appear nervous, saying good morning to a paperboy slinging morning editions from his bicycle.

When I finished, Sam ordered me to hit three nails through a large willow by the side of the house. I strode nonchalantly through the yard, charged with the same deliriously invigorating rush as when I was a teenager siphoning a tankful of gas from our neighbor's car. I forced myself to go slowly, as though I had every right to be here. Peering toward the drawn curtains of the neighbor's second floor window, I was aware that a light could go on at any second. My pace was squeamishly pleasurable, almost sexual in its gratification.

"Atta boy," Sam said, slapping my shoulder as I got back in the truck.

We crossed the Ben Franklin Bridge into New Jersey, meandering through the back roads to the Jersey Shore. We drove past tarpaper shanties and farmer markets whose vegetable stands were stacked with woven baskets brimming with early season fruit. The sleepy boondock hamlets, with rusted-out pickup trucks set side-by-side along gun clubs closed until deer season, reminded me of villages I'd seen on the narrow logging roads leading to the Cascade Mountain ranges. Poor rural living among secrets steeped in incest and witchery, these wilds seemed to hold. Noting the abundance of Italian flags painted on the rickety road signs in Hammonton, I asked my grandfather about the town's historical origins.

"Ever eat a Jersey tomato?" he asked.

Understanding the inference to be drawn by his tone, I

waited for the punch line, zingers he reserved for the Blacks and the Irish.

"Fuckin' dagos grow the best fruit, I tell 'ya Ted," he said. "It's in the soil. Sandy soil. That's all you need to know about Hammonton. That and blueberries. And asparagus, can't forget asparagus."

In Tuckerton, the scent blew warm with the breeze of the tides and the burning of yard fires. We turned right before a narrow drawbridge at the Tuckahoe River, bouncing down a desolate sand road flanked by cattails. We parked the truck at a trailhead that began where the paved road ended and hauled our gear to the banks of a mossy peninsula. Between us we carried two poles, Sam's tackle box, and a styrofoam cooler slithering with live eels we'd purchased from a bait shop in Mays Landing.

Seeming kinder than before, Sam initiated me into the rituals of fishing, showing how to distinguish between a fish biting and the tide pulling at my line. After tying our lines with sinkers, he baited my hook, puncturing a slithering eel through its tail. This way it wouldn't turn into a ball and knot the rigging, he explained. He removed a burlap cloth from his pocket and gripped another eel, holding it away from him. Its slimy green coat glinted in the early light as he knelt down and picked up a paring knife. Flicking at the throat, he gently popped an artery. A stream of blood sluiced down its gill slits, trickling down Sam's wrist. He dropped the fish back into the bucket, where it sloshed for a moment, then lay still. I asked him why he'd done this.

"Bleed it, get the stripers sniffing it. Tenderize the meat a bit, too," he said, the woodsman in him letting the consonants fall lazily off the sentence's tail. He showed how to cast the leaden rig out into the middle of the river. I did as he had, opening the arm on the spinning reel, cradling the line with the crook of my forefinger, letting go the instant I brought the rod over my shoulder. The current moved the rig a bit, drifting it upstream with the tide.

"I understood your grandmother gave you quite a scare yesterday afternoon," he said after a time.

"I had no idea something was the matter. I mean, I did, to the extent that she's always holed up in your bedroom or moping, but I was just too busy to think anything was wrong."

"Lately it's worse," he said, reflecting. "She's getting out patient treatments at Ancora Psychiatric Hospital in Hammonton. There's days she won't get out of bed," he ruefully added. As for Ancora, Sam said it was made infamous by one of its patients, a World War II combat veteran named Howard Unruh, who gunned down thirteen people in the span of ten minutes outside of his Camden, New Jersey home.

I was mystified to learn Dolores was holed up in some lunatic asylum in rural New Jersey, and told Sam so. Knowing she was under the same roof as a mass murderer cast a further gloom over her condition. That she didn't suffer from cancer, he assured, or any other sickness that might signal an alarm that an end was near, didn't temper my inquisitiveness. He said there was a faster route we could have taken to the shore, down the Atlantic City Expressway, but in order to understand how Dolores had fallen ill, I would first need to know the odd direction he had taken to meet her. Standing next to me in the brightening morning haze of his homeland, and with the fish not hitting our lines, Sam revealed his ancestry.

He had just returned home from France in 1918, where he had fought with the 79th Division of the American Expeditionary Forces under General Pershing. He lost the pinkie finger of his right hand to enemy fire while fighting to secure the German observation post atop the Abbey ruins at Montfaucon, and his sense of smell after trooping through one too many lingering clouds of mustard gas. His wartime heroics earned him a bronze medal, and upon his return from overseas a job at a munitions plant deep in the woods of Atlantic County, where he was born.

Sam traced our Scottish roots back as far as Gordon Lemuel Cowell, an ousted tenant farmer who emigrated to the inland rivers of Burlington County, New Jersey from the Isle of Skye in late 1774. A skilled wood craftsman, Gordon immediately found work at a shipyard near the Batsto River, where he crafted the boats the privateers used to sack the British Navy warships sent over to collect tariffs from the colonists. But like other rogues tempted by the lure of easier money, Gordon became a pirate before the one-year anniversary of his arrival here. He roamed the seacoast in a handcrafted schooner, auctioning his pillaged cargo on the Mullica River docks. The journals he left behind were unclear as to why exactly, but Gordon abandoned his work as a merchant smuggler to join up with Joseph Mulliner and the Pine Refugees, a dastardly assortment of outlaws that roved the upland pines in search of homes to plunder and young women to rape. They shot and killed anyone who tried to stop them, retreating to their hideout in the thickets of Mordecai Swamp. One of Gordon's conquests, a fourteen-year-old Baptist girl named Mary Elizabeth Jones, gave birth to Samuel's grandfather, the peaceful Joseph Samuel Cowell, who, like his father, led a vagabond existence in pygmy pines of Burlington County, living in a weatherboard hovel and surviving off rattlesnake meat and snapping turtles he cooked over a smudge pot that kept him warm in the winter.

My grandfather's dad, Samuel Joseph Cowell Sr., was born in 1832, moving two counties south when he grew older, staking a claim in Atlantic County. A bachelor his entire life, he fathered Sam at the age of sixty-six on September 23, 1898, with the seventeen-year-old mother dying of a fever infection while giving birth. His father reared Sam and a mentally retarded brother on the money he earned operating numerous corn whiskey stills along the tributaries of the Great Egg Harbor River. The batch, which he bottled and sold to the fisherman at the Cape May wharves, was said to have mystical properties, much like Mexican tequila, earning him enough money to feed and clothe his growing sons. But in the end the brew proved too potent, engulfing him in flames when he accidentally detonated a boiler.

Upon his return from the war, Sam built himself a cabin on the land that had been his father's, even though a deed was never passed down to him and the title was cloudy. He worked briefly at the Amatol shell-loading plant in nearby Belcoville until it closed down soon after the armistice was signed. He lost everything when his cabin, built on a flood plain, went under in a storm surge. Fortunately his veteran's status continued to pay dividends, earning him a job stacking toilet paper rolls at the Scott Paper Company factory in Chester, Pennsylvania, where he met my grandmother.

Dolores had also just changed jobs. Dismissed from the Angora Baptist Orphanage when she turned sixteen, she found work as a maid for Endicott Reese, the head of a Bryn Mawr family who lived on a horse farm in Kennett Square and owned several of the textile mills that overlooked the tow canals at the foot of the Green Lane Bridge. One night, the owner's wife, May Wilton Reese, a menopausal lush with a preference for straight bourbon, slapped Dolores before a roomful of guests after she dropped the Thanksgiving turkey carvings onto a guest's lap at the Reese's annual "Home for the Holidays" party. Repentant, Dolores begged for Mrs. Wilton's forgiveness. She promised to atone for her sins by staying late at night and teaching the Endicott children how to write cursive, a skill that had been passed down by her own parents, who both taught grammar at the first one-room schoolhouse in Roxborough. One night during an evening blizzard, when the roads were too icy for the butler to drive Dolores home to her West Chester rooming house, May tricked Dolores into staying the night. She was waiting in the guest quarters when Dolores turned in, having her way with her that night and all that week, as Endicott had left for his yearly visit to the Memphis warehouses where he selected the cottons to be used at his mills. Just fifteen, too naïve and submissive to know any better, Dolores endured the woman's gropes until they grew more assaultive. She slipped out one night under the cover of darkness and found work at Scott Paper Company. Distinguishing herself from the other ladies in the steno pool, she landed a full time position, serving under company President Arthur Hoyt Scott as his Gal Friday, which duties included delivering the payroll checks to the floor manager. It was there that she made her acquaintance with my grandfather.

After marrying, Sam and Dolores moved to a tiny row home in Manayunk, where Dolores gave birth to my mother in 1924. To raise the large family Sam expected to father, he built the house on Ridge Road in 1925, back when most of the area was undeveloped farmland. In his spare time he picked up shifts at Valley Green Nurseries across the street. He found working outside in the fresh air invigorating, preferring it to the pulpwood stench of the paper mill. He also discovered a talent for landscape design. Customers began seeking his advice as to what shrubs and flowers would grow best in the shade, which geraniums would die with the first harvest frost, and which mums were most hardy and resilient to October's sudden temperature plunges. Through a network of references acquired at the nursery and with the work he got from his church congregation, his business prospered, spreading into the wealthy sections of Northwest Philadelphia.

*   *   *

As Sam came to the end of his story, it was as though he had thrown on the brake switch to a long and exhilarating coaster ride. I was awed by how he'd pulled himself up by the bootstraps, proud that he and my grandmother had resiliently surmounted every obstacle set in their path.

"Your grandmother is a lost cause," he said, retreating from the heroic shadows he had cast. "She'll never come back from the place where her mind is now." His voice trembled. "Never did get over that old Reese bitch raping her. Stuck in her mind like sludge. She had bad night terrors for a while. When they didn't go away, we decided on the shock therapy. Imagine having volts of electricity piped through your brain. It makes her forget things. Not like what she had for breakfast yesterday, but whole years she can't remember. And then there was her surgery. I mean, imagine for moment you're a woman, and the doctor tells you they have to cut your breast off? It's like the doctor telling you they have to slice off your nuts, and for the rest of your life you can't shoot a load."

I was stunned to hear Sam reveal something so intimate and private about his wife. With his guard down, enfolded in the rapturous momentum of family memories, I decided now would be as good a time as any to ask about my father.

"Did you ever tell my father about all this?" I asked.

"Your dad," he said, bending over to hook more bait, "was an interesting character."

"Interesting how?"

"Well, yes indeed, it was a sad day for all of us when he

died. You couldn't have been more than one when we got the call that his plane had gone down."

"Huh, that's weird. Dolores said I was three when he died. I had heard it was a boating accident."

"One, two, three-years-old, that's a long time ago we're talking about," he said, prying off a can of beer from a six pack, cracking the top and blowing the suds off the opening.

"Was he rich?"

"He came from a fairly well-to-do family out near Lancaster, I think. Was he rich? No. In fact, he and your mother were living at our house when we heard of the accident." He emptied the entire beer down his gullet without a breath, slurping the last drops out the bottom.

"How did they meet?"

"Christ, how the hell do I know how they met, Ted?" he said disgustedly. "And really, who gives a flying shit? You're here, aren't you? You weren't born a retard, you weren't raised in an orphanage. Here, drink this," he said, handing me a warm Schlitz.

I didn't get a nibble on my line the rest of the morning. My hook kept getting tangled in weeds and other aquatic obstructions I mistook for bites. The crabbers on the drawbridge were having better success, reeling in their pots and pouring their catch into fruit baskets and ice chests. By noon we began packing our things, dumping the remaining eels into the river, where they scooted away like minnows darting under bridge shadows. I contained my excitement, for I knew this meant we were on our way to the beach, even if I didn't yet know who we were going there to see.

But instead of following signs toward Cape May, Sam returned in the direction of Camden, stopping for lunch at a crab shack named Timber Doodles, a few miles away. The parking lot of the log cabin restaurant was empty except for a pickup truck. The inside, warm with kitchen heat and smelling like boiled seawater, was set up with wobbly picnic tables lined with red and white checked paper tablecloths. The panelled walls were draped with foam buoys and starfish woven into fishnets. We seated ourselves at a horseshoe-shaped bar that centered the restaurant. The only other customer in the place was a skinny young man outfitted in denim bib overalls and a hooded sweatshirt. Wearing an orange hunting cap worn backwards, he occupied a corner stool at the other end of the bar. He looked up for a moment to eye us as we sat, and I nodded to him. I figured it was wise to be friendly toward these country folk in their own backyard. He returned my gesture, continuing his discussion with the bartender, a chunky middle-aged woman with large eyeglasses. Along with the man, she had been watching the broadcast of the game between the Phillies and Cincinnati Reds on the black and white TV above the bar. She pleasantly greeted us, placing two menus and a roll of silverware before us while rattling off the specials. Sam ordered Yeungling beers and the all-you-can-eat blue claw crab special for us both. The woman disappeared into the kitchen, returning moments later with a platter of steaming crabs.

"Where you boys from?" the young man from across the way asked.

It was just the second time since coming to Philadelphia that anybody had asked where I was from, and I was receptive to such openness. Already forgetting that Sam was raised in these parts, and being a tad groggy with brew, I confessed I was from Seattle, and to our lack of success fishing stripers. He wanted to know the exact location we had been fishing.

"You're too far inland for stripers," he said, speaking in that same twangy dialect Sam had fallen into. "You need to go down into into Cape May County. Try them sod banks in the back bays. Down at the rips last weekend they were beating the shit outta my bucktail. Up here you'll only catch a few stray tog, mostly pickerel. What were you using for bait?" he asked Sam.

"Eel," Sam answered, without looking up from his plate.

"Why'd you use eel? Eel's great in the fall, but not this early in the season. This early in the spring they bite at surf clams and sandworms. Or you could try jiggin'a bucktail with a piece of shedder crab, but they're not in season till July. "

Sam said nothing as the man rode him. I thought it best not to contradict him or bring him into a foolish light by remarking that he had selected the wrong type of bait.

"Nope, you won't catch no stripers here, old timer. You gotta go out to the surf for them," the man continued, his chuckle interrupted by a coughing fit that bulged the veins in his neck. "But not here. Definitely not here."

Sam was deceptively silent, withstanding the dig at his

age with a show of good sportsmanship. I worried his thin smile betrayed his true cunning, a germinating rage he was using to buy time while contemplating a biting comeback. He had stopped eating and was looking straight at the man, who had returned his attention to the ball game. Tony Taylor had muscled a high slider over the left field wall of Veterans Stadium to put the Phillies ahead in the eighth inning. Fearing Sam's reaction, I politely indulged in harmless conversation, attempting to deflect the missiles:

"When's the best time of the year to fish here?" I asked.

"Our striper season usually ends around December," he said. "Twenty-five pound stripers, you might get some stray tog, yeah, catch tog out there. Tog tastes like steak. Great fish, man. Can't go wrong, can't go wrong. Can't buy striper. You can fish it, catch it and eat it, but you can't buy it. No big fish, though. Trawlers, they take all our fish. Law states three miles offshore, they come in close to drag the bottoms. I say 'look, I can see you're doin' it,' but they do it anyway. Down in Cape May they do more trawling."

I told him we had passed a sign for whale watching charters operating out of Cape May.

"Whales? No whales here. Ain't no fucking whales around here! Gulf Stream is thirty, maybe forty miles off coast. When it comes up in summer, all tropical fish come up. Oh, we got fish, we got fish."

I was watching Sam out of the corner of my eye. Squinting, slacking his gaze, then squinting again, he did not take his eyes off the man.

"Are you a hunter?" I asked.

"We hunt, yeah, we hunt deer mostly. My buddy got a ten-pointer on Doe Day. He's got the head in the freezer. Between us, we got twenty-eight deer all cut up into sausages, burgers, pies," he said, heavily salting his fries.

"Last year, right out here I reeled in a thirty-pound striper using grass shrimp," Sam broke in, loudly cracking a shell.

"That's weird, I thought only weakies bit on grass shrimp," the man said, giggling skeptically.

"What did you say your name was?" Sam interrupted.

"James," he mumbled.

"James what?"

"Philpot," he answered louder.

"What?"

"Philpot," he mumbled again.

"Philpot," Sam said. "That sounds like a nice Anglican name. Philpot," he repeated to himself. "And your first name again?"

"Jim. James. Look, it doesn't really matter."

"It doesn't matter what your name is?" Sam asked, loudly sucking the spicy batter off his fingers as he continued to ride the man, now staring blankly at the television. "I'm just trying to understand a little bit about you is all. Do you go to college?"

"Nope."

"Don't go to college. Hmmm. Let's see, how old are you?"

"Twenty-one."

"Twenty-one. Have you registered for the draft?"

"Of course."

"Well if you've registered for the draft, like you say, and you aren't in college, you would be classified as A1, which means you should be in the war fighting for your country like other young men your age, instead of sitting on your keister drinking white Russians, am I right? Am I right?"

The man's face deepened with redness, but he smiled, as though trying to fake the impression that he understood a joke everyone in the room was getting except him.

"Unless, of course, you're evading the draft, right? Am I right? AM I RIGHT???"

The waitress placed her hand on Jim's wrist, stopping him as he started to push from his chair. She opened up a hatch and let herself out from behind the bar, walking up behind him. She hooked her hands under his armpits, saying, "Up, one, two, THREE!" then lowered him down to where I couldn't see him. After a pause, he appeared again, rolling toward us in a wheelchair. He lifted out a dog tag from under his t-shirt, facing it toward Sam, who bent downward, gently turning over the plate and focusing on the stamp-bitten inscription.

"Jesus, son, how'd this happen?" Sam asked, compas-sionately eyeing the legless young man sitting before him. "Land mine get you?"

"Front end of a Camaro."

On leave for two weeks, he was driving home from a bar one night when his car blew a tire. He and a friend were so drunk and the woods so deep and dark, it was too late before they realized they were parked halfway into the middle of the road. Jim was leaning over his trunk, searching for the spare tire jack, when the headlights came up behind him.

"Next thing I know, I'm in a hospital bed," he said, his eyes wetted, distant. "My ex-girlfriend, my parents, and brother were in the room, and my ex was crying hysterically. I knew right then something was bad, really bad, because why would she be in the room, her of all people? Then the doctor came in and sat down on the side of my bed and asked everybody to leave the room. 'There's no easy way to say this, young man,' he said, looking down at my legs. I just sort of went numb when he said they had to come off, could hear my mother shrieking in the hallway when he left the room and told her. Then my dad came in. I could see how he was holding back tears. That hurt worse than the news, because I hadn't ever seen him cry before. But you know what the worst was? It wasn't the realization that my legs had to be amputated, or watching my family agonizing like they were. It was when they wheeled me in for surgery. I was looking up at the lights, and when I saw the anaesthesiologist reach for my arm I had a change of heart, wanted to save my legs after all. But this guy worked so fast, before I could say anything he had already stuck me with the needle and told me to count backwards from ten. I remember that feeling right then; not the fear of having no legs for the rest of my life, but of helplessness, it being too late to change my mind. It'll be a year coming up Memorial Day weekend. I get veteran's benefits, so it's not so bad. I bought my truck with the insurance settlement. Anyhow, I just didn't want you to think we don't serve our country in these parts. I was a ground pounder with the 14th Field Artillery, 6th Battalion. We were headquartered two kilometers south of Phu Cat Airbase."

Without engaging in soldierly camaraderie, or sharing the story of his maiming by enemy fire, Sam hastily terminated the conversation. "Good luck to you, my friend," he muttered, tossing down some bills and hurrying us out the door.

Unsheathing the same knife he had used to slice bait and open his crabs, Sam poked the blade point into the side of the tire on Jim's pickup truck. The escaping gasses hissed loudly as the frame lowered, startling a coyote spying us through the roadside brush. He gashed the other three inner tubes in succession. Then, behaving as though I wasn't there, he jumped into his own truck, turning over the engine. I believe he would have stranded me there had I not hopped in at that moment. I would have let him be, kept silent witness to his crime, had he lived up to his word. But when I saw that we were heading back home instead of going to the shore, as he had promised, I asked, "How could you do that to a cripple?"

"Don't be so naive. He's a lying piece of shit."

"How so?"

"I know as sure as God made green apples that it was the 15th Field Artillery Regiment, not the 14th, which was headquartered at Phu Cat. And it was the 7th Battalion, not the 6th. I know because my buddy Billy Jackson at the Legion, his nephew was in the Fighting 15th and got killed by a sniper near the Bong Son River, just north of there. Which leads me to conclude the prick probably lied about that car accident also."

"For Christ's sake Sam, the guy won't walk for the rest of his life," I said, without admitting that I hadn't seen any shrapnel scars or bullet wounds on Jim's arm either. But what really angered me was Sam's lying about going to the shore. Was there something I said that caused him to change his mind? Or did he never have intentions of taking me to the shore in the first place?

"He lied about serving his country, which is a disgrace more dishonorable than running off to Canada, as far as I'm concerned," he spewed.

"Lying, Captain Sam? What about that boat you were going to buy?"

"No wonder you two faggots were bullshitting it up back there." He turned sharply, avoiding a collision with a bounding deer. "You have draft dodging in common."

"Did I run off to Canada?"

"Then you want to enlist? I can make a call to the draft board in Philly. Or maybe you'd like to go down there yourself? That way you'll get your choice of what division you want. Here, let me give you the address. Write this down." His eyes aglow, he searched excitably for a pen, finding one clipped to the sun visor above his head. "It's called the Armed Forces Examining and Induction Center at 401 North Broad Street." Holding the wheel with one hand, he rapidly scribbled the address on the front side of a prayer card. "I took the liberty of looking it up for you earlier, it'll save you the time so they don't have to come looking for you." He flung the pen at me, nearly losing control of the truck.

I longed to crush his ego. But where were the sore spots on a man who had seen all that Sam had? What words would hurt worst? He had fought heroically, been wounded battling for his country, started a successful business from nothing, and answered to nobody.

"Maybe on my way to being inducted, I'll stop by the American Legion and tell your buddies that you were conspiring to help me avoid the draft," I said. "Better yet, I'll call the Plymouth Township Police Department and let them know about the nails you had me hammer in the tree. How's that sound to you, old timer?"

"And who do you think they'll believe, me or a draft-dodging coward? You did that on your own while I was writing up invoices. Threaten me like that again and I assure you I will rip out your frontal lobe and shove it up your fucking nostrils."

"You're calling *me* a coward, old timer?" I hollered, hanging to the door handle as Sam sped along the narrow turns. "You have me do your dirty work and you have the balls to call *me* a coward?" Laughing bitterly, I didn't hold back, digging deeper. "The sad thing is, old timer, that in two months from now I'll be back in Seattle and you'll still be here, one year closer to your death. How old are you now, anyway? Seventy? Seventy-five? I would think that old ticker of yours could give way at any second, seeing how hard you try to push yourself out there in that sun. When's the last time you've woken with a hard on? When's the last time you've had to stand at a toilet in the middle of the night and wait till your dick goes down so you can piss? Can you remember that far back?"

He curled his upper lip under his front row of teeth, gripping the steering wheel tighter. His knuckles whitened. He turned sharply off the road, knocking my shoulder against the window handle as he slammed on the brakes. Reaching into his front pocket for a book of matches, he had difficulty steadying his hands as he tried to strike a match. As it caught, the blooming white flame drew sparkles across his glimmering eyes. He held match and book out before him, alternately eyeing each piece as if one were a dove, the other his magic hat. He touched the flame to the book, watching mesmerized as the phosphorus flared, stagnating in a rancid sulfur cloud.

"As far as dirty work, this should make us even, don't you think?" he asked, stretching his arm out the window, holding his hand underneath a pine branch until the needles ignited. He said coolly, "One week, Mr. Bundy, you have one week to get out of my house. I knew this was a bad idea from the get go, but I went along with it anyway." He shook his head in disgust, banging it on the steering wheel, muttering as the flames caught the branches. "I knew this was a bad idea, letting you stay here. In your short life, you've really accomplished nothing, as far as I can tell. You're lazy, untrustworthy, disrespectful, sneaky, but most of all you're perverted. Even as a young boy, we could all see there was something very wrong with you. And the awful things you said to that young lady out in Washington, it's a wonder they would even *consider* allowing you back in. But your life is for you to figure out, Ted. I've tried to give you some guidance, and I have failed. You have failed. You have failed me, and you have failed your family. It certainly will be interesting to see what becomes of you."

The cab quickly trapped with wood smoke, burning my eyes. "How will you know what becomes of me?" I asked. "You'll be dead by then, Sam Cowell. A dead old man. Nobody will put flowers on your grave because nobody will care that you're dead. Weeds may grow from your plot, but flowers won't be able to withstand the poison your spirit breathes, Sam Cowell."

His punch struck with the force of a robust street bully. A volcano of stars fuzzed my vision, reverberating waves of pain through my jaw. As my mouth went salty with blood, I spit a shard of tooth into my hand, fascinatedly gazing at it for a few seconds as though it were my appendix preserving in a jar of formaldehyde. A handkerchief fell into my lap. I held it pressed against my gums, swallowing blood. I leaned my head back, less concerned with the increasing throb in my jaws than with the resonance of Sam's declaration. He had set a timetable for me, leaving me but one week to scour the house before I would be turned out. I would have to be craftier, stealthier in my quest for documents, photos, buried information. I would have to press him harder. But how could I, now that I had wedged so great a distance between us?

Eleven

I declared an unspoken truce with Sam, as though bound to silence by our deeds. I slept until dinnertime the day after our altercation, and when I woke, a hot/cold compress was on my night table, along with a bottle of aspirin and a glass of water. I hobbled melodramatically downstairs to the kitchen to fill the compress with ice. A plate of roast beef and mashed potatoes covered in tinfoil was on the table for me. Sam was finishing his meal. Saying nothing, he smiled regretfully, as though together we had endured no more than a decadent night of drinking. I returned his expression, feeling equally remorseful for the disobedient comments that had egged him on to slug me. In some oddly distant way I felt guilty, as though I deserved my chastisement, and even more so, his corporal punishment. Before quietly putting our dishes in the sink, he passed me a section of the *Philadelphia Daily News*. The blaze eclipsed nearly ten acres of forest, burning down a stable and killing a foaling mare. Atlantic County officials were looking into the possibility of arson, but their statement offered no further details.

I made it for my scene study final that Monday afternoon. Our scene went surprisingly well. Though in pain, I mumbled through the lines as best I could remember, impressing my professor enough to receive an A, which he posted outside his door immediately following class.

Though finished with classes, I stayed home from work on Tuesday, offering Sam no explanation for my absence. I used the time to search the hall closet, the attic, Sam's sock drawers, and Dolores's undergarments. I memorized their exact placement, returning each item to the same position. I looked through garbage bags filled with old linens in the basement crawl space, thinking they might contain mementoes still unpacked from when my grandparents had moved here from Ridge Avenue. I found nothing-no toys, coloring books, anything suggesting a boy had once lived there or here.

Giving myself one last chance to pry the truth from Sam, I returned to work on Wednesday morning with the hope that his lingering guilt would bear fruit. We were planting juniper bushes for Eileen Harrison, a kind but fussy coot who'd already come out on her porch two times to monitor our progress. Because she was a neighbor and one of Sam's first clients, he tolerated her demanding prickliness out of a sense of loyalty. I'd heard the weatherman forecast showers in the afternoon, but at noon the sun was blazing, burning Sam's neck and shoulders the color of supermarket ham. My hands were raw from needle stings and my arms were scraped with juniper burns. Overcome by a dizzy spell caused by my aching jaw, I stole to a shady tree in the backyard, resting until the vertigo passed. Sam hollered my name as I was refilling my thermos with spigot water. Reverting to form, he sounded like a grudging desk sergeant. I obediently answered his call and came out front, fully expecting to be berated and ordered to step it up. But when I trod over to him, his tone lightened.

"I need you to go back to the house and get some rock salt," he said. "Eileen is worried about her driveway freezing. She thinks it's gonna snow tonight. I know, I know. She's senile. It's eighty-eight fucking degrees in the shade, but she thinks it'll snow. I'm getting ready to tell this biddy to go take a shit in her hat, but she does remember to pay her bills on time. Maybe this will shut her up. I don't think I have any salt leftover from the winter, but there might be some in the barn." He took the key off its ring and handed it to me. He told me where he thought the rock salt might be, near or around his workbench, or in the chest of drawers he was refinishing. "Bring it back here, and when you walk past her just waggle it in front of her face, that should shut her up." We both laughed conceptualizing this, perhaps quietly rejoicing our unstated reconcilement. Recalling how he had always taken pains to lock up his barn tight as a drum, I played it cool when I accepted the key to his fortress, not giving away my hand. I was well aware that I was running out of time, and that I would soon be moving back to Seattle. Out of nowhere had come the perfect opportunity to do a little snooping.

The dim barn smelled of stale grass clippings and burnt engine oil. I kept the door open, guided by the trembling shadows trickling through the backyard trees. I carefully stepped over mower parts, a detached snowplow, and a metal lathe disassembled across the leak-stained boards. Searching for a light, I had to crick my neck so as not to bang my head on the overhead loft. I found a hanging work lamp swung over a post beam. I switched it on and looked behind stacks of old newspapers bundled in twine, paint cans, in a milk cooler filled with polishing rags, and then underneath his workbench. After searching in the crannies and spaces Sam had suggested, and still not finding any rock salt, I pulled on a rope that let down a folding set of stairs and wriggled up through the opening.

The loft was scattered with fresh mice droppings and crumpled beer cans. I crawled over an old sled lying next to a ten-speed bike balanced upside down in the corner, its spokes cruddy with mummified daddy longlegs. Behind the front wheel were two wooden wine crates packed with Playboy magazines. Each issue, wrinkled from handling and smudged with fingerprints, was dogeared at the *Little Annie Fanny* cartoon strip in the back pages, with the busty blonde's exposed breasts circled in magic marker. A cigar humidor containing film negatives lay underneath a separate pile of centerfolds. Holding up one of the strips to a faint thread of sunlight beaming through a hole in the wall, I could make out the outline of a nude female with long curly hair tumbling over a set of pointy breasts. The picture was grainy and faded by storage, so

I couldn't fathom how old she was. Lying on a bed, her feet in the air behind her ears, she was smiling, her knees locked and toes curled. As she had a fair amount of baby fat and a downy coat of vaginal hair, I thought she might be in her young teens, but her pose was struck by someone more confident in her sexuality. I noticed an object clamped between her labia. It did not seem like a dildo, for it was too thin, stood straight, and had no curve to it.

I went down the stairs, taking the negatives with me for further examination later. The chest of drawers Sam had mentioned was sheeted under a turpentine-stained drop cloth near the barn door. I pulled the covering off the furniture and found the salt in the space between the furniture and the wall, beside a spilled jar of pennies. Curious to see what else might be kept hidden here, I opened one of the top drawers, where I noticed a large Tupperware container. An unmarked, letter-sized manila envelope was inside. I spilled the envelope's contents onto the workbench, finding an old black and white photograph of a large white house. It stood on a small knoll, with a greenhouse of sorts behind it. The second story was shabby, with exposed patches of flaking stucco and crooked black shutters. The house looked familiar, but as to how exactly I couldn't say. A date, *1961,* was sketched in pencil on the back. Another photo was caught in the fold of a book of matches whose cover read *Astor Bar.* It revealed a youngish man in his thirties, with slicked hair and perfect teeth, wearing a three-button suit with a regimental-striped tie. I recognized the buildings behind him from advertisements and movie backdrops, but not the person. I checked the back: *Jack, Astor Hotel, Times Square, 1952.* Who was Jack? A family friend? Perplexed, I placed the negative on the workbench aside the photos of the old house. Checking inside the envelope again to make certain I had missed nothing, I discovered a birth certificate stamped with the Seal of the State of Vermont. The birthplace was the City of Burlington, County of Chittenden. Because I was reading from left to right, not top to bottom, I didn't notice right away what I should've seen first. As such, I wasn't physically prepared to absorb what hit me next:

2. *NAME OF CHILD: Theodore Robert Bundy (ILLEGITIMATE)*

I skimmed down, astounded by what I read. I learned that my father was Jack Worthington, a Caucasian whose birthplace was New York City, New York, 1914. My mother's address was listed as 7202 Ridge Drive, Philadelphia, Pennsylvania. I read the document's Certification of Issuing Office section confirming that it was no forgery. Signed by the Registrar and City Clerk of Burlington, and dated November 24, 1946, it read: *I hereby certify that the foregoing certificate is issued pursuant to Chapter 183, Vermont Statutes.* I continued searching feverishly, eyeing a small silver keepsake box stowed in the back of the bottom drawer. Inside I found a tooth, a lock of blond hair, a teething rattler, and my baby book. I learned that I was born at ten o'clock on a gusty autumn evening under a waxing crescent that shone as bright as a full moon." I had slept peacefully and cried only once, when I was hungry. Most distressing was the line under *Birthplace,* which read, *Elizabeth*

Lund Home for Unwed Mothers, 76 Glen Road, Burlington, Vermont. My hands shook terribly. What was the Vermont connection to this all? I was told my mother had been widowed, that my father had died when I was three. Yet the photo of him was taken when I was six. I remembered Sam telling me that my father was a local boy. Had he also lied about his accidental death? What else was my family not telling me? I recalled what a teacher in high school had once recommended as I struggled to solve a confounding geometry proof: "See the forest through the trees, Ted, see the forest through the trees." Sweeping aside metal shavings, I placed the items next to one another and stepped back to view them. Consumed by the freakish thrill of my discovery, it was no small wonder I was caught completely off-guard by the velocity with which the memories I'd been seeking all along converged into my consciousness. Or was it the tactile reinforcement of my own baby hair that sent me back in time? I had presumed incorrectly that I could peel back my repressed memories layer by layer, leisurely excavating them at my discretion, like an archeological dig where the dinosaur bones are meticulously dusted and tagged for later observation. And precisely because it was a memory I was resuscitating and not a dream distortion, the motives of each character were clearly defined, not polluted by the corrosive residue of my subconscious. In a moment of recognition I recalled the people, the places, the house in the photograph. I stared at my hands in wonderment, realizing I was reinhabiting the tender years I came in search of. There I was, sitting on the cellar floor of my grandparents' old home at 7202 Ridge Avenue, when I heard a voice call from upstairs.

"Teddddeeeeeeee!!" my grandmother calls to me. "The doctor is here!!"

I am playing with my Lincoln logs, constructing a cabin to house my toy soldiers. Frustrated by the pounding throb that booms from my left ear, I trudge dizzily up the stairs, but not before stomping on the soldiers, disjointing the cabin with a swift kick of my Buster Browns.

"Commmiiinnnnng!" I answer.

Upstairs, a smiling woman is seated on the sofa in my grandparents' living room. I recognize her as our widowed neighbor, Dr. Cecelia Farnsworth. She is wearing a brown skirt and a tight white sweater with a purple and cream-colored silk scarf tied high up her throat. Her black hair, pulled tightly from her scalp, is balled in a high bun skewered with a wooden needle. She has watery green eyes and marionette lines slit down her cheeks. I walk into the den as I am told.

"Come here, Teddy," she says kindly.

I do as ordered, bashfully looking down at my feet.

She unhasps the gleaming brass buckles to her doctor's bag and slips open the combination. "Sit here," she says, patting the space next to her on the sofa. She opens her bag and methodically searches through her instruments. "Inch closer, sweetheart." She removes a stethoscope, flashlight, reflex hammer, and a wooden dispenser. Gently lifting my chin to face her, I hold out my tongue while she gently examines my tonsils. I smell her sweet perfume. She draws closer. I squint as a blinding beam of light shoots into each eye. Lightly, she steadies my trembling knee.

"Put your head on my lap," she orders softly, hiking up her skirt a bit.

I rest my cheek on her plump thighs. Her skin feels warm on my cheek and smells like damp baby powder.

She ratchets the head of a metal instrument and places it into my ear, warming my drum with a soothing beam. From a distant street a Mister Softee ice cream truck's jangling refrain sounds like a windup toy.

"You have a case of *otitis media,*" she says. "In other words, young man, it is nothing more than an ear infection."

As I get up off her lap, my grandfather walks in through the back door. His black hair is oiled back and he is wearing a white t-shirt. A loose forelock droops over his brow. He carries a newspaper in one hand, a thermos in his other. He approaches me and places the back of his hand against my forehead. "Not feeling so well, my boy?" he asks, a look of concern knotting his forehead. I shake my head.

"Hey there handsome," Dr. Farnsworth says to my grandfather. "Your little boy here has a mild ear infection. He should be okay, though. He's not running a fever." She breaks into a smile. "His grandfather, on the other hand, is a different story." She gets up off the sofa and goes over to him, pushing him against the wall, circling her arms around his neck. She lifts a stockinged foot out of her shoe and begins kissing him while rocking the shoe back and forth on its heel. Still seated on the sofa, I hear them giggle as they start to undo their clothing.

"My wife," my grandfather whispers, playfully pushing her off of him. She turns her head to gaze down at me, and then to her right, where the corners of the den wall hide them from a straightaway view through the screen to the backyard. There I see my grandmother, hunched down, cultivating her garden.

"She knows the arrangement, Sam."

"I know, but…"

"But what?"

"She's right outside."

"You go downstairs and play for a while, Teddy, Dr. Farnsworth and I have to talk," my grandfather says. He swats her rump, taking her hand in his as they leave the room together, walking through the kitchen.

I go back downstairs into the basement and resume playing with my toys, but am too curious to concentrate, wanting to further explore the odd behavior I've just seen. After a few moments, I slink through the kitchen and living room, stopping at the bottom of the staircase to listen to the noises coming from the upstairs bedroom. Fascinated, I hear the same noises grow louder as I sneak upstairs to listen closer. A door is opened a crack and I peek inside. Dr. Farnsworth is naked, lying on her back in a large bed canopied in soft white cloths that flutter in the wind blowing through an open window. Her legs are spread wide up in the air, knees locked. She holds her ankles behind her ears. Laughing, my grandfather is on his knees, leaning over her, snapping pictures of her crotch while playfully inserting a frozen hot dog between her legs with his free hand.

"Put down that camera and knock me up!" she yells.

"You want me to knock you up? I'll give you a baby, woman, I'll give you a baby," he says through clenched teeth, tossing aside the hot dog and camera. In one swift motion he flips her over onto her stomach, holding her wrists together with one hand, with the other angrily grasping a handful of her hair. Her head is to the side and she is smiling at me. My grandfather reaches for a pillow and rolls it into a ball, placing it under her hips.

"That's it, that's it," she urges him. "Give Olivia a sister, come on, you can do it," she says, peeking at me from the corner of her eye, smiling. My grandfather notices me but doesn't release his hold on her. I run outside, anxious to tell my grandmother what I've seen.

Still on her knees, she's pulling weeds from her flowerbed. She has taught me to read by the message stamped into the iron sign impaled in the middle of the garden:

The kiss of the sun for pardon,
The song of the birds for mirth,
One is nearer God's heart in a garden
Than anywhere else on earth

I run to her. "Grandma, grandma, grandpa is upstairs hurting Dr. Farnsworth!" I hear their yells coming from the upstairs window.

"That's your imagination, Teddy. There's nobody upstairs," she calmly assures me, without looking up from her work.

"No, I heard it, I saw them, I did, I did."

"Teddy, sometimes we think we hear and see things that we really don't. We hear noises that are silent and see things that aren't there. Just like in your dreams, sweetheart, what you think you are hearing and seeing now is all in the land of make believe."

It is Christmastime, cold, but warm enough to play outside. My grandmother has sent me to play outside with Dr. Farnsworth's daughter, Olivia. I am wearing a wool cap with earflaps tied underneath my chin. We are playing hide-and-seek in the Farnsworths' backyard at the end of the block. An only child, Olivia has thick glasses, pigtails, and perpetually congested airways that leave two raw snot-crusted tracks chapping the cleft under her nostrils. Crouching behind a bush, I watch Olivia, her hands pressed over her eyes as she counts to ten: "One, two, three…"

Already bored by the game, I sneak up on her and tickle her ribs until I feel the warm flow of water dampening her knickers. She cries and I let her up and she runs inside her house.

She comes outside to play with me again later in the afternoon, wearing a fresh change of clothes. Refusing to let me play with a pedal car she has received as a present, she steers in circles around my legs, taunting, "This car is mine and you can't haaaaave it." She repeats this annoying mantra until I decide I have had enough. I push her to the ground and lunge for her throat. I squeeze harder and harder, joyfully watching her face turn blue while Lucas, the Farnsworths' pet Rottweiler, standing nearby on his hind legs, ferociously barks.

I don't see Dr. Farnsworth coming. She tears me off her daughter. My scalp burns as she yanks me by my hair, dragging me to our porch stoop. While we wait for somebody to answer the front door, she hisses, "The next time you lay a hand on my girl, I'll kill you, Teddy Cowell, do you hear me?" Thrilled, it seems, when I begin sobbing in gushing torrents, she says, "Or better yet, I'll come over and get you out of your bed in the middle of the night is what I'll do, then I'll feed you to Lucas. How would like that, young man?"

I bawl, hoping to be rescued, but our house is silent and nobody answers the door.

"In fact," she says, evilly smiling, "what do you say we go and visit Lucas right now?" She drags me by my wrist across the lawn. "Luuuuucas," she calls, her voice echoing through the yards around us, "come here my sweet, look what I have for you!!!"

I gaze dizzily up to the sky, wincing into the blinding sun as my back bounces off the ground. I hyperventilate the nearer we come to Lucas. Dr. Farnsworth roughly turns me over to my knees so my face is just out of reach of the hound's muzzle, yet near enough so I brush the cold wetness of his snout, feel the heat of his sour breath and the warmth of his flung slobber. His hackles raised like porcupine spines, he stands flexed on his hind legs, bouncing onto his forepaws as the chain pulls taut at his collar. The doctor jerks back my hair so my throat is exposed to Lucas' snapping fangs. I close my eyes and recite my bedtime prayers, waiting for my eyes to be gouged and my neck to be torn open. Yet after a few more minutes Lucas' vocal chords grow hoarse, diminishing into a succession of whimpering yelps when the force of his bark can no longer be sustained. He doesn't see me as a conquest now, but as a game he is growing bored with. Dr. Farnsworth lets go of my hair and I sink limply to the ground, curling up. I hear Lucas take one last sniff of me before trotting lazily into his doghouse. His collar tags clank as he turns in circles, then settles on a cool spot of ground. Terrified, I don't move again until I hear his resigned sigh of contentment.

When I open my eyes again Dr. Farnsworth is gone. With the coast clear and Lucas safely resting, I race to our backyard, where my grandmother is busily clothespinning a bedspread to the laundry line hung between a tree and a greenhouse. Catching my breath between sobs, I frantically tell her the story. I soon grow frustrated, for she does not believe that her neighbor would dare consider harming me.

"That's just your imagination, Teddy," she says. "Remember when you thought you heard your grandfather hurting Dr. Farnsworth? And do you remember me telling you it was just your imagination playing tricks on you, like when you have those scary dreams? This is the same thing. Lucas never bit anybody. He probably just wanted you to play with him is all," she says, busily folding the corners of a bed sheet and placing it in a wicker basket by her feet.

Exasperated, I drop to my knees, frustratedly hammering my fists into the ground. My grandmother laughs, stepping away, allowing me room to thrash. Dr. Farnsworth, in bare feet, stomps into our backyard. I rise quickly and scamper into the house, watching crouched behind a screen door.

"Dolores, that boy should be put behind bars and kept there!" Dr. Farnsworth screams, her hair riled into wild ends.

My grandmother nods vigorously in wholehearted agreement with her neighbor's condemnation of me as heathen spawn. She apologizes profusely for my behavior and promises that my evil deeds will be more properly addressed when my grandfather comes home from work.

"I can't have this brat coming over and trying to harm my child, Dolores. Last week he yanked her down off the tree house by her ankles and practically broke her neck!" She jabs a finger toward my grandmother. "Then he tackled her in Lucas' dog crap, and tickled her till she peed herself. Are you hearing what I'm telling you? I have a practice to run and Olivia to care for and I can't have Teddy coming over and behaving like this! Keep him on your property," she exclaims, her chest heaving. "Or should I say, *my* property!"

"I agree, Cecilia, he's terribly misbehaved, but I have a house to take care of also, as a well as Sam and Ted. I can't watch him every second. His mother is taking him back to Washington this autumn. He'll be gone by then, I promise. Please, I'm begging you, there's no way we can afford a place like this on our own. We're spread too thin as it is, but Sam needs the greenhouse, this land. Just a while more, until he can afford to rent a shop of his own. Please, just a while more, Cecilia. After this spring he should have enough clients to rent his own space. Please, Cecilia," she begs, clutching a blanket her chest. "What can I do? What do you want me to do? I'll do anything for my family, anything you want, just don't kick us out of this house."

Dr. Farnsworth pauses for a moment, considering the offer. "Well, there is something you could do. It might seem a tad inappropriate."

"Name it," my grandmother says.

"You know I want to conceive again, and at forty, how many years do I have left? I don't want to have to go through an adoption agency again. I want a child of my own."

"I don't understand…you want me to be your midwife, or," my grandmother says, staring dumbfounded, then realizing the implications of what she's already agreed to. "Oh, no, you wouldn't make me agree to that, not that," she says, shaking her head, holding her hands over her mouth in horror.

"Why not?" Dr. Farnsworth laughs. "Sam's a healthy virile man. Don't you think he wants a son? And wouldn't you agree you're being a little selfish by not giving him the chance to try for one, since it's too late with you?" She steps forward and puts her arm around my grandmother's shoulder, muffling her sobs. "Now, now," she says, shushing her, consoling her as though she were a boy with a skimmed knee to whom she is about to apply a drip of iodine. "It won't be that bad,

Dolores," she coolly says. "I'll just need him for a few days a month, then he's all yours." My grandmother sobs harder. Dr. Farnsworth assuringly pats her back, kisses her forehead, then looks toward the door. She catches me gawking. "Shhhhhh, it's OK," she says, smiling at me the same way as when she was under my grandfather. "Shhhhh."

I am seated in Dr. Farnsworth's office on the first floor of their home. The waiting area smells of alcohol and ether. It is early morning, sometime near Easter, I think, for daisies wrapped in colored tinfoil decorate the windowsills. I am burning with fever. After hanging our coats, my grandmother sets me down in a tiny corner desk set aside for children. Next to the desk is a wooden rack filled with *Highlights* maga zines. She opens a magazine for me, turning to one of those braintcasers where you try and locate the utensils hidden in a picture of a kitchen. Just as I circle a spatula, the receptionist slides open the glass window partition and announces that the doctor is ready to see us.

I hold my grandmother's hand tightly as we follow the receptionist down the hall. My grandmother stops to peek inside Dr. Farnsworth's office, beaming when she sees Olivia seated behind her mother's desk.

"Look, Teddy, it's Olivia!" my grandmother says.

I bashfully eye Olivia, uncertain how I am expected to behave, the incident with Lucas still fresh in my mind. She is drawing in her coloring book and doesn't look up at us.

"Don't you think it'd be nice for you to say you're sorry

to Olivia?" my grandmother asks, casting a stern gaze down at me.

I do not wish to, but again do as I am told, shamefacedly hanging my head, looking at my feet as I mumble forth an apology. We follow the receptionist into the examination room, where the doctor will see us shortly. My grandmother lifts me onto the examination table and sits in a corner chair. Olivia quickly enters behind us, followed by Dr. Farnsworth. She is wearing a lab coat, her hair done in a long single braid. I recall the terrorizing standoff with her dog and begin bawling.

"I see you have a young assistant today," my grandmother says, proudly looking at Olivia as though she were one of her own.

"Olivia says she wants to be a doctor for women, isn't that right sweetheart?" Dr. Farnsworth asks as she draws the shades closed.

"That's correct," Olivia answers primly.

"And what do we call a doctor that sees only female patients?" Dr. Farnsworth asks.

"A gynecologist," Olivia announces.

"Do you think you can tell Mrs. Cowell and Teddy how to spell gynecologist?"

"G-Y-N-E-C-O-L-O-G-I-S-T," she boasts.

"Very good, sweetheart," my grandmother sings in praise.

"I can spell that, too," I offer, envious of the sudden attention bestowed upon Olivia.

"Of course you can, dummy, I just spelled it for you,"

Olivia says. Everyone laughs but me. I glare at Olivia, wanting to return my thumbs to her throat.

"Thanks for seeing us on such short notice, Cecilia," my grandmother says.

"I'm always happy to take care of my neighbors, especially those who are my friends. And we're all friends here, aren't we, Teddy?" Dr. Farnsworth asks, standing before me.

"Yes," I answer obediently, hugging myself against fever chills.

"Don't you think you owe my daughter an apology?" she asks.

"No."

"You don't? Well, I should beg to differ. But I tell you what, Teddy, we'll make a bargain, you and I: If you tell Olivia that you're sorry for hurting her, I'll make that tummy ache and fever of yours feel all better. Deal?"

I look for my grandmother to speak on my behalf, but she just stands there like everybody else, waiting for my apology. Olivia, standing with her hands wrapped around her mother's knees, sticks her tongue out at me, slyly so that nobody else notices.

"I'm sorry," I mumble.

"I think we can do better than that, don't you, Dolores?"

"Absolutely. Dr. Farnsworth is correct, Teddy. Be sincere and look at Olivia when you speak to her."

"I'm sorry, Olivia."

"That was very sweet, Teddy. Now, let's check your heart," Dr. Farnsworth says, positioning her stethoscope on my chest.

She reaches the cold metal disk up my back and has me inhale.

"That's a good boy," she says, placing a footstool on my feet. As she unbuckles my pants, I start to cry. She pulls them down to my knees, touching me, asking me to cough. Olivia is beside herself with laughter. What I thought was a carton of Kleenex tissues are actually surgical gloves. The doctor slaps on a pair, working each finger into them, snapping the elastic around her wrists.

"Okay, Teddy, remember when I had you lie down on your stomach last time? Do you think you can do that for me again, so I can take your temperature?"

I feel the paper crinkle against my stomach as I lie down on the table. Olivia is eyeing me intently. "Why can't I have the thermometer in my mouth?" I plead with my grandmother, who is seated in a corner chair. Quivering with humiliation, I begin to cry again.

"I know you don't like it, Teddy, but you're not big enough to have a thermometer in your mouth. You might bite on it," my grandmother says.

"And then you could die of mercury poisoning," Olivia adds, her eyes fixed below my waist. She holds her hand to her mouth, stifling a giggle.

"That's right, Olivia," my grandmother says. The doctor reaches for a white tube, dabbing some lukewarm jelly on her fingertips. Slowly she inserts the thermometer inside me. The cold steel shivers up my spine as though her finger is reaching all the way through my intestines and poking out my throat.

"A hundred and one," she reads to my grandmother, who rises from her chair, helping me put my pants back on. "I'll prescribe him some penicillin. He should be fine."

As the examination concludes, I slowly get down off the table and sit with my arms crossed. Too ashamed to face Olivia, I keep my eyes pinned to the floor, counting the wood boards. Consumed by my thoughts, I don't pay any attention to the conversation between my grandmother and Dr. Farnsworth until she walks over to the doctor. I look up and notice my grandmother pointing to an area on her own shoulder.

"Hmmmm. I'd like Dave to have a look at this. Do you mind?" Dr. Farnsworth asks, feeling the area, instructing her to sit up on the examination table.

"Not at all," my grandmother answers uncertainly. The doctor exits the room, returning seconds later with a tall, mustached young man wearing spectacles. A stethoscope dangles from his neck.

"This is Reed Tucker, Dolores," Dr. Farnsworth introduces the unsmiling man, now standing to her side. "Reed is interning for me on a rotating basis. He goes to Penn."

Unsmiling, he does not look at Olivia or me, and proceeds toward my grandmother. He pauses before her, placing a hand on her shoulder.

"Reed, this is a forty-eight-year-old pre-menopausal patient with mild breast tenderness," Dr. Farnsworth explains, stepping back to observe his technique. Her tone is clinical; she speaks about my grandmother as though she were inhuman, a cadaver about to be cut open.

"Breast examination?" he asks.

"That's right. Dolores, do you mind unbuttoning your shirt for me?" Slowly, my grandmother removes her blouse and hands it to Dr. Farnsworth, who carefully places it on a chair.

"Could you lie down for me, ma'am?" the man asks.

"Raise your right arm for me now, Dolores," Dr. Farnsworth instructs. "Now lay it flat down at a right angle behind your neck." She guides the intern's hand under my grandmother's armpit, where he probes around her hair bristles. She flinches when he hits a ticklish spot. Dr. Farnsworth lowers the bra straps off my grandmother's shoulders, pulling down the chest band. "What you want to do is start near the nipple and make small circles with the pads of your fingers. Check the tissue for pre-cancerous lumps. Give it a shot," she says, standing aside to monitor.

I look down at the floor again. I feel ashamed, powerless, wishing my grandfather would break through the door and rescue us from this stranger touching my half-naked grandmother. But as usual my curiosity gets the better of me, and I peek again. The intern stays at one place on her chest, continuing to press his fingers there. He furrows his brow. Noting his concern, Dr. Farnsworth gently moves him aside and places her hand where his was. A look of grave apprehension passes across her face.

"I'd like to have Reed assist in a full examination, if that's okay with you, Dolores?"

"Why don't you go outside and play for a while, Teddy?"

my grandmother suggests. I desperately want to stay and protect her. I am scared for her, frightened what might happen when I leave the room. My grandmother reaches behind her, unzipping her skirt, letting it fall past her slip.

"Go on now, Teddy, you and Olivia go play outside for a while," Dr. Farsnworth says sweetly. "And you may tell the receptionist, if she is not too busy, that I said you may each have one piece of Easter candy for behaving so nicely."

Twelve

An approaching wind surged outside the barn door, unhitching a scatter of helicopter seeds across the floor planks. I was unclear for how long I'd been standing in Sam's dusty barn, absorbed in the fuzzy haze between recollection and actuality. It could have been a few seconds, moments, an hour perhaps. I was bewildered by the relative ease by which I was able to travel backward in time, eclipsing its remoteness, reliving my early childhood with such extraordinary vividness. Oddly calm, and trying to harness everything I had seen, I noticed a figure looming in the doorway, casting a shadow on my feet.

"Where the hell have you been?" Sam asked, huffing expectantly, his thunderous demand springing off the walls. A raging vein ballooned down the middle of his forehead. His nose tip and cheeks were dark red, his gray chest hairs streaked with peat moss dust.

"So if I'm to understand correctly," I said, still disillusioned, as though hearing the sound of my own voice for the first time after a prolonged period of isolation, "Cecelia Farnsworth owned 7202 Ridge, and to stay there rent-free you fucked her right under Dolores's nose? Is that right?" I held my stance, awaiting his reply.

As he glimpsed the mementoes laid out on his work area, his shoulders sank, the color draining from his face.

"And you allowed this same woman to slice off your wife's breast?" I asked.

"A surgeon operated on your grandmother. What the hell does Cecilia Farnsworth have to do with anything?"

"And to think you told me *I* was sick. Perverted, if I remember correctly. How would you define two people who get off being watched by a four-year-old? Do you like being watched, Sam? Do you? Was that the thrill?"

"What the fuck are you talking about?"

"I saw you and her upstairs in your bedroom, Sam. Care to explain this?" I held up the negative.

He tore it from my hand and examined it, shrugging. "This is a nudie picture you probably found in some pile of shit left here by the old owners. So what?"

"You're telling me that's not Cecelia Farnsworth?"

"Cecelia Farnsworth, when she was alive, weighed about three hundred pounds," he said, laughing.

"Then why did you move?"

"You wanna know why we moved here? Because Cecelia made us leave. See, what you selectively forget is that you tried to *kill* her daughter, Ted. Do you remember that? We're talking about attempted murder here. Murder is murder, whether you're four or twenty-four. You nearly crushed her larynx. Cecelia owned the land and the house. It was either leave or she would call the Department of Human Services. I had, still have, a reputation in the community. You think I wanted people to find out? You should be thanking me, because instead of being sent to live in Seattle, you'd have grown up in an orphanage, just like your grandmother. And look how she turned out."

"And what about Jack Worthington?" I asked, saying his name aloud for the first time.

"What about him? He wanted nothing to do with you or our family after you were born," he said. "He told us he didn't give a shit about you, that we were Pennsylvania trash. Is that what this is all about?"

"Is he alive?"

"I hear he still might be working in New York City, I don't know exactly where, though."

I removed the picture of my father from the bench and put it in my back pocket. I calmly folded my birth certificate, taking it along as well. The other relics, dissembled into a collage by the wind, I left in plain view for Sam to further contemplate.

"Here's your rocksalt," I said, dropping the bag at his feet and tossing him the key. Downcast, he said nothing as I walked past him out the barn door. As I shuffled absentmindedly through the yard, I heard him call out to me.

"Hey Ted!"

"What is it, old timer?"

"Your dad had the right idea." He circled the side of his head with his pointer finger, smiling. "We should've just left you in Vermont."

Later the same evening, I sorted through what wickedness I had seen. I no longer knew what or who to believe. Would I forever be haunted by my past? Had my intensive self-hypnosis caused further damage to my psyche? The only way to know for certain, I deduced, was to find the remaining pieces of this sordid puzzle by retrieving my birth records in Vermont, hoping they contained critical information, such as my father's address. I needed to find him, wherever in the country he might be, knock on his door, and confront him with these questions: As I lay swaddled in the delivery room, what prompted him to leave that instant and forever abandon his paternal responsibilities? Was my mother a one-night stand for him, no more than a test to see if he was man enough to father a child? I needed something more substantial than pictures, anecdotes, and deceptions to learn the full story of my origins.

With Sam off working early the next morning, I packed a change of clothes, remembering to bring along my Freud text. I slung my backpack over my shoulder and headed toward Sam's bedroom. His billfold was on his bureau, amid a few pennies, fluffs of pocket lint, and business cards from landscaping wholesalers. I guiltlessly emptied it of three crisp hundred-dollar bills, walked out the front door, and down Columbus Avenue for the last time.

PART III

NEW YORK CITY

THIRTEEN

I got lucky five minutes into my journey, scoring a ride into Center City Philadelphia from a trio of seniors from Plymouth-Whitemarsh High School on their way to the town of Margate, at the Jersey Shore. Had I heard of it? It was between Ocean City and Atlantic City, they said, just over the Longport Bridge from Somers Point. At the mention of their destination, I suddenly conjured a picture of Avery Dwyer slathered in tanning oils on some exotic beach. I told them I was a songwriter on my way to New York City to hand deliver some new music sheets I had written for Bob Dylan, who, I secretively assured them, was scheduled to perform at a Times Square nightclub that evening. Could they direct me to the area? Fortuitously, one of the boys was familiar with the locale. He drew a map of Broadway, showing me where it intersected with Seventh Avenue, and how to walk there from Port Authority Bus Terminal. When they begged for a few verses, I balked, saying it was bad luck for a novice composer to hear how a song sounds before it is first played on an instrument.

At the bus depot in Philadelphia I bought a ticket for the morning ride to New York City, with a four p.m. connecting route to Burlington, Vermont. The little oxygen that circulatated in the bus blew feebly in warm recycled drafts from a vent below my window. The half-emptied seats were filled with theatregoers and jacketless men wearing loosened neckties and hats. Made dopey by the insidious rise in the mercury, several people had nodded off in a groggy doze. Those who couldn't sleep stared vacantly out the window, fanning their foreheads with newspaper sections. I wrestled in my seat like an insomniac battling fatigue, trying to get comfortable as we plowed along the northernmost stretches of the New Jersey Turnpike. Although it was a great leap of faith to think I was making headway toward accurately diagnosing my illness by conducting my own haphazard form of Freudian analysis, there were simply too many interesting and coincidental parallels to his theories that begged further exploration. Despite what might linger dormant in my subconscious, and fearing what prophetic insights I might tap by reading Freud, I couldn't resist the urge to remove his text from my satchel and seek more explanations. I found an interesting passage in *Three Contributions to the Theory of Sex,* under a chapter titled *Infantile Sexuality*, subchapter *Sadistic Conception of the Sexual Act:* "If children at so tender an age witness the sexual act between adults, for which an occasion is furnished by the conviction of the adults that little children cannot understand anything sexual, they cannot help conceiving the sexual act as a kind of maltreating or overpowering, that it impresses them in a sadistic sense. Psychoanalysis teaches us also that such an early childhood impression contributes much to the disposition for a later sadistic displacement of the sexual aim."

Though on point with what I had seen, the passage made little sense to me. I couldn't imagine how sex combined with animosity or violence would produce any sort of addictive pleasures for me, as the only perversion I conceded to was a kinky predilection for exhibitionism. Nor could I draw the conclusion that any noticeable harm had come from witnessing my grandfather's philandering escapades. But had I really witnessed anything, or was Sam right about me, that I was going nuts?

We hit traffic at Secaucus. The right lane was shut down a quarter-mile ahead, and a cavalcade of cars and trucks fell in behind the passing lane. A cluster of flashing yellow emergency truck lights flickered soundlessly through the bus interior as we approached the pileup. A New Jersey state trooper directed traffic around the wreckage as it came into view, while another lit a boundary of road flares and fluorescent cones around the breakdown lane.

Two cars had overturned, one stacked perpendicularly over the other. The car on top, with Pennsylvania tags, was twisted upside down in a smoky mass of metal, its back end facing the road. Like the other morbid rubberneckers, I craned for a glimpse of the bodies. Traffic had come to a complete halt behind and in front of us, and even our driver was stretching his neck for a better view of the carnage. Both trunks were popped open and a suitcase of clothes had spilled onto the road. The hood of the vehicle on the bottom was crushed flat, as though it had been compacted and piled in a junkyard scrap heap. The blood-spattered windshield, still intact, hung limply from the roof frame in fragmented shreds. The emergency personnel worked in tandem, sawing to free a trapped passenger in the bottom car while the other shielded her face from spark burns. I watched with fascination as they lifted her unresponsive body from the window and placed her on a stretcher, collapsing the gurney into the waiting doors of the ambulance.

As the traffic cleared, I couldn't shake the lasting image of the dead woman, the way her lifeless eyes gazed quizzically up to the sky as the medics shrouded her face. I wondered what she had been doing, what she had been planning to serve her family for dinner, when the impact occurred. What was *I* thinking, doing, when her car crashed? An hour ago she was alive, and now she was dead. *Fifteen minutes* ago she was alive, and now she was dead. While continuing to embrace the alluring recency of her mortality, I glimpsed the lower Manhattan skyline, surfacing in the distance through a part in the graffiti-sprayed boulders topping the Secaucus cliffs. The building towers and luminous skyscraper windows mirrored glints of sun down through the haze clouding the Hudson River, drawing closer as we descended the high narrow turns circling Weehawken. Wondering what strange adventures the massive city might hold, I felt a tug in the pit of my gut when I realized that the view was a mere mirage obscuring the true purpose of my trip. Furthermore, it served as a reminder that I was completely on my own now, with only my survival instincts to rely upon.

Two old ladies chattered excitably across the aisle, pointing to the view we shared. They had tickets for the matinee showing of *Hair* playing at the Biltmore Theatre. I heard them mention Broadway several times, whisper something about the theatre being near Times Square. Reminded of my father, and that a map of the area had been drawn for me, I removed the photo from my pocket and examined it again. With a three-hour layover until the next bus left for Burlington, I wondered why I shouldn't take a shot at tracking down this finely dressed executive, despite the remote chances of finding him.

We followed a trail of other buses in our lane through Lincoln Tunnel, plunging through the dank yellow-tiled corridors under the Hudson River. Before letting us out into the Port Authority garage, the driver turned to face us, asking that we remain seated as he spoke. He was built stoutly, with black brylcreemed hair and a red nose the texture of a cauliflower. He clicked on his hand piece, clearing phlegm from his windpipe.

"Welcome to New York City," he said, his breathy voice struggling forth in an asthmatic wheeze. "Hold your pocketbooks with your life," he continued, grinning as the ladies with the theatre tickets looked aghast at one another. Raking back a curl the swelter had loosened, he warned, "Trust nobody until you're east of Fifth Avenue. Pick pockets work in pairs on Forty-second Street, and they're on the lookout for dangling purses."

With absolutely no idea where I was going, and too prideful to ask the driver for directions upstairs, I followed the people off the bus as they went through the metal doors into the transit hub. The Port Authority basement was bustling with passengers standing in long lines, waiting to board the commuter buses. I stayed within the pedestrian flow heading up a set of escalator stairs leading up to street level. I sensed a collective swiftness among the people, like they were hurrying to place racehorse bets seconds before post time. Not wishing to appear like some wide-eyed bumpkin from Appalachia ripe for muggers and thieves, I assumed their quickness, outpacing the moving escalators, briskly walking as though I, too, had someplace more important to be. I saw how easily one might get lost here, remembering the hard lessons of going off-trail and getting lost in the dense camp woods once when I was a Boy Scout. I marked the trail of my steps by the newspaper kiosks I passed on the mezzanine, as if they were mountain signposts. *Just keep moving*, I told myself, making my way up to the Forty-second Street entrance.

FOURTEEN

A swift pace of foot traffic thronged in opposite directions down the Eighth Avenue sidewalk. A fanfare of squealing brakes, horns honking, and distant police sirens echoed off the skyscrapers. Safely clutching my backpack from the crowds bursting through a row of doors behind me, I spotted an un occupied square of space a few yards away, a sanctum where I could stand for a moment and attain my bearings while regaining the sudden loss of direction spurred by the city's immense proportions. If I didn't quickly make up my mind which way to proceed, I risked accidentally colliding with a pickpocket, or worse, being confronted by one of the jaundiced panhandlers loitering under the alcove shadows. From among the awestruck tourists gazing uptown at the soaring building towers while waiting their turn for a taxi, I recognized a frail young woman I had seen on the bus. She had a map opened and was struggling to concentrate on it as the sidewalk crowd swerved to avoid her. A mute amputee gimped toward her on one crutch, his pant leg flapping like a windsock over his stump as he tried to keep time with his good leg. She shooed him off her, but he was insistent, jiggling his tin cup over her map. A police officer overseeing the disturbance sat idly on his mare for a few seconds, then cantered toward them when the bum would not leave her be. When his presence failed to budge the man, the officer buckled his helmet strap and dismounted. He casually unleashed his nightstick, placing it under the man's ribs, guiding him gently back under the alcove. Though amused by the vagrant's brazen indifference, I could understand the policeman's offhandedness. After all, what purpose would be served by making an arrest, or even issuing a citation? In a city this large, crime would have to be prioritized, with felonies like murder and grand theft having precedent over petty larcenists and beggars. What one could get away with here, I devilishly thought, taking out my directions. A scribbled arrow pointed in the near distance to my left, across the walkway stripes. Eying the sign for West Forty-second Street through a thick blue haze shimmering over the midtown traffic, I fell in alongside the mass of people waiting for the traffic light to change at the corner of Forty-second and Eighth Avenue.

A smell of brake dust fouled the air. Catching sight of a telephone booth across the street, I decided to begin my search for Jack Worthington within the millions of listed numbers. Thrown into relief by the bright noonday sunlight, the XXX movie theatre marquees, along with neon massage parlor silhouettes blinking under the giant noonday shadows, gave the initial impression that Forty-second Street was no more than a honky-tonk strip that had seen better days. But there was something eerily unique about this block that I couldn't put my finger on yet. Something other than its placement in the center of a giant city which differentiated it from the garden-variety red light districts of go-go bars and adult theatres I'd frequented in Tacoma and Seattle. Crossing the street, I made it a point to grasp the distinction.

There was no telephone book in the freshly urinated booth, rather, a shredded binder dangling off a torn metal chord and an empty bottle of rum fermenting in the corner. Leaning slumped outside the booth, a man in soiled plaid pants torn away at the knees wore a sandwich board warning *Sinners Repent, Your Time is Near.* I asked the swarthy attendant working the corner newspaper stand to confirm I was going in the right direction toward Times Square. He paused to consider my question, as if wondering defensively whether some perverted meaning sullied my intentions. Without looking in my eyes, he pointed his thumb in the direction behind him, mumbling something I took to mean I should resume west on Forty-second.

Mindful of our bus driver's stern warning, I avoided eye contact as I continued down the sidewalk. This seemed like a street where you could easily fall victim if you were minding your business and a grifter locked you on his radar, sensing by your wonderstruck expression or narcoleptic gaze that you were lost or in desperate need of a lay or a heroin fix. The degrees of iniquity appealing to the fiendish, darker side of the human spirit grew severer the farther down the block I ventured. Over the Victory Theater, a giant billboard read *WEL-COME TO 42 ST. The World's Greatest MOVIE CENTER.* But at the Apollo next door, the billing for the film *Loving Couples* read *MORAL DECAY EROTICALLY REVEALED IN ZEIT-ERLING'S BOLD SHOCKER.* And farther down near Seventh Avenue, a gorily violent double feature, *Blood Feast* and *The Gruesome Twosome,* was showing at the Rialto I.

"Hey soldier boy, you wanna fuck my ass?" a large bald transvestite offered to a duo of seamen trolling the block for action in their starched white petty officer uniforms. Lingering outside a blood bank, he wore a stocking cap over his head and a tight fitting sequinned white dress accenting his pectoral muscles. The more I tried to ignore his presence as I walked by him, the harder it became to seem as though I were not. "What about you, mister blue eyes?" he asked, effortlessly prancing over to me in his platform heels. Malodorous fumes of failing deodorant, melting talcum powder, and cheap perfume drew out from the perspiration running down the jut of his chin. He wouldn't accept being ignored and became belligerent when I didn't answer him. Quickening my stride, I tried to outpace him, when another man wearing nothing but a Superman cape and tight red underwear hurtled past us on roller skates, screaming as he whizzed by, "I am nachyo niggah!! Jesus Christ iz yo filthy white niggah!!!"

"I know you hear me, you Clark Kent lookin' mother fucker," the transvestite hissed in my ear. "I know your secrets. I know your secrets," he blurted, spitting at my feet. Yet, as if the gum-spotted sidewalk were a booth at some outdoor bazaar where he hawked his wares, he understood the boundaries of his commerce, and ceased harassing me as I slowed to read the sun-curled magazine covers pasted in an adult bookstore window. With tawdry titles like *Adult Movies Illustrated, Cinema Scorchers,* and *Cinerotic,* each cover displayed erotic still shots clipped from kinky foreign movies. Beautiful and nude, the actresses were bent submissively over chairs, their hands bound by rope and mouths stuffed with ball gags by a harem of lustful women. Intrigued, I took a look inside, where I saw racks upon racks of X-rated books and shelves displayed with fetish toys. Another room offered instruments of extreme perversion such as nipple clamps, enema hoses, and large veiny dildos sold in clear plastic packages, like chew toys at a pet store. A blinking sign above a connecting door enticed *25 cents all day peep, live 24/7!* A semi-circle of peep booths stood like bathroom stalls in the center of a dimly-lit room, where a worker was mopping the curling linoleum floor tiles.

I stepped into one of the booths, fastening the latch behind me. The space was tiny and smelled like strawberry-scented air freshener. With little shoulder room to maneuver, I put a quarter in a slot and the light above me went out. A small black screen lifted, revealing a scratched glass partition smeared with jism streaks and lipstick stains. A buxom black woman, wearing a bright orange g-string, pointy heels, and a see-through plastic halter-top, was dancing in the middle of a raised plywood floor. She was heavy, thick through shank and buttocks, with a butterfly's wings tattooed halfway up her spine. She swayed to the beat of the instrumental house music, a spacey organ solo layered with horns and funky sitar riffs blaring from a crackling speaker on the booth ceiling. Her dark skin glistened beneath the thumping stage lights as she whipped one leg around a brass pole, sliding her bottom to the stage. She stood when she noticed me, prancing over to the window and pulling down her g-string to the bottom of her full hips. Raunchily jiggling her ass, she tucked her head between her legs and began fingering herself. I put in another quarter as the screen closed, but by the time it rose again I had lost the dancer's attention to another customer. Her teasing piqued my appetite. I wanted to see more, get closer.

I stood in a line of men waiting for the dancers. They were seated inside a row of old telephone booths converted into private areas for dirty talk. When my turn came, I tipped a worker five dollars. He recommended one of the girls. Not necessarily pretty, he said, but offers the filthiest talk for your money. I went behind her booth when the light out front turned green and the curtain opened. Through the glass she appeared to be around forty-years-old, with large breasts spilling out the sides of her clingy negligee. She was sipping on a bottle of grape soda which she placed on a ledge in order to pick up the phone. Her eyes were crescented with turquoise eye shadows and her lashes clung together in gluey clumps, like a spider's furry paws. Though not what I had in mind, I picked up the receiver anyway.

"Have you ever done this sort of thing before?" she asked.

I said I hadn't.

She explained that each dollar bought me a minute of talk time. She pushed a button and a tray came out onto my side of the wall. I put in five dollars and she asked my name.

"Willard," I said.

"So what sort of things do you like to do, Willard?" she asked, saucily slipping off the negligee strap, drawing a circle around her aureole.

"Such as?"

"Such as, what are you into?"

"I like spanking," I said.

"Do you like to give or receive?"

"Give, of course."

"Have you ever-" she asked, when our conversation was cut off.

Excited by where this was leading, I placed a few more dollars on the tray and slid them through.

"-been spanked?" she continued.

"Never," I said.

"Would you like to be?"

"No, I'd like to spank you, though."

"What would you like for me to do now?" she asked.

I relished the uninhibited freedom of being able to say any filthy thought that came to mind, acting out the kinky commands I could only fantasize delivering to clean girls like Caroline. "Spread your legs," I said. "Let's see your pussy."

She pulled down her panties and lay them aside, stirruping her feet on the sides of the glass. She massaged between her legs, but showed no reaction.

"Do you like it from behind?" I asked.

"From behind is okay."

"What about mirrors?"

"Mirrors are fine, as long as you don't get your head shoved through one," she said, laughing harshly.

"Now get up and turn around," I said. "And spread your legs."

She did as commanded. "Where do you think this comes from?" she asked, looking at me upside-down.

"Does what comes from?"

"This need for men to dominate, be in control," she said.

"I think it's Nostradamus. Or Kumasatra, something like that," I said. I was growing bored. My time was running out. I couldn't see the point of putting any more money underneath the glass. I needed more closeness, to touch a woman, smell her skin.

I paid five bucks for a private lap dance, following a Latina named Peaches down an adjoining hallway to a set of pasteboard doors painted bright pink. I sat on a plastic chair and waited until she came in through a rear door. She wore a long strawberry-red wig and a matching gold-tasseled bustier and g-string, her skin pasted with sparkling glitter. She pushed the play button on a tape deck and opened her robe, belly dancing against my crotch. I nuzzled her chest, drawing in the scent of cinnamon cloves. When I reached for her breasts, she batted away my hands.

"Ten extra to touch my tits," she whispered sternly. I slipped a ten-dollar bill under her g-string, lightly snapping the band. Slowly gyrating, she reached her hands behind her back and unhooked her bra, letting it collapse softly off her shoulders. I caressed her for a moment, resisting the urge to squeeze. My heart was beating rapidly as she went to turn off the tape player. She sauntered over and pulled out her g-string, forming a basket.

"One for the kitty?" she asked, smiling.

I folded a twenty and placed it down her crotch, aggressively pressing it against her mound. She jumped back friskily, like a cat having its stomach rubbed. I took out another ten dollars. "Let's see your ass."

She grinned sassily and turned around, sliding her bottoms down to the middle of her thighs, then quickly pulling them up.

"How much for a blow job?" I asked.

"I'm not for sale, sugar," she said, lighting a Pall Mall. "But I know someone who is that might like a cute young guy like you. You don't have any diseases, do you? Genital warts, herpes, nothing like that, right?"

"Of course not," I said, riveted to learn who I was about to meet, as if I was being set up on a blind date.

"Her name is Candy. She's a cute young redhead, hangs between Nedick's and the camera store next to it. If you don't see her, look for Desiree across the street. She's a little longer in the tooth but gives better head. Blonde. Works the sidewalk where the old Hubert's Museum used to be. Good Luck. Keep smiling."

It was nearly one o'clock when I poured back out into the sweltering afternoon sun, hungry for a sexual conquest. In search of Candy, I was about to cross the street when my path was blocked by a performing midget. Wearing a cavalry bugle slung across his shoulder, he was a freakishly short cripple born with a large, bulb-shaped cranium he covered with a felt beret. He hit forcefully at a large bass drum hanging from his neck while drawing from a repertoire of Civil War anthems. He hobbled a few steps here, a few steps there, passionately tootling "Oh, Susanna!" then working into Reveille, as though rousing a dispirited cavalry regiment for one last charge. As he bent down to retrieve the silver tossed at him, I wondered why he chose to live like an organ grinder's monkey. Wasn't death a more sensible option, simple as walking in front of a speeding delivery truck, stepping in front of a hurtling subway train, or sucking the exhaust pipe of an idling car engine? Though deeply interested in understanding what forces had led him here, I was more fascinated in knowing who had given up on him. Had he been a ward of the state, a psychiatric patient, perhaps a transient imbecile shipped cross-country to where he would be another facility's charge? Or was he a refugee of a traveling circus, fired when the grotesqueries that earned him a living ceased appealing to his curiosity seekers? Contemplating the shallow depths of his gene pool, I was beleaguered with further questions about my own mysterious past. How could my father have any connection to this street? What would a person of such undiluted bloodlines be doing here, among these outcasts? Had I been abandoned by my family, might the trails of my despair have led me to fend for myself here also?

I walked anxiously toward Broadway, removing the picture of Jack. I held it up high, giving it scale against the electric-lit signs stacked over the others on the Times Square Building. An advertisement for Admiral Television Appliances had been replaced with one for Castro Convertibles. But the flashing red Coke sign and the cursive script of the Canadian Club Whiskey signature, standing watch over the traffic island at the intersection of Broadway and Seventh Avenue, were the same. I had always figured Times Square to be the same glittering place where women and men by the thousands, soused on champagne, withstood the bitter cold winds on New Year's Eve waiting for the ball to drop. I had envisioned Broadway theatres and grand penthouse apartments where rich people like my father lived. Yet as I gazed at an excavation site between Forty-forth and Forty-fifth Streets, I was struck with a profound sense of disappointment. The opulent hotel in front of which my father had posed eighteen-years ago had been reduced to demolition rubble, fenced off by sidewalk scaffolding. An office building to be named One Astor Place was being built there. Though frustrated I might have succumbed to false hope, I was determined not to be victimized by defeatism. I had one last chance in this city, one more hope to find my father: The New York City Library. Somewhere in their vast repository of public records, I reasoned, I'd find my father's address on a roll of microfilm or some other recent technological advancement that would direct me to him.

But the library, I somberly noted, had been closed for renovations. A construction permit tacked to the thick oak doors was taped to a brief notice that the branch would reopen again in July. The wanderlust for answers deserted me suddenly, tweaking a sense of loneliness and desperation far worse than what Caroline's break-up or Sam's mistreatment had incited. I paused, reflecting on the grim consequences spawned by my misdeeds. Consumed with self-doubt, I staggered down the granite stairs of the library in a pathetic stupor. I wasn't any better off, I glumly concluded, than the paralytics and jaundiced zombies whom I had earlier judged with superior contempt. I couldn't go on in my present state. I thought how easy it might be to dispose of myself, take an elevator up to the top floor of one of these buildings and jump off. Don't all the answers come to you right before you die anyway? Though my brains would splatter on the pavement, at least I would be at peace with myself. I recognized the insidious trickery of Merton's prophecy taking shape right before my eyes. I regretted how gullibly I had enthused over the false hope of traveling to a new location, only to find that all hope was lost. I feared that any more misery would backwash like a surging tide, reabsorbing into my arteries, killing me slowly if I didn't go berserk first. And if I didn't die then, or find some way to shift this blame outward, I would surely end up here, among these mutated imbeciles, destined to walk the streets and sell my asshole to whoever wanted to pay the most to bugger it.

Dejectedly shuffling back the way I came, I saw where a lurid slasher film, *The Wizard of Gore,* was playing at the Rialto II Theatre. I was drawn toward the sickening description in the glass case beside the box office: *MANIAC MAGICIAN WHOSE MONSTROUS TRICKS ACTUALLY WORK! SCENES SO FAR BEYOND ANY THAT YOU'VE EVER SEEN THAT NO DESCRIPTION IS POSSIBLE. IN DEVASTATING COLOR!* The illustration depicted a woman's corpse slunk into a giant magician hat, her lifeless arms dripping into a pool of blood. I bought tickets to see a double feature instead, *Blood Feast* and *The Gruesome Twosome*, playing at the Rialto I next door, for it was starting in five minutes and I couldn't wait any longer, possessed with the need to find an immediate outlet for the accrual of my bitter sorrow.

Blood Feast was as gruesome as its billing promised. The film was about a gimp serial murderer on the loose in Florida. He begins his carnage by hacking the leg off a woman in a bathtub, then scalps a girl on the beach, watching with sadistic glee as her blood pours out into the sand. He kills the next woman in her hotel room, cutting out her tongue and roasting her leg in a pizza oven in preparation for a cannibalistic Egyptian feast. His comeuppance is just, for he is crushed to death in a garbage compactor while desperately trying to outfox his pursuers. Despite the horrendous acting and campy script, I was transfixed by the film's graphic violence and anxiously awaited the second movie.

The Gruesome Twosome: A retarded oaf named Rodney Pringle lures in coeds from a local Florida college under the guise of a room for rent, then scalps them, providing the hair for his mother's wig shop. The setting was surreal, with all those women being killed among the exotic foliage and turquoise seashore waters. Although there were a few teasingly innocuous breast shots, the director had them fuzzed out. Teased, I left a quarter of the way into the movie, walking two doors down to the Lyric Theater to see *99 Women,* about a sadistic warden overseeing a women's penitentiary on an island known as Castillo de la Muerte, "Castle of Death." Undeserving of its X-rating, this movie tantalized also, with the director rushing through the scenes with the nude caged women in favor of a tedious, glacially moving plot line that failed to keep my attention for more than a half-hour.

Hungering for more explicitness, I went across the street and saw *Venus In Furs* showing at the Harris Theater. Although there was more nudity, most notably a breast-fondling scene between two lesbians, by now I was groggy from moving in and out of the air-conditioned theatres and baking hot streets, and grew sleepy during the movie. I slipped into a surreal landscape Freud would describe as a lucid dream, a peacefully altered state where the dream's narrative is subject to the whimsy of outside elements invading your consciousness. I listened with eyes closed as my mind interpreted its own warped narrative of what was transpiring onscreen. Instead of seeing the actors, I pictured Caroline stepping out of a silk nightie and crawling under the sheets with Kevin. A titillating inertia pinned me to my seat, forcing me to see her being fucked by him, drawing her sharp long nails down his spine, giggling as he tickled her with his beard scruff. "Come for me, Kevin. Fill me with your babies," Caroline whispered, but in the voice of Cecilia Farnsworth wrestling with my grandfather. With my anguished memories suddenly indistinguishable from my dream, the spell broke, releasing its hold over me. Terrified that I was losing my sanity, yet aroused also, I jumped out of my seat. I hurried out from between the sparsely filled seats and began my search for a prostitute, hoping a rough tryst with a lusty streetwalker would avenge my loss of Caroline and release what pent up anger the violent imagery had fueled.

Candy was where Peaches said she would be, but not at all what I expected. Clutching a rhinestone-studded purse while lingering outside Nedick's restaurant, she was about fourteen-years-years old, with a bright red wig and Irish-pale skin. Sporting a roll of baby fat under her chin, she was much too heavy for my liking, with bulky legs and a big belly that strained the buttons of her miniskirt. I figured she was strung out on drugs by the listless way she shuffled back and forth against the restaurant window, so I avoided her. That I might catch a venereal disease if I had sex with one of these whores didn't deter me from seeking out Desiree. I was in a far too agitated state of arousal to care about anything beyond purchasing two rubbers from a novelty store dispenser.

Desiree was standing with one leg up against a restaurant window. She had peroxided blonde hair worn short, parted on the side in a shag-type cut, like Twiggy. About thirty, she wore skin-tight velvet short-shorts and a hot-pink halter. She smiled and came forward, apprehensively clutching her purse.

"Desiree?" I asked.

"Who wants to know?" she said, snapping her gum.

"Peaches sent me. You come highly recommended."

"Peaches sent you, heh?" She walked up close to me, blowing a bubble. Her cheeks were dusted with thick pancake makeup that partly hid acne pustules.

"How much?" I whispered.

"Fifty for an undercover officer."

"I'm a pharmacist from Queens," I said, peeking suspiciously both directions down the block, as though fearing capture by my wife. "What does twenty get me?"

"Half and half."

"Which is what?"

"Suck and fuck."

"How about ten?"

"How about fucking yourself, asshole, and quit wasting my time," she said, grinning sassily at a businessman eyeing her.

"How much for head, your pussy, and your ass?" I asked.

"An around-the-world is thirty."

"Deal."

"Are you staying at the Dixie?" she asked, referring to the seedy hotel I recalled from one of my frenetic jaunts between theatres.

"Just in for the day," I said.

"Follow me."

I followed her into an alley next to the Anco Theatre, then through a side door leading into a small, unmercifully hot dressing room smelling of Ajax cleanser. She wheeled aside a clothing rack hung with empty wire hangers and old Henry VIII costumes. Next she pulled down a stained mattress that had been leaning against a row of broken stools and dusty makeup mirrors. It splashed into a puddle of leaked water as it collapsed to the floor, releasing a stink of insecticides. She stood waiting, her hand held out. I cautiously stepped over a soiled French tickler as I came toward her. I peeled off thirty dollars, which she stuck down her bra. I should have been turned on, but didn't feel the faintest warmth in my jeans as I looked disdainfully at the squalid mattress. "I'm not getting down on that," I said, firmly turning her around.

She complied, securing her hands on the edge of the long table in front of the mirrors, scattered with wigs and rusty curling irons. A cockroach flitted out an empty rouge container. I heard the muffled percussions of booming cannons, the whistle of falling trench mortars from the war movie playing in the theatre behind the wall. She pressed out her pelvis as I lifted her skirt. I pulled down her g-string to below her cheeks, pimpled with heat rash. I took out the condom and fumbled with the wrapper, fighting to tear it open. Sensing my embarrassment when I couldn't get hard, she reached over to her purse and removed a tube of lubricating jelly. I closed my eyes and tried to concentrate as she rubbed some on me. I focused on perverted thoughts- Caroline with Kevin in all their unbridled carnal lust, Sam schtupping our neighbor-but nothing worked. Desiree awkwardly jerked my shaft, unpeeling the rubber and attempting to fit it on me, but it slipped off and fell to the floor. She giggled, inciting a burst of humiliating anger. I ground my hips into her, holding up her head so she saw herself in the mirror.

"You think that's funny, whore?" I whispered angrily.

"Let me go!" she screamed.

My excitement surged as she squirmed to free herself. I pinned her thrashing arms down on the table and snatched a tube of red lipstick off the table, smearing her lips like a clown's mask. But she was simply too strong to hold onto, and when I went to pull up her bra, she broke free.

"You just wait!" she screamed, lunging for her purse. Believing our interlude to be no more than a bout of playful domination, I stood and laughed.

"You just wait, you fucking maniac! You won't be fucking laughing long," she said, feverishly sifting. Fearing she might have a pimp, or was searching for a gun, a switchblade, or a can of mace to blind me with, I grabbed my backpack and bolted out the door. I calmly jaywalked across the Eighth Avenue walkway, slowing my pace so as not to appear suspicious to the mounted policeman guarding the entrance to Port Authority.

My heart was racing as I stepped into the bus terminal. The mezzanine was buzzing with people. I hurried to the ticket window, but not before checking the time. It was five minutes after four. I had missed the bus to Vermont. Before the stinging misery hooked into me, I looked up at the clicking times on the destination board. A bus was departing for Ocean City, New Jersey at four-fifteen, the last one of the day.

Avery Dwyer, I thought. Momentarily exhilarated, with five minutes to make the bus, I dashed between people to get to my gate, hopping down the escalators to the downstairs loading platform, where the bus driver was tearing out tickets slips and helping old ladies board.

PART IV

THE JERSEY SHORE

FIFTEEN

My sadistic tendencies on Forty-second Street revealed a perverse feature of my personality I never imagined existed. If Merton's hypothesis of the self-fulfilling prophecy was true, as we drove south along the tidal waters bounding the Garden State Parkway, it should have logically followed that I'd now be staring into a crystal ball of some truly unique vista of horror, one that would spell the final doom for me. Yet as I gazed out over the grassy channels and inlets of the Great Egg Harbor Bay, their marshes green as a deep rise of ripening cane fields, I didn't sense a creeping fear of the unknown, nor was I bogged down with the unsettling preoccupation with death that had dogged me throughout my visit to New York City. I expected the culminating dread to wash over me as we rode over the Ninth Street Bridge into Ocean City, but it never came. I was certain the sensation would catch up with me as we drove onto the island, but it did not. Even though all I had left was my identity-Theodore Robert Bundy, born out of wedlock in a state home for unwed mothers-this knowledge wasn't accompanied by a smothering loneliness or self-destructive premonition. As I was going to a place where nobody but Avery knew me, I felt a rejuvenating moment of revelation in knowing I could be whoever I wanted to and could begin my life as if reincarnated, liberated from the constraints of my dark family secrets.

The island avenues were sectioned into quaint shops and grand three-story Victorian homes converted into boarding houses. Room-for-rent placards leaned under faded green window awnings, and on porch stoops American flags were raised in observance of Memorial Day weekend. On the corners of the blocks stood old seashore hotels, cottages of yellow, aqua, and lilac pastels, white stucco motor lodges with *NO VACANCY* signs stenciled in lights above their lobby carports. Drawn to the salty air, I headed toward the boardwalk after the bus unloaded, climbing one of the two walking ramps between Shriver's Fudge Shop and the Strand Movie Theatre. The steamy ocean breeze was rich with the scents of kettle-churned fudge and caramel corn. From a distance I heard the playful echoing shrieks of young teenage girls as they thundered around a rollercoaster turn. On the boardwalk, freshly washed tow-headed children, astir with the bursting excitability of a dog toweled after a bath, scampered gleefully ahead of their parents on the wooden planks humming underfoot. Despite my fresh arrival, I felt well-acquainted, like an animal returned to its natural habitat. The island's purity, its very enticement, stood in such stark contrast to the gritty mangle of New York

City that I felt cleansed from the inside out. Were my troubles once and for all a part of the past, invaluable moral lessons whose painful resonance was a reminder not to repeat them? Or was the enchanting mystique of this place indicative of some greater religious significance, an oasis as a reward for what I had suffered through to get here? A sacrament, yes, that was what I needed, a salt bath to rinse off the lingering sweetness of the whore's perfume, a baptismal cleansing to finalize the resurrection of my forlorn spirit before I set out to find Avery Dwyer.

I walked down a set of stairs leading to the beach, cutting through the dunes. The faint roar of the crashing ocean swallowed the noisy boardwalk babble, leaving an abrupt silence in its absence, like the hissing echo inside a hollow conch. Using my t-shirt as a towel, I placed my bag in front of the Shriver's rest pavilion and stripped down to my boxer shorts, heading straight for the Atlantic.

After a dip in the icy surf, I sat down on my t-shirt to drip dry. In the few moments I was gone, two young women had set down their towels in front of a beached lifeguard rowboat on the Tenth Street side of the beach, a few feet from the pavilion stilts. One was thin and wore a navy one-piece swimsuit. She was lying on her side, using her denim cutoffs to pad her propped elbow. She rolled onto her back, removing her sunglasses to examine her long brown hair up against the evening sun. Her companion, wearing a clingy hot-pink bikini, had just returned from the water also. Glistening, she reached down into a straw purse for a comb and leaned at her waist, raking out her blonde, sea-tangled hair. She caught me admiring her as she swung her hair back up. She subtly nodded at the brunette, who by now had stopped fussing with a transistor radio antenna to have a look back over her shoulder at me. For an instant before the blonde sat, I thought she could be Avery. I was relieved to feel no surge of disappointment, however, when I approached them and saw she was not.

"Good afternoon. I didn't mean to disturb either of you, but may I bother you with a question?" I asked. My words issued smoothly. I was zooming with confidence.

They sat up and smiled at one another. The brunette was tan with light brown eyes and thick, cleanly plucked eyebrows. She looked down self-consciously, quickly sweeping away a thin strip of sand from her suit before squinting up at me again.

"Sure, okay," the blonde said hesitantly. Clenching her comb, she hugged her knees to her chest.

"I'm in town on assignment for a magazine, and was wondering if you could tell me where I might find the Coral Sands Motel." I remembered seeing the quaint white motel somewhere on Ninth Street while riding into town. Or was it called the Sifting Sands? "I'm supposed to meet my assistant there. By the way, I'm Ted."

"Sue Grenier," the blonde offered. Gap-toothed, she concealed a slight overbite with her upper lip as she smiled, introducing her friend. "This is Elizabeth Haysbert, but her nickname is 'Ibby.' The Coral Sands is actually at the corner of Ninth and Atlantic. It's right across the street from where we're staying."

"What sort of assignment are you on?" Ibby asked.

"I'm a photojournalist."

"Really? Far out," Sue said. "Do you work for a magazine, are you freelance, or…"

"I work for *National Geographic*. Actually it's the *National Geographic Society*, if you wanted to get technical. How'd you get the nickname Ibby, Elizabeth? It's pretty."

"My nickname was Libby, you know, short for Elizabeth. When I was a baby, I couldn't pronounce the letter L when I started talking." She spoke shyly, with a Midwestern accent.

"Are you both from the area?" I asked Sue, who seemed chattier than her shyer friend. Though not wanting to resort to the common denominator, geographic origins, I needed to keep the ball rolling, and told them I was from Seattle. Sue was from Camp Hill, Pennsylvania, on the banks of the Susquehanna River. She was majoring in art.

"Really. Who's your favorite artist?" I asked.

"Ciambue."

"Cenni di Pepo Ciambue. From the Byzantine period. Painter of Madonnas. Mentioned in Dante's Purgatory in *The Divine Comedy*, wasn't he?"

Sue smiled again, cocking her head. "Impressive. Were you an art major too?" she asked.

"No, but my old girlfriend was."

"That's funny, my old boyfriend was a photographer," she said. Encouraged by the accidental coincidence, I waited an instant for her to address the occupation of her current boy-friend, but I gathered there was none.

"What about you, Ibby?" I asked, not wanting to cut my chances in two by excluding her.

"Minnesota," she said quietly.

They attended Monticello Junior College in Godfrey, Illinois, a two-year all-girls school near St. Louis. Ibby had just completed her first year. Sue had graduated the Sunday past. Both were nineteen, and had arrived in town on Tuesday, renting a room at a Ninth Street boarding house. They were leaving tomorrow, off to visit Sue's family in Pennsylvania.

Though I had lied in the past about my station in life, until now I never had the liberty to create my history like this, inventing truths, constructing interesting aspects and stories while allowing myself to expound at great length over my accomplishments.

Ibby leaned slightly forward, inching her bottom closer to me. "So what brings you all the way here from Seattle?" she asked.

"Actually our offices are in Washington, D.C.," I remarked, further diverting, "I live in Georgetown and took the bus up." But what she really wanted to know, I gathered, was what interest such an esteemed publication would have in dispatching a writer to New Jersey, of all locations. I gazed out to the water's edge, following a crooked trail of riptide froth drawing out to the ocean. In the distance, the masts of a galleon under full sail broke through a grainy veil of humidity obscuring the horizon. Part of a flotilla entering port for some holiday festival, the tall ship called to mind one of Sam's pirate tales.

"Sorry about that, I spaced for a minute there," I said, shaking my head as though clearing cobwebs. "To get back to your question, I'm doing an article about sunken treasure off the coast of New Jersey." I added, "I'm writing the story of Blackbeard. Supposedly he buried his treasure right around here, in the coastal rivers near Griscom Swamp, after sailing up from Jamaica on the *Queen Anne's Revenge*. I know, I know, it sounds crazy, but it's true."

"Really? How interesting. I never knew there were pirates in New Jersey, and I grew up in Pennsylvania," Sue said.

"Where's all your equipment?" Ibby chirped.

"My assistant, Larry, was scheduled to meet me out here at four o'clock, when the sunlight is best. He was also supposed to get here before me and make hotel reservations, but he's not here yet, and it's almost six-thirty. But that's just like Larry."

"Have you been on safaris and stuff like that?" Sue asked.

An oil tanker spurred a recollection of foreign destinations, exotic ports of call I'd fantasized of visiting while mulling by my window over the Seattle waterways. A story came to me instantaneously. "Two years ago, I had the good fortune of being sent to cover Richard Leakey on an expedition to Africa. The Omo River in Southern Ethiopia, near a site called Omo Kibish, is where he discovered the oldest known human fossils ever found. The articles editor woke me from sleep and sent me there the day after they were uncovered. Although I wasn't present at the river when they extracted the bones out of the bank sediment, I met up with Dr. Leakey's crew a day later to take the pictures.

"I had an all night flight into Nairobi, and at customs they wanted to confiscate my cameras," I said. "I was more scared, if you want to know the truth, as we drove out to the site. We were bouncing around in that jeep through the grown-over jungle roads, getting stopped and checked for documents at every Checkpoint Charlie. But my driver, his name was Mfaki-Swahili for 'exalted'-knew his roads like the back of his hand, and mercifully he delivered me there in one piece. All this is in the forthcoming July issue, by the way."

I had more photojournalism exploits to tell, as they were coming to me faster than I could embellish them-walks across treacherously hot deserts, going days without clean drinking water, being ensconced in a snow cave in the Himalayan ranges-but decided to save these and other goodies for later. Little did they know I'd never operated a camera more intricate than a Kodak Instamatic. Although it was incredibly fulfilling to hold their attention, I knew I must proceed cautiously, for the farther I strayed from the truth, the harder it would be to keep the stories straight. The more extravagant the fibs, the greater the chances an astute observer might note my reckless-ness and call me on it as the night wore on. Tell one too many improbable tales, you're regarded as a bullshitter, and nobody will believe any of the stories you tell after that, with even the true ones disregarded.

"Well," Sue said, turning to look at Ibby, who was still eyeing me, her head tilted slightly, as though contemplating her initial impressions and arriving at a counterintuitive conclusion, "Ibby and I were going to go over to Somers Point later on, if you and your friend want to meet up with us."

From a speaker strung above a great hacienda-style pavilion standing out over the end of a distant pier, a faraway voice carried over the water, where a scattering of surfers in glistening wetsuits sat contemplatively on their boards, patiently waiting for rideable swells to curl out from the dusk-flattened sea: "Ladies and gentleman, welcome once again to Ocean City, New Jersey, America's playground and greatest family resort. In fifteen minutes, please join us here at the Ocean City Music Pier, where the Ocean City Orchestra, led by conductor Clarence Furhman, will be performing in another of the nightly concerts sponsored by the Ocean City Chamber of Commerce. The Recreation Department is sponsoring a 'Bermuda Mixer' this Saturday evening at eight o'clock, to be held at Convention Hall, for the college set…"

"Yippee," Ibby remarked.

Gleaning from her sarcasm that she harbored a darker sense of humor than her more personable counterpart, I dryly wisecracked, "Yeah, that sounds exciting, doesn't it?"

"You definitely need to go across the bay to Somers Point for any fun around here," Sue said cheerily, in accordance with the collective thread of humor bonding us. She had assumed the role of hostess for the weekend, it seemed, compelled to show us a good time, and not wanting to disappoint. "Ocean City is dry," she explained. "There's really nothing to do at night."

"What goes on in Somers Point?" I asked. I hadn't seen any indication of a vibrant nightlife when the bus rounded the traffic circle on the ride down, just a few liquor stores and a historic home on a bluff overlooking the bay.

"They have bars and nightclubs along Bay Avenue," Sue said. "Tony Mart's is one of the places. They have like three bands playing there at once. Plus, there's no cover from Monday thru Thursday. It's where everyone starts out, and then they go across the street to Bay Shores, and then to an all-night hole called The Dunes, near Longport, after the other bars close at two. Ibby and I can't stay out that late, though. We have to leave early in the morning."

It was too soon to accurately conjecture the meaning of her qualifier. Was she saying I could dismiss the thought of any late night hanky panky? Or was this the scrupulous persona she was trying to convey-that fun, not drinking, was her primary motivation, and that the two were rightly distinguishable? I didn't buy it in any event, nor was I deterred, if that was her intent.

"I'd love to go. And I tell you what," I said, ready to cement our plans, though slightly concerned I hadn't yet won over her more skeptical friend. "I'll do you one better: How about I buy dinner?"

"My gosh, you don't have to do that," Sue said. Both their eyes lit up at my suggestion.

"Don't worry, the magazine will reimburse me. I'll say I was dining with two natives with an inestimable knowledge of the local history. The only thing is, I don't have a car."

"We can come by and pick you up," Sue said. "Where was it again that you and your friend were staying?"

I had forgotten about the fictitious Larry. How would I account for his absence, erase him from the equation? I would need to be more careful from now on and memorize my fabrications, which were bound to keep piling up as the night wore on.

"I think it was the Lincoln Hotel," I deflected. "I'll go back there and check in, in any event, and I'll leave a note for him to meet us out. But you don't need to pick me up. I can come to your place. I'll just take a shower in the meantime and finish up some writing. What's your address?"

They were staying at 712 Ninth Street, just a few hundred yards from where we were sitting, Sue said. We made plans to meet at their place at eight.

As I rose to say goodbye, my mind sped with designs for the evening. What kinds of things might I say to further my chances of scoring with one of them? I was so proud of myself that I wanted to race down the beach and scream my lungs out in exaltation, holler joyous greetings to the pilot of the low-flying propeller airplane trailing a netted sign for Coppertone sun lotion out over the reef. I restrained my impulses, however, sauntering casually back toward my knapsack lest I appear too excited. Before sitting, I gave one last look over at the girls to see if they were looking at me. They were, smiling as they shook the sand from their towels. Sue fitted a pair of tight denim cutoffs over her bikini bottoms, wiggling her slender hips to fit into them. Ibby slipped her purse over her shoulder and waved as they walked away.

Reminded of my own meager solvency, I checked my knapsack to see how much of Sam's fortune I should allot for the forthcoming night of debauchery. My deliriousness at the prospect of a sexual encounter turned to panic when I couldn't find my money. Forcing myself to remain calm, I checked the side pocket, as I noticed the flap had been opened. This in and of itself was not cause for alarm, for in venturing in and out of the peep shows and removing my wad of bills several times, I couldn't say for certain whether I had returned it to that pocket and simply neglected to refasten the buckle. I fished through the inside lining, anxiously turning my jean pockets inside out. I went through the silly ritual of reviewing in my mind where I had been, though I knew in my heart that my efforts were silly and for naught. I had counted all two hundred and three dollars on the bus before leaving Port Authority, and kept my bag next to me the whole ride down. Gone, I thought despondently. Swindled, not in the dungeons of Hell's Kitchen, but here, of all places, the sugary white beaches of Southern New Jersey. It was not the stolen currency that concerned me, as I glumly conceded its theft, nor the bitter, resonant sting of irony, as much as the familiar sense of disillusionment and attendant despair my instincts had duped me into believing had been cured when I arrived here. I looked up, futilely searching up and down the beach for suspects. In the time I had spoken with the girls, most of the families had left for the day. The only remaining people were an old man sweeping for coins with a metal detector, a boy paddling on a raft in a gully, and a young girl struggling to haul a plastic bucket filled with seawater. A soggy ten-dollar bill was all I had left to show for months of hard labor. My lone source of consolation came from knowing that I'd been through much worse, and that I couldn't afford to taint the evening's optimism by falling prey once again to my fluctuating moods.

The grease-spattered clock on the wall of a pizza stand read seven o'clock. I had an hour to scrape together enough money to buy us dinner. Gathering my things, I put my jeans back on and strode the north end of the boardwalk. Rather than mope, I accepted the setback as a challenge. Cash was what I needed, so I went in search of it, preparing to steal back what I'd rightfully earned.

I mistakenly thought it would be easy to thieve on this boardwalk filled with fathers flush with vacation pay. Seasonal workers manned the food stands, with no counter left unattended this busy holiday weekend. Part-time security guards watchfully strolled the boards. I perused gift shops, but all they sold were nautical souvenirs such as shark tooth necklaces, woven rope bracelets, and painted hermit crabs. Even if I were able to filch something, how could I pawn a giveaway lava lamp or a useless stuffed toy? I wove stealthily through the arcades and shooting galleries, looking for pockets to pick, but the pop of fake gunfire, the slap of metal ducks being shot down by teenage marksmen, and the thudding roll of skee-balls interfered with my concentration. Besides, the space in these game rooms was far too constricting. I saw no real room to maneuver, nor a viable getaway path. The only way out was through the front entranceway, and I stood a slim chance of outrunning the spry legs of a fleet-footed teen who probably wouldn't have more than a few quarters or allowance dollars in his possession anyway.

I switched directions, continuing past Moorlyn Terrace, trying my luck at the Wonderland Amusement Pier. With arched entranceways and flagged turrets fronting the boardwalk, the pier was constructed to resemble a Renaissance castle whose courtyard housed kiddie rides and carousels. The terraced portion opened onto Seventh Street, offering multiple escape routes if I got cornered and had to make a run for it. But I saw no opportunity to pickpocket here either, I discouragingly noted. Many of those same dads I had seen strolling the boardwalk stood vigilant guard over their broods, assisting their toddlers in boarding the bumper cars, tea cup rides, and tilt-a-whirls. With time running down and my frustration mounting, I decided to abandon the boardwalk and try my luck at the shops in the center of town.

Within minutes the inland sky rolled with dark thunderclouds and the winds picked up. Thick raindrops plopped on my forehead. I hurried to outrace them but the sky opened quickly. A thundershower, brief but violent, cracked white streaks of lightning over the sea, slapping gusts of water sheeting down the windows of the Chatterbox, a restaurant on Ninth and Central, where I took cover until the front passed.

I stood under the tiled eaves as the rain tapered to a patter, then ceased altogether. The raging squall blew out to sea and the dusk was cool with marshy bay winds. With less than a half-hour until I was scheduled to meet Sue and Ibby, I was mulling over my diminishing options when I saw a station wagon pull under the carport to the Sifting Sands Motel, down the street. As the family unpiled from the car, an idea came to me.

The red-faced patriarch, dressed in plaid shirtsleeves and loose-fitting khaki pants, stretched his long arms skyward as he stepped out from behind the wheel. He let forth a long, tired sigh, then strolled lazily toward the rear of the vehicle. Bursting from the tailgate, his two children raced toward the courtyard swimming pool and tested the water with their hands. Their father, I noticed, was without the services of a wife to help with them. His children, however, fell in line under his stern command when ordered back to the car to start unloading the suitcases and beach toys bungee-chorded to the luggage rack.

Hopscotching over the steaming street puddles, I followed the man into the motel lobby, decorated with hanging plant baskets and aerial photographs of the boardwalk damaged after a hurricane. A chamber of commerce calendar was tacked to the panelled wall, and a small stack of the *Weekly Guide of Ocean City*, compliments of management, was piled next to a swivel rack of AAA guides. The father rang the bell on the front desk. He tucked his shirtfront into his pants while waiting for the arrival of an attendant. To appear busy and purposeful, I opened one of the guides and skimmed through tasteful outdoor photographs of beautiful young college women like

Sue and Ibby, either posing on a jetty rock or leaning against the boardwalk handrail, their long hair aflutter in the wind. I familiarized myself with the alphabetically listed restaurants where we could eat.

"Long trip?" I asked the man as I flipped through the pages. I figured he was tired from being cooped in a car all day with his screaming kids and might be in a mood for some adult conversation.

"Ohio," he responded, flashing an affable smile. He removed his billfold from his back pocket and handed over his American Express card to the clerk, an elderly man wearing a wide-brimmed cattle rancher's hat and a bolo tie.

"I just came in from Seattle," I said.

"Vacation?"

"Honeymoon," I said, watching the clerk make an imprint of the card. He handed over a set of room keys. I momentarily lost the father's attention while the clerk directed him to his room, explaining where to find the ice machine. Hesitating by the doorway, the Ohioan seemed thrown by the motel layout. The clerk came out slowly from behind the counter, pointing out an idle maid's cart on the upper landing as a reference point, but the man still didn't follow.

"I'll be right with you, sir," the clerk hospitably reassured me, leading the man outside the door and under the carport. He put a hand on his meaty shoulder and pointed directly toward a door on the second floor terrace, adjacent to a sundeck.

I glanced back at the card sitting atop the metal punches,

then outside. The man still wasn't grasping the directions, and I judged by the level of his apparent confusion that the clerk would be a while explaining things. Keeping one eye on them both, I casually stepped backward toward the lobby desk, blindly feeling behind me for the card imprinter. I slipped the card and the carbon slip in my back pocket before quietly sliding out a side door. I didn't look back as I hightailed it toward the center of town, listening amusedly for either of them to give chase.

I went about looking for a fresh change of clothes, for my shirt was soggy with sweat and rainwater. I chose stores selectively, casing those establishments with lazy teenagers that didn't look up or bother to say hello when I walked in. Though I was energized and had an overwhelming desire to charge everything in sight, I shopped prudently, uncertain how long it would be before the tourist realized his card was missing and called it in as stolen. Moreover, I only had a half hour until I was to meet the girls.

The establishments on Asbury Avenue were mostly women's dress shops and boutiques staffed by sharp-eyed old ladies. However, I found a fancy clothier, Talese Town Shop, near Seventh Street. After trying on a yellow short-sleeved turtleneck and admiring myself in the dressing mirror, I simply strolled out the door wearing it as the gracious storeowner, a short Italian man wearing a measuring tape around his neck, was walking into the storeroom to find me another size. I waltzed into the Surf & Sand Dive Shop at the corner of Eighth Street and Atlantic and charged a $29.95 waterproof Belforte Sea

Diver watch and a Greg Noll Surfboards t-shirt that I stuffed into my bag. I gained a justified, derivative sense of revenge with each crime, convincing myself that by working gratis for Sam I had earned the right to these goods, much as a person earns the right to vote on his eighteenth birthday. I was also evening the score against the anonymous bandits who had stolen the money out of my sack. Infused with pride by my resourcefulness, I circuited the block, searching for a place to wash the saltwater scurf from my hair and the gray patches of sand pasted to the inside of my ankles. Aware of my rank odor, I also sought a place where I could wash up.

A backyard holiday clambake was being held at a home on Sixteenth Street. Cars were parked bumper to bumper out front. Standing beneath the leafy sidewalk elms, I heard the faint sound of laughter and the smell of charcoal fumes wafting over the backyard fence. I noticed an outdoor shower stall in a narrow shadowed alley between the house and the cottage next to it. The stall door was stuck, however, and the salt-corroded latch would not slide. Rather than fight to open it, I turned on the spigot connected to a garden hose coiled next to the stall. I stripped out of my clothes, slowly hosing myself down. I didn't rush, for I was thrilled by the possibility of being seen by woman, catching her by surprise as she passed by on the sidewalk. I continued to be amazed by the seeming naiveté of this town, that I could be standing here naked, washing myself unnoticed outside a stranger's home while a party was taking place just a few yards away.

SIXTEEN

I bounded up the porch stairs to 712 Ninth Street after washing off. The girls were staying at one of a cluster of similarly constructed Dutch Colonials framed arm's length from one another. Grooved with a router into a slab of pine the size of a fraternity paddle, the inlaid letters nailed above the threshold read *Boys Wait Here*. Cautiously observing the firm warning, I leaned my face to the screen door, cupping my hands to survey the entrance hall. The hallway opened onto a living room decorated with seashore prints and wooden mallard decoys. In the rear appeared to be a kitchen light, and from its direction sounded the gush of rushing water. I knocked. The water shut off and the faint shadow of a huddled woman, presumably the landlady, waddled through the shadows to answer the door. Though her face was smooth, the skin of her chest was rough and leathery against the scoop of her yellow dress, like the inside of a roll of salami. I smiled deeply into her light Nordic-blue eyes.

"Good evening, I hope I haven't interrupted your dinner. I'm Ted Bundy," I said. "I'm here for Elizabeth Haysbert and Susan Grenier."

"From the magazine, correct?" she asked in a thick Scandinavian accent, opening the door a little wider.

"Yes ma'am. In the flesh."

"We've heard so much about you already. Come in, come in, please," she said, widening the door to allow me inside. Standing inside the alcove, I breathed deep, audibly.

"Mmmmmm....chicken?"

"Stew," she answered, holding for support against the banister as she called up the staircase. "And you are from our nation's capitol, I'm told?" she asked.

"Seattle, originally, but actually I'm here in town on a photo shoot."

"Come in, come in," she urged.

I followed her stumpy, waddling frame into the kitchen. She shuffled next to the stove range, where a large tureen was boiling. I leaned over, slurping a wooden spoonful of the chicken broth she ladled out for me. It was a bit salty and too heavily saturated with celery in my estimation, but I closed my eyes and lapped my tongue anyway, humming my approval. I heard Sue and Ibby talking as they walked toward the kitchen, but kept my eyes closed, pretending to be so entranced by the deliciousness of the soup that I could focus on nothing else.

"I thought I heard you," Sue said. "You've met Mrs. Syben, I see."

"And experienced the fineries of her culinary expertise, I

might add," I said, faking a look of surprise as I turned to face her and Ibby. Sue wore a green blouse, faded bellbottom jeans and leather sandals. A straw purse was slung over her shoulder. Her long wet hair, freshly shampooed, smelled wet and clean, like morning air in a garden. Decked out in a swirl-patterned dress and silver hoop earrings, Ibby stood taller than her friend, with pink burn lines on her shoulders and raccoon stripes where her sunglasses had left their mark. As I stood admiring them, I still couldn't decide who was prettier, or which of the two I might like to go after if given the opportunity.

"Loving the outfits, ladies," I said. "Both of you, very sharp. Very sharp."

"Why, thank you," Sue said, beaming. "Pauline's Dress Shop. Not bad for downtown Godfrey, Illinois, right?"

"I'll say."

"Where's Larry?" Ibby asked.

"Larry won't be joining us till later on. He got hung up in traffic on the Atlantic City Expressway and will meet up with us at Tony Mart's around ten," I said with the familiarity of one who visits the bar regularly. "If he doesn't show by then, I'll call the hotel and see if he got lost. He'll meet us out, I promise."

Pouting, Ibby gave a slight shrug. She turned hastily, flouncing out the kitchen and down the hall.

"Shall we go?" Sue asked merrily.

"Let's do it," I said, also pretending to ignore what I had seen, worried Ibby's sulking might put a damper on the evening's pleasantness.

"Ted, can I trust you to have these young ladies back home by one-thirty?" Mrs. Syben asked, fidgeting with the leash fastened to her eyeglasses. "They have to be up with the roosters tomorrow morning."

"We'll be back by curfew, Mrs. Syben," Sue reassuringly answered down the hall, preceding me out onto the porch. I was proud to be appointed their chaperone, entrusted with the chivalrous responsibility for the girls' safety. I hoped they accepted their landlady's insightfulness as a clue to trust me.

Sue's car, a powder blue Chevy Impala convertible, was parked a block down the street, in the lot of Watson's Restaurant. Her dad had bought it last year for her eighteenth birthday, a fact she bashfully admitted when I asked how long it had been hers. She asked if I wanted to sit up front after I crawled into the backseat. I was touched by the selflessness of such a polite gesture. But she swiftly caught how her suggestion might be perceived, saying, "I mean, with your long legs and all."

"Long, yes, long and skinny," I blurted, in hopes Ibby might find the humor in my self-deprecation. But she didn't turn to notice them, or return my glance.

"They're not skinny," Sue assured me, flipping her hair from her shoulder as she pulled out of the driveway, turning north in the direction of the Ninth Street Bridge. Waiting in traffic for the drawbridge to close, my attention was drawn below the busy outdoor deck of Hogate's Restaurant. On a fuel dock below the restaurant seawall, a skewered swordfish swung by its tail on a rickety wooden scale hook, spinning like a man swinging from the gallows. A boat captain was flaying its tender white belly and tossing the oily guts into the water, where two sharks jostled.

"Bull sharks," I said. "I should have brought along my camera."

I was about to launch into another tale when Ibby turned to me, sharply asking, "Where to?"

I didn't care for her expectant tone. As penance for my friend indirectly standing her up, and by me foolishly guaranteeing his appearance later on, she seemed to have removed the task of playing host for the evening from her friend and placed the burden squarely on my shoulders. The success or failure of the night, her tone seemed to imply, rested with my choice of restaurants.

"Harry's Inn looked nice," I said, recalling the tourist guide. "They have a piano player, I read somewhere."

We drove off the island and out onto the causeway. The twilit sky, sketched with jet vapor, was an atmospheric shade of dark blue, throwing into relief the marsh grasses tipping sideways under the bend of the sulfurous crosswinds. A pinkish rim of half-fallen sunlight beamed from under the horizon, glowing low atop the swamp woods, like the view to a distant forest fire. The channels, lightly rippled by the storm, shimmered with the Bay Avenue dock lights entering our view as we went up a second bridge. As we looked for a place to park, I suggested we have drinks on the small stretch of secluded beach behind the liquor store lot, where we could take in the romantic sunset and enjoy our own little cocktail party before hitting the strip. And where I could try to grasp a better understanding of Ibby's supercilious attitude.

I went inside Circle Liquors, charging a bottle of rum, a cooler, a stack of plastic cups, and a six-pack of Cokes. I also grabbed a bag of ice from an outside chest, hoisting it on my shoulder as the girls followed me down a pathway leading to the beach. Sue pointed toward a secluded cove of bayberry scrub and wild beach heather. They kicked off their sandals as we took seats facing the yellow Ferris wheel lights, refracting over the Ocean City skyline on the far shores of the bay. I set up my bar on top of the cooler and mixed our drinks, giving a long pour of rum into each cup.

"Cheers," I said. We clicked cups, and with our hands still outheld, I proposed a toast: "Sue, here's to your success at Ithaca College, may it not overshadow your illustrious art career thereafter."

"Ibby was a great swimmer in high school," Sue interposed. "She was on the swim team at 'Cello."

"Well then, Miss Haysbert, here's to your winning us a gold medal at the Munich games."

"Cheers," Sue said. We held eyes for an instant.

"To Ocean City," I announced.

"To Ocean City," Sue said, a look of concern betraying her cheerfulness as she looked toward Ibby.

"Cheers," Ibby obligingly muttered. For a second she stared at me with a look of judgmental inquiry, as though again readjusting whatever earlier perspective she had formed. She gave a half-hearted lift of her cup, barely taking a sip. I tried giving her the benefit of the doubt, thinking that she was not as easily wooed as her friend, or maybe couldn't drink too much and was watching her intake, pacing herself for the night ahead. Neither rude nor impolite, she displayed a begrudgingly indifferent attitude, silently thwarting our enthusiasm. As she was a newcomer, and Sue more familiar with these towns, I hoped she might be playing the role of the politely deferring houseguest, or was miffed, perceiving herself as a third wheel. Sue tried including her in the conversation, but Ibby offered little, just that Minnesota mosquitoes grew giant in the summertime, and winters with the lake-effect snow were far too windy and cold for her liking. She had dreams of transferring to someplace warmer, a campus like UCLA or Arizona State, or maybe even Pepperdine, she said, squinting eastward across the bay. Sue, who until now had done a splendid job ignoring her friend's sullenness, seemed to sense Ibby's conspicuous silence stealing away the evening's jolly mood, and sought to keep her entertained.

"Are you getting excited about tomorrow, Ibby?" Sue asked.

"Like you can't imagine," Ibby answered, brightening for the first time all evening. "I've just been sitting here thinking about how nice it must be to go to a school like Davidson."

"Davidson?" I asked, eager to understand their connection to that noble Southern institution.

"Ibby and I are driving back to Philadelphia early tomorrow, and then we're going down there to see my cousin graduate," Sue said.

I resented how Ibby had so craftily manipulated her way back into the fold. News of their plans made me jealous. In what was to be my first evening out in some time, I was now learning that the exciting night I had hoped lay ahead was an insubstantial prelude to greater events in store for them.

The sun went under the dimming sky and the gnats started biting. A breeze shifted a black patch of clouds, shadowing the moon. I used the threat of bad weather as an excuse to move on, saying I had heard a marine advisory issue a small craft warning to vessels out at sea, and that another round of boomers was on the way. I was hungry, disappointed, and anxious to drink some more to quell the creeping disenchantment that news of their plans had incited. I wondered if coming to Somers Point had been a mistake, if I was being used, to be discarded like a fast food bag along the parkway when my services as a chaperone were no longer needed. I guzzled a last numbing swallow of rum before suggesting we get a move on, lest Sue's car be towed.

Crowds of college-aged friends, mostly young men and paired-off young couples, tramped over the lawn in the middle of the traffic circle and veered off down the side streets intersecting Bay Avenue. Without asking my preference, Ibby leaped in the front seat as we made the short drive down Shore Road toward the restaurant. She had been smiling broadly ever since Sue reminded her of their plans tomorrow. She threw back her head in deferential laughter at something Sue said, then peeked at me, making the inconvenience of my presence subtly known. Her mannerisms, although bratty, were alluring, almost playful, like she was somehow challenging me, tempting me to explore her further.

Harry's Inn was close by, on Maryland Avenue, just past Somers Point Hospital. The hostess led us to a quiet corner table with a view of the starlit deltas and dune bluffs spanning the distance between Somers Point and Longport. As advertised, there was a pianist, Nick Nickerson, a nattily spiffed crooner of older years attired in a white dinner jacket. Deferring to our waiter's expertise, I ordered two bottles of white wine without bothering to look at their price or vintage. I made a show of savoring the bouquet, swirling the wine in my mouth with my eyes closed before accepting his selection. Ibby ordered nothing to eat, not even a salad, even after I reassured her that I was treating. She snacked on a buttered roll and sipped at her water as I devoured my lobster, and Sue her prime rib. Indulging Sue's chatter with nods and gestures, I wondered what Ibby was thinking, why she paid me no mind. I couldn't take my eyes off her as we ate, admiring the smooth glow of her tanned shoulders, the shine of her long pretty hair in the candlelight.

I was taken aback when the bill arrived. It was nearly a hundred dollars. The chattering girls fell silent as I patiently studied it. Sue offered her share, but I declined her offer. I was careful not to seem as though I was disputing the total, just making certain I hadn't been unnecessarily charged. I returned the card to the waiter in the closed receipt folder while the girls sipped their coffee. A few more moments passed, and when our waiter did not return, I grew quiet and edgy.

"So Ted, let's hear another one of your stories," Sue said.

Suddenly less confident than earlier, I told them the one about being suspended on a rope bridge over a waterfall, then stopped, promising to continue the story once we got into the car. I asked the girls if they had seen our waiter. Ibby pointed him out. He was talking on the phone in the service area, near the heat lamps, looking in our direction. *They're dialing it in*, I thought. Acting quickly, I stood, tossing my napkin on my chair.

"Ready to hit the town?" I asked, expanding my chest, letting out a satisfied yawn.

"What about the bill?" Sue asked.

"Don't you worry about that," I said. Hurrying them along, I asked, "Why don't you two get the car started?"

"Are you sure? Here, let me give you some money," Sue offered in a proudly self-reliant tone.

"Please, girls, I can't take your money. It'd be like stealing. I'll expense it," I assured them. "Plus, there was something on the check I needed to talk about with the manager. I think we were overcharged on that sour grape juice they call wine." I took another sip, confirming my disapproval with a wincing scowl. "Go ahead, you two pull the car around. I'll be out in no longer than five minutes, I promise."

I timed their dismissal perfectly. The manager, a squirrel-ish, bespectacled man in a silk vest made a beeline toward our table. Anticipating his approach, I stood and hastened toward the front doors. He interrupted me halfway across the dining room as I tried passing him. Though acknowledging him, I didn't stop to speak with him, continuing toward the hostess stand as though I had some business to conduct there. He changed directions, following alongside me as he spoke.

"Mr. Healey? Randall Healey? I'm sorry, but there must be some mistake, your card has been reported as stolen."

Galled, I stood close to him and bore directly into his eyeglasses. "I'm not following," I said.

"I'm truly sorry, this sometimes happens."

"Call it in again," I sharply ordered, coolly clenching my fingers behind my back.

"Did you want to pay with another card this evening? We accept Diner's Club, of course, or…"

I reached over to a dish on the hostess stand and peeled open a dinner mint, casually slipping it into my mouth. I helped myself to a book of matches as well.

"Did you have cash with you?" he asked.

I remarked loudly, "If I had cash on me, I would have used it to pay the bill, wouldn't I? I'm appalled by your insinuation." I sucked hard on the mint, loudly slurping its juices through my teeth.

He was unrattled by the severity of my indignation, modulating his voice so it didn't rise above a low whisper. "Nobody's insinuating anything, sir. As I said, I'm terribly sorry, but I'll need some alternate form of payment for your meal."

"Call it in again. I can wait all night." I rocked on my heels. "Are you going to call them, or do I have to?"

"Very well," he said curtly. He walked over to the phone by the service area and began dialing. The waiters passed around him, balancing coffee pots and wheeling desert trays. I smiled at the young blonde hostess erasing and sketching the seating chart, gazing the length of her body as she pretended to look busy.

The manager nodded, staring at me. "He's right here," he said with a smug grin, handing over the receiver.

"Hello, who am I speaking with?" asked a lady on the other line.

"This is Randall Healey," I answered, intermittently nodding.

"Mr. Healey, for verification purposes, could you please tell me your date of birth?"

"November the twenty-sixth," I said, then muttering, "Nineteen twenty-seven." I turned around to face the manager.

"I'm sorry, sir, but that's not the date of birth we have in our records for a Mr. Healey," she said. "What is your home address, sir?"

"No, no, I understand you have to do your job," I said, talking over her. "Just a simple misunderstanding is all…no, there's no need to apologize, these things happen. Okay, I'll tell him. Would you like to talk to him? No? Sure, I'll tell him, you have a nice evening as well. No, that's okay, I completely understand, no apology is necessary."

"She said to call in the account number one last time as a formality," I told the manager. "It should work this time. I have to use your men's room, if you'll excuse me." Acting as though I hadn't a care in the world, I went into the stall, making certain the door was locked behind me. I ripped out a roll of toilet paper from the dispenser and hurriedly unravelled it, bunching it on the floor tiles near the door so that it would not ignite anything else. Crouching, I lit the bundle, momentarily spellbound by the rapid ascension of flames unwinding from the pile, the scorched fabric floating upward in charred flakes. As the bathroom quickly fogged with gray puffy smoke, I stood and calmly walked out.

The manager had just hung up the phone when I returned. He stood poised, as though ready to intercept my flight were I to try for the exit. I asked a table of four yammering old ladies, "Do you smell something burning?"

There was a gradual quieting. Dishes stopped chinking. Voices lowered, displaced by a nervous murmur. *Fire? Did somebody say fire? Where?* Bewildered, people looked to the ceiling, out the windows, behind them in search of smoke. Some of the men stood halfway from their chairs, making audible sniffing sounds in the surrounding air. Seeking to defuse the rumbling agitation, the manager stood befuddled for a second, directing his nose toward the source of the smell. He motioned one way, then another, trying to sort through the confusing bombardment of priorities, as if seized by which took precedent. Before leaving his post for an extinguisher on the opposite wall, he looked at me with a sportsmanlike grin, as if conceding he had been outwitted.

Sue had pulled the car around front, where she and Ibby were waiting. "What happened with the check?" Sue asked.

"He took the wine off our bill," I said, sitting low in the

back. I felt no euphoric aftermath to this crime, not even a smug satisfying sense of justification that in some distant way I could attribute to Sam. The fright of being apprehended scared me sober. Stealing a credit card was one thing, arson something entirely different, a crime that would necessitate notifying the police and fire department and prompt an active search for a culprit. I had made a scene and my theatrical diversions were witnessed by many. As we drove to Tony Mart's bar, somewhere out in the night I heard the distant wail of a fire engine grow louder as a searchlight swept back and forth across the sky. I thirsted for another drink to deaden my nerves, fearing what imperiling consequences awaited me at my next destination.

SEVENTEEN

FOLLOW THE ARROW TO TONY MART- Were it not for the loud display of this neon roof sign, consisting of a spastically blinking red arrow pointing downward to its sidewalk entrance, Tony Mart's nightclub might have been mistaken for a small fish cannery. The three-story, flat-roofed building, built overlooking a dirt parking lot, occupied the corner of Bay and Goll Avenues. The outside walls were painted in alternating shamrock-green and white checkerboard squares. Brushed in faded strokes across the cinder walls of an outbuilding were the words *SHOWPLACE OF THE WORLD* and on a blue ribbon beneath it, *Thru our doors walk the most beautiful girls in the world.* People in the parking lot were pouring out of cars, their shrill laughter echoing across the seashore night. Droves ventured merrily down the streets toward the building's sidewalk entrance, beneath a marquee posting the bands headlining that evening: Gunther's Bus, Papa Rising, and Tears of the Sun.

We stood under the green awning above the doors, joining the line of people waiting to get inside. I managed to convince myself that I was needlessly worrying and mimed all outward appearances of contentment. I smiled, laughing at a harmless joke Sue cracked about the Three Wise Men in a bar, when in actuality I betrayed a gnawing fear of being arrested. I imagined what it might be like to be handcuffed and put to answer before a New Jersey judge, sentenced to hard time, being forced to work on a chain gang. Having a criminal record. I could run from here, as I had from Seattle, Roxborough, and New York City, but where would I go with no money and no place to stay? The line nudged forward a bit as a large group was let inside. I adjusted my position to where Ibby and Sue screened me from the view of the Bay Avenue traffic. I wanted to provide Ibby and Sue access to the convivial laughter surrounding us, to be part of a familiarity the other people in line enjoyed, which I was unable to provide. I reminded myself of the persona I had created; I could be whomever I wanted to, and that I would be having sex with one of these two beautiful women before the night ended. But this freedom did not eradicate my insecurities. With my newly formed identity came the confinement of playing a role that grew more difficult the more I worried about recriminations for my unlawful acts. Right now, the restaurant manager was surely describing me to the police, and the wagons would soon begin circling. It was too late to concede defeat and admit to the girls that the business about *National Geographic* had all been an elaborately designed hoax. That news would surely scare Ibby and Sue into abandoning me in this distant town where nobody knew me.

The inside of the crowded bar was steamy and smelled of evaporating beer, sweat, and perfume. There were two small rectangular bars at either side of the entrance. A trio of clowning undergraduate men stood singing their fraternity fight song, hungrily looking to make eye contact with each woman who entered. Along the paneled walls, fluorescent zodiac prints hung above the glowing jukebox lights, and miniature felt pennants from schools such as Princeton and Lafayette were tacked along the ceiling beams. We shambled down a congested aisle ending at the three stages in the rear. Cigarette coals bobbed underneath a formless black outline of heads swaying under the stage lights. A sweaty crowd was grooving under a smoky haze to the band Gunther's Bus, whose members, clad in matching beige tunics, strummed an Iron Butterly cover tune. A go-go dancer in a Cleopatra wig danced solo on a raised circular platform between two stages. Wearing a shiny silver minidress that looked like it came from the set of a sci-fi movie, she seemed to be carving an imaginary figure with her hands, shaking her tambourine wildly as if under a Pentecostal spell. Sue, sensing my most immediate needs, leaned over and screamed into my ear, asking what I'd like to drink.

As she went to fetch beers I was left standing alone with Ibby. We spent several uncomfortable moments alongside each other, watching the band from within our confining silence. One sector of my brain wondered what Ibby was thinking, the other feared that the authorities were sweeping the area, going from bar to bar in search of a brown-haired young man passing himself off as Randall Healey from Elyria, Ohio. Finally working up the nerve to say what had been bothering her all evening, Ibby moved to face me.

"Do you really work for *National Geographic?*" she asked, staring me in the eye. For the first time I noticed one of her pupils was slightly askance and wandered, an intriguing feature I hadn't noticed earlier.

"Of course. Why do you ask?"

"I was just thinking about something you said earlier, is all."

"Which was?"

"Well, first you asked where the Tradewinds Motel was. Maybe it's my imagination, but then you said that you were meeting Barry, or Larry, I forget what his name was. But then right before we left the beach, when Sue asked where you were staying, you said the Lincoln Hotel. And then after you came to pick us up, and we were driving, you said something like, 'I should have brought along my camera,' when we saw those sharks near the bridge. I remember thinking, Didn't he say he was a writer?"

"His name is Larry, not Barry," I said incredulously.

"It's just that there are all sorts of stray men that have been coming up to Sue all weekend, telling lies. She's a little naïve. I'm just looking out for her best interests," she said, returning her attention to the band with a look of irrefutable satisfaction.

I was blistered by her forthrightness, but kept my cool. "Why would I lie about where I worked?"

"Maybe you were trying to impress us."

"Maybe I was trying to impress you? That's mighty presumptuous of you, don't you think? What reason would there be for me to impress you?"

"None. Look, that's not what I'm saying, Ted, that's not what I meant. I shouldn't have said anything, but it just seems a little strange that you would come down here by yourself is all," she said. "Everybody else here seems to have come with somebody, a friend or something, and you're here alone," she continued, pitying my loneliness, a facet of my personality I thought was impenetrably hidden as a time capsule. Worse, she had cavalierly sized me up, exposing me as the aimless drifter I was. And she was dead-on accurate, that was the most cutting aspect of her damning appraisal, the part of the blade that struck bone. Her usage of the manipulative tricks I thought only I was privy to deepened my desire to take her.

"Didn't I say Larry was going to meet up with us later on?" I asked. While still enrolled in classes at Washington, I had done a research paper on "The Barnum Effect," based upon a personality theory developed by psychologist Bertram Forer. Highly skeptical of psychics and astrologers claiming to have paranormal insights into the human mind, he argued that people subjectively validate personality tests of themselves as highly accurate, but which they do not realize are universally predictable. I borrowed directly from Dr. Forer in attempting to break Ibby's resolute spirit. "Your quietness doesn't fool me, Elizabeth Haysbert. I have you all figured out."

"Oh, you do?"

"You have a great need for other people to like and admire you. You have a tendency to be critical of yourself. While you have some personality weaknesses, you are generally able to compensate for them. Though you're disciplined and self-controlled outside, you tend to be worrisome and insecure inside. At times you have serious doubts as to whether you've made the right decision or done the right thing. You pride yourself as an independent thinker and don't accept others' statements without satisfactory proof. You've found it unwise to be too frank in revealing yourself to others. At times you're extroverted, affable and sociable, while at other times you're introverted. Am I right, Ibby? Be honest."

"Let's just drop it, OK?" she said, pouting regretfully, as though she had been severely reprimanded.

"I'm just teasing you, sweetheart." I smiled, gaping down the front scoop of her dress, then back up at her, making certain she'd seen me.

"We're back," Sue announced cheerily, standing beside a pair of tall young men. "You guys, this is Ronnie Walden, from Cairo, Georgia. And his friend, Ethan."

Darkly tanned, Ronnie was athletically postured, with sleepy blue eyes and long blond hair. The whiskery scruff on his chin partly camouflaged the traces of an abandoned goatee. Underneath an open leather vest he wore a purple silk shirt unbuttoned to the middle of his smooth, thickly muscled chest.

A green string of jangling love beads swung from his neck as we leaned in to shake hands. He was the type of man handsome enough to stir glances of competitive mistrust in other good-looking men. I'd seen his sort before, cockily clumping his ski boots through the lodges in Washington, watching to see which women turned to admire him. Acutely aware of his presence, I could see where some of the women in the bar were giggling and whispering to one another, subtly elbowing their friends to have a look. Unable to deflect the attention from him, I felt inadequate and put at a disadvantage. As a worldly journalist from a famous magazine, shouldn't I be the one deserving of such adulation? By contrast, his even taller friend had a drawn face, thin lips, and an oily protruding chin. Pale, with long black hair and bushy muttonchops, he was wearing an aqua-print Hawaiian shirt tucked too deeply into a pair of new blue jeans. Uncomfortable, it seemed, in his thin gangly frame, he nervously twirled a pinky ring, as if aware I was taking note of all his superficial imperfections.

"I'd like you to meet my best friend Ibby Haysbert, and this is Ted...I'm sorry, I've already forgotten your last name," Sue laughed.

"Bundy," I said, quietly seething. I saw myself as no more than an insignificant tagalong without credentials, just as Ibby had inferred.

"Ted is a photographer for *National Geographic*," she said flatly, as though no longer believing it herself.

I stood faithfully by my lie, sheepishly acknowledging her modest introduction. But the sting was not removed from the embarrassing linger. I caught the tail end of an eye roll Ibby made toward Sue. My self-restraint continued to evoke a frustrating resentment erotically stimulated by Ibby's flagrant disbelief, and my desire to have her deepened correspondingly. I suddenly fantasized dragging her back to the same beach where we had had our cocktails and having my way with her, teaching her a lesson in humility.

"Ronnie has an absolutely wild story he just told me," Sue said. "Why don't you tell Ted and Ibby what you just told me?" she asked. "Ibby is a huge Doors fan."

"I met Jim Morrison yesterday in Greenwich Village," he said with a deep Southern drawl, taking a huge swig of beer as he surveyed our reaction. He seemed to read my skeptical gaze, addressing me in particular even though we were all listening. "I can't believe it myself, Ted." He had the knack salesman have of making you feel good about yourself by repeating your first name. "Hey Ted, have you ever heard of the Café Au Go-Go?"

I hadn't. "Of course," I said.

"Then you know it's this place in Greenwich Village, right? Dig this: I was visiting a musician friend of mine from Cairo High School, Ellery Potter. He lives with a bunch of roommates in a walkup above a Chinese restaurant on Bleecker Street, right next to the nightclub. It was like three in the morning. Ellery was having a little soirée, you know, like four or five people were over, nothing big, just casual, everybody smoking and drinking, hanging out and listening to Ellery play guitar. We were smoking opium out of this huge wooden-carved hookah pipe that Vikran Rajdeep, this Indian cat who was a friend of Ellery's, brought back from a visit to Bangladesh. I got stoned real fast, that weird, mellowy opium high, and wanted to crash, but everybody was still up. We were all sitting in a circle in the floor, and Vikran says to this skinny blonde girl named Pam zoning out in a beanbag chair near the front door, 'Didn't Jim say he was stopping by later?' I didn't think anything of it. Like an hour or two later, I was zonked and passed out on the floor. There was no air-conditioning in the place. I was sweating my ass off. You know what it's like when you're tanked and you wake up and it's real hot and stuffy, you can't sleep? That's what it was like, only hotter. Stifling, man, stifling. Anyway, when I woke up, everybody was gone.

"I needed to cut out and get some fresh air," he continued, "and so I went downstairs to take a walk, to see if I could find a place to get some cigarettes, a joint that would be open at that hour of the night, or morning, I guess. Dig it-I walk downstairs, and who do I meet coming up?" He huddled us together, as though he was the quarterback calling the final play on a last-minute drive. We all pressed in to listen. "Jim Morrison," he said, pulling back to gauge our expressions.

"Get out of here!" Ibby exclaimed.

"No shit," Ronnie said. "Remember last week, Friday night, when him and the rest of the Doors were on that PBS show *The Critique?*"

"I read about that," Ibby said. "But we couldn't get the station in Godfrey."

Ronnie was a captivating storyteller, almost as good as Sam. He continued to read my eyes, as if sensing that I doubted him. "They filmed that episode at the Channel 13 studios on West Thirty-third Street, I heard later on," he said. "So it made sense that he would be in the city. Like I said, he was walking up the stairs as I was on my way down. At first I didn't recognize him, with that funky brown beard he wears nowadays. He had on those same big sunglasses he wore on the show, so I couldn't see his eyes. 'Hey, man' he says, and nods at me. I put two and two together when I heard that low monotone voice of his. 'Smoke?' he asks me. I didn't know whether he was offering one or wanted one. He reached behind his ear, where he had a cigar tucked, then he goes into his shirt pocket for a lighter. He must have had that little gauge on the lighter set at high, because the flame that shot out of it was so enormous I thought it might catch his beard. He started twirling the cigar to get it lit. I told him that I was a big fan, that I had had tickets to the April show at the Spectrum in Philly that got cancelled because of the Miami incident. With those sunglasses on I couldn't see his eyes, read what he was thinking, or tell whether he was listening. Real strange cat, though. He said that he was getting ready to publish a book of poetry. 'Ummm…Philly..ever hear of Thomas Eakins?' I told him I hadn't. 'Ummmmm…he used to take pictures of the primates at the Philadelphia Zoo.' He recites a few poems which I can't think of right now, and then he goes, 'Is Pam here?' I say, 'No, it's just me and my buddy Ellery, this is his pad,' then I ask him if he wants to come upstairs and hang out, and he just shakes his head, walks down the stairs and splits into the night, like it was no big thing. Is that wild or what?"

"Who's Thomas Eakins?" I asked, unconvinced.

"A famous nineteenth-century artist," Sue said. "A photographer also."

"Morrison is a fan of Eakins? What a trip!" Ibby said.

My face burned with embarrassment. How could a photojournalist not have heard of such a well-known photographer?

Her eyes wide open, Ibby stood in quiet amazement, casting Ronnie a look of heroic devotion she hadn't given to my legends of swashbuckling pirates roaming the high seas, or the story of careening through the jungle to document the discovery of early man. Although I still suspected he was lying, I didn't call him on it for fear I would appear like a spoilsport, jealous of being outshined. More so, I risked blowing my cover if Ronnie decided to counterpunch with a few probing questions of his own, an interrogation Ibby would certainly join in on if invited.

A light show commenced onstage. The footlights changed from yellow to red, then went green, purple. A liquid projector lit a kaleidoscopic swirl of psychedelic bubbles on the ceiling above the drummer's head. He broke into a freaky solo in the middle of "In-A-Gadda-Da-Vida," contorting his mouth into a series of odd facial tics. Ronnie took Sue and Ibby by their hands, leading them to the floor in front of the stage, where they merged into the swarm of people dancing.

I was left standing with Ethan. The bar had a seven-glasses-for-the-price-of-one special. I noticed him ogling Sue as he relayed a glass to me.

"Ronnie's so full of it," he said, laughing. "That bit about Jim Morrison, he made it all up."

"I figured as much," I said.

"He told the last group of girls we met that he was from the backwoods of Florida, studying the teachings of the Jehovah's Witnesses in preparation for a mission."

"How old are you?" I asked.

"Eighteen."

"What about Ronnie?"

"I think he's like twenty-two, or at least that's what he told me," he said.

"How do you know each other?" I asked.

"I hitchhiked down here from Norristown two days ago, just to hang out for the weekend and see if I could meet some girls. We just met earlier tonight, at an olive oil party we were both crashing. Ronnie said he was on his way to California."

"An olive oil party?"

"It's like a swingers' party," he said. "It's sort of like a tradition down here, from what I've heard. What happens is, somebody throws a house party, and in one of the rooms are all these Twister mats covered in olive oil. It's like a big Roman orgy, with people dressed in togas and drinking red wine and swapping wives and girlfriends." He laughed excitedly, saying, "Ronnie and me got to talking because we were the youngest guys there and didn't know anybody, and we seemed out of place because we weren't dressed up in costumes. This lady, you know, a middle-aged housewife type, comes up to us and starts telling Ronnie how cute he is, and how she just *loves* his accent. Then she takes him down the hall and into this room. I go outside onto the deck to get high, when the music shuts off all of a sudden. I hear two people screaming at each other. Something weird must have happened between Ronnie and this lady, maybe he got rough with her or something, because when I went back inside, he was going at it with the host, who turned out to be the lady's husband. We split before the guy could call the cops on us."

"How'd you wind up here?" I asked.

"After we left the party I was all ready to hitch a ride back to Norristown. Then Ronnie pulled out this wad of cash he said he found on the beach today and talked me into staying and going out drinking with him."

"That's some story," I said, laughing along with him. "And where did Ronnie find the money, again? Sorry, the music's too loud, I can't hear myself think."

"On the beach."

"Where on the beach?" I caught the eagerness in my tone and momentarily backed off from a further inquisition when he didn't answer. I resisted the impulse to immediately confront Ronnie. He was doing the monkey with Sue and Ibby, their fists moving up and down, hair flailing. I sensed an empowering sense of control over him, my jealousy replaced by a compelling urge to manipulate him into blathering his secrets, to hear how well he could lie when faced by an accuser who knew the truth about him.

While deciding how I would congratulate Ronnie on his fortuitous discovery, I saw a vaguely familiar woman seated at an L-shaped bar that wrapped around the stage. She was seated no more than twenty feet away from where we were standing. I stood watching her for some time through the twirling spots reflecting off the mirror ball above the dance floor. The light beams carouseled off her face in colorous speckles, making it difficult to maintain focus and recall where I had last seen her. Seattle? Tacoma? Circles of swiftly moving images spiraled sideways past my vision, like terrains seen streaking past a boxcar door. Then a swell of relief gushed through me, as I finally recognized Avery Dwyer.

She was talking to a man seated on the stool next to her. Dressed to party, she presented an entirely different image from the pristine girl I remembered bending to put her car top down in her parents' driveway. She wore her long blonde hair held back with a paisley headscarf. A pea-green halter-top was held together around her neck by a thin metal choker. In between turning in her stool to look at the entranced drummer and talking to the man seated next to her, she flashed me a glance, as though she remembered me also but was confused by when we might have met. Pondering what mode of introduction might work best, I left Ethan by himself and wound through a commotion of sweaty bodies to reach her.

"Your name's Lauren, right?" I politely asked. She stared at me without batting a lash, as if she hadn't a clue what I was talking about. Her spring tan had begun to peel, flaking into tautly yanked roots where her scalp began. Her eyes, washed colorless by the spiked lashes shadowing them, were difficult to read.

"Sorry, you've got the wrong person," she said.

"I didn't mean to stare at you like that, but for a second there I thought you were someone I knew. That was rude of me. I apologize." I briskly drew back after delivering the misdirected compliment, as though suddenly uninterested. I hoped she would detect the insincerity of my apology, the falseness of my dejection. I knew from experience that a young woman such as Avery, accustomed to flattery and attention in all its permutations, couldn't help being intrigued by such brazen indifference to her prepossessing beauty, or accept being mistaken for someone else.

"Where did you think you knew me from?" she answered, spinning in her stool to face me. Although she was courteous, her voice was stern with reproachful insistence. Her unamused tone let me know she had little time for playing, that if I hadn't summoned her to offer a drink or present a come-on, then I'd better be prepared to finish whatever I thought had been important enough to interrupt her. I considered telling her I was finishing up my last year of medical school, but backed off when I sensed by her assertiveness that she wasn't the sort who would fall for such bullshit, and that she'd soon remember me and call my bluff. I didn't wish to be in a position where I'd have to explain my remarks, but I went ahead and lied despite myself.

"For a second there I thought you were the T.A. for my

anatomy lab at Penn, but you're not," I said. "I've mistaken you for somebody else. You're far prettier, though."

"Why, thank you," she impatiently commented.

I smacked my forehead with the heel of my hand, laughing loudly.

"Did I miss something?" she asked.

"I remember you now. You're Avery Dwyer, right? Sam Cowell is my grandfather. Remember, we cut your lawn?"

"Oh yeah, I'm sorry. I remember now, right, right! Who are you here with?" she asked, lightening suddenly, seemingly atoning for her standoffishness. As she reached for her cup of beer, I noticed her diamond engagement ring, the round cut stone aglitter under the stage lights. A profound dispiritedness recycled itself, an emotion I realized had always been with me, hiding in remission like a rare cancer cell a patient is deluded into thinking he has successfully radiated, but which returns years later, strengthened in its mutated form.

Breathing heavily, her forehead flushed from dancing, Ibby suddenly stood before us. Strangely, her presence was rescuing. I put my arm around her and introduced her to Avery. Hoping to instigate a little jealousy in Avery, I gave Ibby's shoulder a tight squeeze. She seemed oblivious to my freshness, zeroing in instead on the discourse she had just interrupted. She didn't stiffen as I pulled her to me, but neither did she reciprocate my embrace, or waver her focus from Avery.

"Do you work at *National Geographic* also?" Ibby asked, seemingly very interested to learn how we knew one other, anxious to verify my credentials. Frantically in search of a history between Avery and me, I felt the squeeze of claustrophobia setting in. I fell silent, shamed with fearful embarrassment for having underestimated the possibility of a chance run-in like this.

"*National Geographic*?" Avery asked. "I thought you were pre-law at the University of Washington." Befuddled, she glanced uncertainly at us both, as though we would need to fill her in on the secret. "Wait, didn't you just say you went to Penn and were in an anatomy lab or something?"

Pretending not to hear her question over the music, I shrugged and drew back my head, pointing to my ear. Dizzily contemplating modes of disentanglement, I decided it best to say nothing, to force each woman to ponder her own interpretation of what she'd just heard. My chest tightened. The more oxygen I drew in, the harder it was to breathe.

Avery tapped the man sitting next to her. "This is my fiancé, Chase," she said. He was tall with raked black hair, and smiled disarmingly as he shook my hand. While under different circumstances such an introduction to her betrothed might have devastated me, by this point I didn't care, just felt the need to get out of here, step outside and reassess my dilemma. "Ted and his grandfather cut our grass," she said, matter-of-factly referring to me as the help. I felt Ibby's sidelong glance, imagined her silent ridicule.

Sue joined us. "I just came over to tell you that we're leaving, Ted," she said. "We have to get up early to leave tomorrow. It was nice meeting you, though." She leaned over and kissed my cheek. Smirking, as if inviting me to imagine what she was thinking, Ibby turned to look at me one last time. Preceding Sue, she ducked out one of the side exit doors near us without saying goodbye to me. I scanned the dance floor for Ethan and Ronnie, but they had left as well. Of all the humiliating consequences, I never imagined the girls would leave so soon, and without me. I was suddenly on my own, with ten dollars in my pocket and a backpack filled with stolen clothing. *My backpack*, I suddenly remembered.

I abruptly excused myself and hustled outside, but Sue's car was gone. With my head low, I self-consciously trod back over the traffic circle, remembering the rum on the beach behind the liquor store. It remained in a stand of dunes where I had left it. I took a long quenching swallow to ease my anger and silence the distant cries of band music and street laughter echoing in the night. A lulling hum of car tires thumped over the buckles of the Ship Channel Bridge. The streetlights and neon parking lot signs and boat lights and channel markers swirled before my eyes as I finished off the bottle. Entombed in a nearsighted haze, I lost my sense of place, wondering from which point I had begun. Backtracking to the bar, I zigzagged through dirt parking lots, drunkenly staggering through rain puddles gullied at the uneven spots. The bright white glare cast from the Bay Shores Café sign swerved and bobbed in blurry circles against the night sky. I took a long arcing piss, dousing the passenger-side seat of a Mustang convertible. Swaying, I was unable to aim straight, splattering onto the side of the car. A group of hippies leaning against a yellow microbus parked at the edge of the seawall were filling a balloon from a nitrous oxide tank. Witness to my shenanigans, one of them looked up at me, laughing hysterically when he realized what I was doing.

"Partner," he called out, offering me the balloon.

Weaving, I took a hit, inhaling deeply.

"Hold it in," he urged.

Gripping the balloon, I went dizzy suddenly, like a child at a birthday party blindfolded and spun in different directions as he tries to whack open the piñata. I caught my balance against the van. A sound similar to shattering crystals reverberated throughout my brain, followed by a noise like rubber hands pinging back and forth, going *winga winga winga,* building to a crescendo. I began giggling uncontrollably when I thought I heard a bottle smash across the street, a pocket of distant laughter, the echo of my name cocooned within the noise.

Eighteen

It was dark and I could see nothing. I reached into the blackness in front of my face and touched a flat wooden board. For a horrifying instant I feared I had been buried alive, laid in a coffin six feet under the cold hard ground. Seized with panic, I wriggled about until I felt the sand underneath me. As my equilibrium evened, I came to realize I was in Ocean City again, under the boardwalk.

I crawled out from under the boards and checked my watch. Four a.m. Sucking on a balloon was the last thing I remembered. Dizzy, I shook the sand from my head, wiping a broken shell from my elbow. The sudden rise in elevation rocketed my blood pressure, spinning me off balance. I went down on all fours and vomited, splashing hot streams of bile onto the sand. My esophagus burned with caustic sodas tasting like rum and stale tap beer. The throes of my lurching spasms caused the pounding in my head to grow louder, more resonant.

Recuperating between purges, I wiped my lips with the back of my hand. I curled into a fetal position, pressing my fingers to my temple, palpating the clammy skin in circular motions. I pressed hard as I could, unknitting the tired knots. A sedating remission followed, the grinding from my fingers bursting a wallow of self-medicating opiates upon my storm-ravaged belly.

When I felt well enough to stand, I stripped out of my clothes and staggered toward the ocean. The moonlit surf, aglow with plankton, lay flat as a millpond. The rhythmic break of the ankle-high surf hissed feebly as its suds withdrew into the hard sand. Needing to think clearly, I dove under the icy black water, felt its undertow sweep the back of my knees. The sobering cold pried a wider glimpse into my recent memory. Doubtless rescued by instincts of self-preservation, I remembered Sue saying that she and Ibby would be leaving for home at five o'clock this morning. Convulsing with shivers, I checked my watch again. It was four-fifteen, which left me forty-five minutes to get to the Somers Point traffic circle if I stood any chance of meeting them and getting a ride home. I would put aside my pride, anger, shame and resentment, confess my lies, hope they were sympathetic to my plight and take pity on me. Beholden to them, I would ask for a ride to the train station in Philadelphia, call my mother, beg her forgiveness, then have her Western Union me enough dough for the train fare back to Seattle. My mother, who by now would know about the money I had stolen from her parents.

Nude and shivering, I trotted back to my clothes, drawing

humorous stares from two early morning surfcasters strolling with their rods and minnow buckets in the direction of the pier. I gazed up after putting on my clothes. Above the overcast sky a streaking comet flared out like a dud round of tracer fire. The Wonderland Pier Ferris wheel stood motionless at a half- crescent, the ride chairs silent in the darkness, the movie theatre lights shut off. Ashamed to be awake at an hour of the morning those who led holier lives slept through, I shuffled guiltily down Ninth Street with my head down and my hands tucked in my pockets. The avenues were silent except for the electrical transformers buzzing through the telephone wires and the whir of air conditioner units blowing in the alleyways. I contemplated stealing a car, joyriding it to Philadelphia, then abandoning it in a North Philly ghetto. But it was too quiet in the streets, and I was in too fragile a condition to unscrew a steering column and splice ignition wires, even if I'd had the necessary tools with me.

I trudged over the Ninth Street Bridge, then along the causeway shoulder where old black men fished off the levee rocks. The bay was overspread with a mist thick as lake smoke. A soft chime of junction buoys tolled mournfully in the distance, like church tower bells signaling the close to a minister's sunrise benediction; deceivingly peaceful nautical sounds that no longer fooled me with their illusory optimism, as the glorious sights of this town had gulled me when I first crossed its boundaries.

Hearing a car come up behind me, I turned and held out my thumb. A Buick whistled by without stopping to offer a ride to this exiled male straggler cast off into the night. I turned forward again as it sped away, solemnly watching its muted taillights narrowing into the dark haze. If I were a beautiful woman like Ibby or Sue, surely they would stop and pick me up, I angrily concluded, reminding myself of their betrayal. A simple beggar, a half-wit dependent on the whimsical benevolence of the public, that's all I am, no better off than the Forty-second Street imbeciles whose filthy, meaningless insignificance I'd so haughtily demeaned. Wrestling with the bitter indignation gnawing at my soul, I fantasized what vengeance I would wreak upon the girls if I saw them again, especially Ibby. Believing it was my duty to dispossess them of their sense of entitlement, rape crossed my mind. But how could I carry out such a dastardly act when I needed something from them yet? As my motivations simmered, a brisk wind scented with smoke and washed up fish gusted in from the west. I suddenly remembered setting the toilet paper ablaze, running out on the check, memories the rum had blanked. Although it was night yet, darkness was thinning. I stepped up the pace. When the sun came up I would be easier to find, conspicuous out here all alone, in plain sight of roaming squad cars searching for an arsonist who also fit the description of a credit card thief.

Footsore from the long walk across the bay, I arrived at the circle, scoping behind stores and restaurants for a dark secluded sanctuary where I could rest and watch for Sue's Chevrolet as she drove over the bridge. The smoke of baked fries and grilled pancakes wafted from the Somers Point Diner, the only establishment with its lights on. I checked the lot, but Sue's car was not there. The time was four-forty-five. I had only fifteen minutes until they were scheduled to arrive.

I snuck onto the dew-soaked grounds of Somers Mansion, a historical site on a hilltop occupying the town's highest point. The patchy, moonshadowed lawn, wet with silvery dew, offered a clear sightline to the drawbridge towers. Cars were starting to spill down into the traffic circle, emptying into the arteries east toward Mays Landing and Philadelphia, west toward Longport and Atlantic City.

Somers Mansion was closed for the night. Certain there must be a cash box for donations somewhere inside, I peeked through the windows, following a bluish stripe of moonbeam illuminating the stone mantelpiece and the scorched chimney flue. The windows wouldn't budge, their sashes molded shut with cracked layers of bubbling house paint. I considered breaking a pane, but saw nothing on display worth the risk of waking a sleeping hound attuned to suspicious night movements, or a senior citizen volunteering watch. The storm cellar doors near the front door were padlocked. I finally gave up, turning to face the circle and await my ride.

I crept several paces to my left and then to my right, peeking through the hollowed spaces between the shrubs for the best vantage point of the cars as they descended the bridge. I crept low to the ground so I could spot Sue's convertible as it entered the circle, and so the other motorists would not see me. Stooped behind a glossy cluster of magnolia leaves, I watched one, two, three cars pass over the bridge. The fourth was Sue's Impala.

The girls' manes flew aloft above the windshield glass, lifting high off their necks in the tousling bridge winds. I hurriedly burst through the shrubbery, leaping down the cracked cement rampart separating the property from the Jolly Roger cocktail lounge parking lot. I mistimed their arrival. They sped past me, the rear lights swishing around the circle, leaving peyote-like trails before my tired eyes. Much to my relief, instead of taking the MacCarthur Boulevard artery leading out toward the Garden State Parkway, Sue continued three-quarters of the way around the circle, pulling into the diner. I watched to make certain she and Ibby went inside before I returned to my spot, waiting.

Thirty minutes later they emerged from the diner's shiny chrome doors. But they weren't by themselves this time. Although I was too far away to see their faces, I didn't need binoculars to identify Ronnie, with Ethan walking behind him in close order. Jealousy clouded my judgment. I fought to compose myself. I desperately needed a ride out of here, but out of nowhere had come the chance to get my money back. Had they left the bar together? Where had they all slept? I grabbed a broken branch off the ground and stood under a street lamp, determined to be seen. Sue sped around the turn, flashing tunnels of light the intensity of weakened flashlight beams through the slowly purpling sky. I leaned on the branch as though it was a walking stick, favoring my ankle. Catching sight of me, Sue pulled over alongside a telephone pole and backed up. Wincing, I hopped over to the passenger side, pretending I couldn't place any weight on my foot. The four of them gazed at me with apprehensive expressions, as though they had expected to see me, but weren't overjoyed.

"What happened to your leg?" Sue asked tentatively. She and Ibby looked refreshed and had changed outfits. The driver of a GTO filled with homebound revelers impatiently blared his horn at Sue, shouting obscenities as his tires screeched around her.

Ibby's arm was resting on the car door. She tapped her nails along the door, then reached to the car floor and handed me my backpack. My injury didn't rouse her sympathies. "Where's Larry?" she asked dubiously. She awaited my reply with a glare. Her look seemed to say that if it were up to her, I'd still be thumbing it on the side of the road.

"Larry was in a bad car accident last night on his way here," I said, somberly staring at her. She quickly turned to Sue, who appeared skeptical.

"What happened?" Sue asked.

"I'm still trying to find out," I said. "He's in intensive care at a hospital in Cape May, is the last I heard. When I got back to the hotel last night there was a message waiting for me at the front desk. It was from my boss, saying Larry was in critical condition. Apparently he's stabilized, and they're transferring him to Jefferson Hospital in Philadelphia for spleen surgery. I tripped running to get here. I couldn't find a cab to take me all the way to Philadelphia and the first bus doesn't leave the

Ninth Street station until nine this morning. I hate to ask, Sue, but I really need a lift to Center City."

Ronnie lethargically moved aside to make room for me, hoisting his legs onto the drive-train hump. His eyes were at half-mast, his pupils dilated. Grinning idiotically, he appeared in the midst of a psychedelic trip, on what hallucinogen I couldn't say. He bumped shoulders with Ethan, whose head bobbed to the sway of the car's momentum as Sue set off down MacArthur Boulevard.

A cryptic silence lingered in the car. I intuitively sensed they had been talking about me in my absence, and that I had done something to earn their silence. Slow to understand, Ronnie and Ethan gazed at me with stupid uncomprehending grins, as though in the quagmire of their seesawing minds they didn't know how to appropriately articulate condolences or adequately express their bereavement. Liquor and fried bacon soured Ronnie's breath.

"You get in your car and turn over the engine," he said so that everyone heard him, "and you wind up flat on your back in a hospital bed, your guts opened up, with the grim reaper vying for your soul."

His remarks set Ethan off in a cackling laughter. "You can say that again, man."

Ibby shot them both a look. "You think that's funny, Ethan?"

"What? I didn't say it, Ronnie did," Ethan said flippantly, crossing his arms. His inflection had acquired a snappy abrasiveness since I'd last spoken to him.

"Actually, Jim Morrison wrote it in a poem," Ronnie interrupted.

I'd forgotten about his peculiar obsession. I had to keep reminding myself that all of this was a continuation of their sleepless night. As we drove out into the leafier suburbs, I allowed the serious mood to insulate me from further inquiry. Ronnie, however, used the grim news of Larry's dire condition as an excuse to reveal more into Morrison's macabre visions. "He also said, 'It's wasteful to worry about pain. In the end it's nothing more than a pawn in the game of death. Sometimes it's best to embrace dying.'"

"That's sick, Ronnie," Sue said from under the dank yellow tollbooth corridor light at the parkway entrance. I couldn't grasp why Ronnie would say something so inappropriate and was making a spectacle of himself. Even if he was tripping, he should've known expulsion was imminent, that we were at the mercy of the girls' benevolence. I had no choice but to keep my mouth shut about the money I suspected Ronnie had stolen, for making a scene might get us kicked out onto the side of the road. We followed the turn of the service road as it merged into the northbound traffic lanes. The moon sparkled through the pines and the river lights shimmered through the reeds and cattails bordering the desolate hinterlands. For a while it seemed ours was the only vehicle on the road. The glare of safety reflectors and yellow road signs warning of terrapins and deer crossings punctuated the silent rural darkness. The temperature dropped abruptly the farther we drove out into the bayous and estuaries of the Great Egg Harbor Bay, as if I had swum into a cold spring shooting up from the bottom of a lake. Seeking shelter from the blustery winds, I slumped farther down into my seat. I found a towel on the car floor. It smelled of coconut oil and was still damp from the ocean, but had been warmed by the heat of the car floor. I scrunched it into a ball and placed it behind my neck. The cushioning warmth soothed my tired neck muscles. I grew sleepy, waiting to slip into the sanctuary of a lucid dream more secure in its uncertainty than a new day I could not bear to face, and a night I desperately needed to escape from.

"It's spooky out here," Ibby said to Sue

Lost in a drugged fog, Ronnie gazed at Venus aglow in the stratosphere, as if contemplating its significance in relation to a certain planetary alignment. He sat up a bit and leaned between the front seats, expertly imitating Morrison again. "The worst kind of fear is the fear not realized."

"That's enough, Ronnie," Sue sternly ordered, sounding like a mother issuing an edict of silence to a station wagon full of feuding siblings.

"Just because we let you buy us breakfast doesn't give you permission to creep us out, Ronnie," Ibby said. "You're starting to scare us."

"Yeah, Ronnie, you're starting to scare us," Ethan parroted, laughing himself out of breath.

I took perverse joy in hearing Ibby protest and was secretly pleased by how skillfully Ronnie baited her. I intuited some sort of strange transcendent symbiosis between us, as though he sensed Jim Morrison's beguiling poetry altering my psyche and working me over with its black magic. His tone grew darker, more somber. "Jim also said, 'Fear inevitably leads to a most vile, gruesome death.'"

The yellow light of the instrument panel glowed dimly against Sue's silhouette. She reached over Ibby's lap and into the glovebox for a Zippo and a pack of cigarettes. Keeping her eyes on the road, she leaned forward to light one but the spark wouldn't catch. Ibby reached and took the cigarette from her, bending near the steering column to light it, sucking until the coals burned evenly. She drew a puff and returned it to Sue, who revealed the details of their itinerary.

"First we'll have lunch with my parents, then we'll sit out by our pool and get some sun," she said to Ibby, admiring Sue with the fawn-like glance of a little girl just invited to a sleepover. Sue went right on talking, smugly indifferent of our presence. "My brother has all sorts of parties lined up for us to go to. I can't wait."

"I can't wait either," Ibby said excitedly. Her pewter bracelets jingled on her wrists as she fussed with the tuner. She tucked a loose wisp of hair behind her ear, stealing a glance toward me. She quickly looked away when she caught me, enjoying, it seemed, the barrier separating my world from theirs. The disc jockey, speaking through an echo chamber, was allowing a caller to dedicate a song to a serviceman in Vietnam.

"Looking forward to meeting you in Hawaii," the girlfriend answered tearfully when asked what she'd like to say to her fiancé, whom she would soon visit during his forthcoming leave.

"Let's go back two years for this one," the disc jockey hurriedly improvised, as if trying to de-ice the melancholic tone left dangling in the on-air silence. The rhythmic notes of a cowbell were followed by the throaty, hypnotic voices of the Chambers Brothers singing "Time Has Come Today." Sue and Ibby immediately looked toward one another, smiling in recognition. Ibby turned up the volume. She pointed her finger at Susan, who thumped her hands on the steering wheel. They shouted the chorus in unison, alternating verses. Ibby's voice screeched, cracking as she tried reaching an unattainable octave.

I closed my eyes. Plagued with nervous exhaustion, I succumbed to Lester Chambers' soothing pipes, allowing them to pull me under into the dark caverns of my netherworld. As though disembodied, I morosely recalled the gruesome movies I'd seen on Forty-second Street, sitting in the theatre seats, my feet sticking to the floor, the faint lurid whispers and dark shapes of hunched men scurrying down the aisles, coming and going. I remembered the blood and sex, nudity. Hacked limbs. Seeing Caroline naked on the screen, facing the camera, mouth open, Kevin on her, behind her. Oscillating between lucid dreams and the singer's voice, my head floated, adrift in a morphine-like delirium. I saw the eyeless sea captain laughing at me again as I went under the ocean's surface one last time.

"Hey Sue, it's dangerous to pick up hitchhikers!" Ronnie suddenly hollered, jolting me awake.

Sue briefly lost control of the wheel, swerving across the broken white line to avoid running over a snake crossing the parkway. For a second I was uncertain into what dimension I had arrived, dream or reality. Sue decelerated, pushing on the hazard signals. Stones pinged off the quarter panel as she slowed onto the sandy gravel of the shoulder. Her headlights, illuminating swirls of hazy tidal mist, shone at a reflective green mile marker, 31.9. Below it, a grass ditch lay between the road and the edge of the woods. *It's yesterday already*, I thought, seeing the first strands of purple light bleeding through the oaks as the car rolled to a stop. She threw the gear into park, leaving the engine running, then stepped out of the car and turned to face us, leaving the door open.

"Get out!" she fumed, pointing outside the car, her eyes bulging brightly. Ethan pushed up the driver seat and climbed out. He slammed his fist on the hood, where he waited for his friend.

"Fuck you, cunt," he said icily to Sue, towering over her. "And quit talking to my friend like he's a three-year-old. Let's go, Ronnie. They're not gonna fuck us. I'll take my chances hitching a lift rather than ride with these spoiled cunts any more."

"All of you!" Sue screamed at Ronnie and me.

Ronnie slowly bent forward and folded the seat over, unraveling out the driver's side door. He had something concealed in his right hand, behind his hip, but I couldn't see what it was. Flipping his middle finger at Sue, he joined Ethan, and together they crossed over the median.. I lost sight of them over a rise in the road on the other side of the parkway. Suddenly I was faced with a final decision: Either pursue my money, or beg not to be tossed out their car.

"You too, Ted," Sue ordered.

As I had done nothing to instigate Sue's eruption, I sat rooted, refusing to be let loose on the side of the road without explanation. "What did I do?" I asked. "You're going to turn me out in the night like this? How am I supposed to get to the hospital?"

"Oh, that's right, the mysterious Larry," Ibby said. "Did you really think any of us ever believed you worked for *National Geographic*, Ted? Before you answer, let me ask you this: How did you get home last night?"

I could recall as far as the nitrous oxide hits. "After you two left, I got a ride home from a couple of surfers in a Volkswagen bus. Why?"

"*We* drove you home, Ted," Sue said. "After we left Tony Mart's, we went with Ronnie and Ethan to a bar called The Dunes. Ronnie conned us into going, saying his brother was bartending there, and that he was their only ride home." She rolled her eyes at Ibby. "On our way back from The Dunes we found you passed out on the grass in the middle of the traffic circle. People were walking over you, pouring beer on you and laughing at you. Ronnie wanted to leave you there, but we made him and Ethan lift you into the car. Ibby remembered you saying you were staying at the Lincoln. We drove you there. The lobby clerk said nobody named Bundy had checked in all weekend. So we tried the Coral Sands, another place you had mentioned. We woke the manager. He said he hadn't heard of you either and asked us to describe you. He said you fit the description of a young man who had stolen a credit card from one of his customers at another motel he owned, earlier in the night. He was calling the police as we left. When we went back out to the car, you were gone. Ethan said you'd climbed out of the backseat, went up the boardwalk ramps, and that was the last they saw of you. He and Ronnie waited for us out on the front steps of our place while we showered and changed, and then we went to breakfast."

"Which brings us to now," Ibby said.

"I just don't feel comfortable with you in the car, Ted," Sue said. "Nothing personal, I'm sure you're a great guy and all, but all this involvement with the police is something we'd rather not expose ourselves to. I think it's best if we just say our goodbyes here. And good luck, really, with everything."

"It's almost daylight," Ibby chirped. "I'm sure someone else will come along soon and pick you up."

I felt a tranquilizing release, like a pressure valve had been opened and all the anger, frustration, and anxiety that had been building in me hissed out its opening, leaving me painlessly deflated. I reached into my bag and took hold of my Boy Scout penknife, which I hadn't opened in years. Holding it, feeling its cold rusty metal, precipitated a prepubescent excitation I remembered feeling as a boy, once while balancing myself atop a floating beach ball at Lake Sammamish.

Ibby stepped out of the car and flipped the seat up for me. I slowly slipped on both backpack straps. Crouched in position, I sprung out of the back seat and lunged for her throat. I clamped a hand over her windpipe and dug, relishing the stricken look of terror in her wide-open eyes. Holding her in position, I flicked open the knife and pointed it toward Sue.

"Oh please, oh please Ted, let her go!" Sue cried, holding one hand over her mouth, waving the other at me, trying vainly to rescue her friend.

Ignoring Sue's pleas, I pulled Ibby roughly down the grass slope toward the woods. Her larynx spasmed as she fought for air. Tripping over herself, she clawed at my wrists to balance herself, but her feet went out from under her. As I lifted her, she gouged a sharp nail into my wrist and my watch flew off. I let go of her hand and she tried to run away, but I easily caught up to her. Overtaking her again, I dragged her farther into the woods, out of the first light of day. I gripped her hair and threw her forward, where she struck against a tree. Reeling, she fell backward onto her tailbone. She began a spastic retreating crabwalk, backing into a briar patch. Sue leaped on my back. I threw her over my shoulder with ease, then stabbed her belly. She fell to the ground quietly and clutched her wound. As Ibby tried to stand, I pushed her down again.

"Please God, no, no…." Ibby begged, holding her palms up over her face to ward off the knife arched over my head. I snatched her wrist with one hand, but the blood from her wounds made my grip slippery and she pulled away. I hit her head against the ground to stun her. Squeezing the knife with all my strength, I sunk the blade deeply into her neck, then into her solar plexus, spraying blood in every direction. She grimaced with each blow, holding her flapping skin in place. I pulled her close to my face once again, forcing her to look in my eyes so she could see what pleasure this brought me, when I felt a swift, painful blow to my head, and went out.

NINETEEN

During the first moments of consciousness, before understanding where I was, or that I had crossed over into a new day, I stayed flat on my back, staring up into the half-light of the wooded early morning darkness.

I was uncertain whether I had fallen asleep, passed out, or merely dozed off. I kept perfectly still, unaware of how I'd come to be lost within this unrecognizable forest. Drunken and suffering from bed spins, I allowed myself several seconds to adjust to my surroundings before moving the slightest bit. I gazed up through an opening in the trees, where shimmering halos of fading constellations flickered against the purplish sky, extinguishing one by one, like evaporating wicks of unattended lanterns left behind in a suddenly deserted encampment. Am I in Washington State, on the Hall of Mosses Trail? My hand went reflexively to my side in a phantom motion as I attempted to unzip the flannel cover of the dew-soaked sleeping bag I presumed covered me. I felt my chest and anxiously groped my jeans when I realized my bedding was not there, as though I had lost something vital, like my wallet, a set of keys, or an important phone number.

I sat upright, unpinning my shoulder blades from the ground, brushing a shivering trickle of sandy grit down my neck. A humid, brackish-smelling mist lingered in the trees. Above the din of night insects chirruping in the underbrush, a pond toad groaned in throaty, mating gasps, like a blast of wintry air singing under the rattling aluminum strip of a storm door. Its cadence soon faded, overtaken by a chorus of tapping woodpeckers drilling at some termite-rotted hollow in a distant marsh. I was in the vicinity of an ocean, I concluded, one far from home.

My forehead thumped with painful beats as I slowly rose to survey the frontier. Groggy, I braced one hand firmly against a tree to gather my balance, twisting my midsection, adjusting my contorted spine, popping my neck bones. My stiff limbs felt sore and my lower back burned as I repositioned myself, as though I was a convalescent allowed his first steps after weeks spent locked in a body cast. I peered through frosted columns of moonlight funneling through the tree shadows. A narrow winding footpath marked with fresh deer tracks lay several feet ahead of a scattering of crashed beer bottles. I followed the trail to the edge of the forest, which ended at a grassy embankment. I figured the clearing to be a shoulder on the outer loops of a national forest highway. Because of its steep ascent, I was unable to see beyond this landing. Plus it was early yet, too dark to see very far into the surrounding wilds.

As the seconds passed, gray traces of daylight began to creep into the perimeters of my sightline, enlargening the tree branches into sternly hewn fists, greening the delicate leaves outstretched among their limbs. Despite the encouragement of a new day beginning, the night's proximity lurked timelessly in the morning darkness, as though unwilling to relinquish its perspective on the events it had recently witnessed. My uncertainty intensified as my sights grew clearer. In the distance I heard the gravelly rumble of an approaching truck. A speeding pair of headlights flared into the clearing the path led to, lighting up the tapering darkness like a photographic negative. A faint breeze whipped by the truck's propulsion scattered a tornado of pebbles flung from its tire grooves down onto the shoulder, whisking the dead leaves encrusting the forest bottom. The truck must have been hauling the morning catch, for the tailing fumes smelled vaguely of fish crated in ice, freshening my recollections of the day before.

As the noise faded I went over in my mind what I knew for certain, what memories I could recall from the last twenty-four hours. I had arrived in Ocean City yesterday afternoon. While on the beach, posing as a journalist on assignment for *National Geographic* magazine, I met Sue Grenier and Elizabeth Haysbert, college roommates who early the same evening escorted me across the bridge to the nightspots in Somers Point, where we cavorted until the early morning hours. The circumstances of my journey's finish remained vague and suspect, however, and my recollection of what transpired between then and now lacked specificity. Where were the girls now, and could they somehow be connected to my waking under these trees?

I yearned for a swallow of cool water; my throat was parched and I trembled with dehydration. I couldn't have been more than a few hours removed from the episodes of my night, I thought, checking the time. A bloody scratch marked where my watch should have been. The wound's jagged surface tweaked my suspicions. It looked as though it might have been torn by the edges of a broken fingernail, but I couldn't recall getting into any fistfights that might have knocked it loose. Had I simply walked up the embankment then and hitched a ride home, I could have written off this episode as mere foolery, a drunken odyssey needing no explanation or cause for long bouts of introspection. Instead, I went down on my knees and searched around me, unearthing the dead leaves, feeling down into the cold wet layers of compost. I resumed sweeping the ground with my hands until I finally came upon the timepiece, embedded in a grove of moonlit ferns near the grass, an area the darkness must have hidden when I'd first seen the trail moments earlier. The glow-in-the-dark-numerals showed five-forty-five. I stood, strapping the band to my wrist, when a burst of air shot from my lungs, causing me to topple backwards, as if knocked senseless from a blow. To my left, no more than ten feet beyond the grove, tented under the flimsy shoot of a pine sapling, I saw the bodies of Sue and Elizabeth.

For a moment, as I stood disorientedly trying to piece this scene together, I thought I'd risen from a car crash or some other disabling malady. This would explain my infirmity, the symptoms of amnesia. But there were no signs of wreckage, no flames or burning smell of oily smoke to justify my denial. And the truck that had passed by seconds earlier-wouldn't its driver, upon seeing an automobile accident, have stopped to offer assistance? Although I sensed they were dead, I refused to believe what I was seeing, and because I also refused to consider that I could be mixed up in something so terrible, for a moment I was able to study the women with an attitude of childlike fascination, like a boy on a walk through the woods stumbling upon an animal giving birth.

Sprinkled with decomposed leaves, the friends were separated a few feet from one another, their faces turned from me. Sue, closest to me, was nude and sprawled facedown. I recognized her long blond hair spread out on the ground. A blue summer dress was piled neatly beside her, under a straw purse. Hunched fetally beside her was Elizabeth, her knees drawn to her chest. A dirtied green minidress lay sagged about her crumpled limbs. The shoulder straps had collapsed off her tanned shoulders and a leather sandal dangled off one toe. The other sandal was missing.

I tiptoed closer, spreading open the branches and looking down. I tried my best to remain calm, clinging desperately to the hope they'd had too much to drink and in passing out had instinctively snuggled next to one another to keep warm. The understanding that my actions were futile didn't discourage me from trying to wake them. Holding the branches away from my face, I tickled Sue's toes, but my touch didn't rouse the faintest stir or drowsy mumble. A shore wind roared slowly through the treetops, raining acorn nuts onto the ground by her feet, blowing a leaf off her shoulder. A twig pelted Elizabeth's thigh, drawing no reaction either. I reached under the leaves covering Sue and nudged her pelvic bone. Her skin was warm with a sticky liquid, a residue thicker than the melting dew that had clung to the leaves I'd dug. As I drew them back, my fingers were warm with fresh blood.

A part of the night returned to me, bringing me to my knees, catapulting me backwards into distant tunnels of repressed memory. Without warning, a vivid emergence of coherent images evolved instantaneously beneath my eyelids, transporting me to places deep and remote. I recalled hitchhiking for a ride at the Somers Point traffic circle, being picked up by the girls and loading myself into the back seat of Sue's convertible, then heading north with them on the parkway toward Philadelphia. I remembered Sue pulling over to the side of the road, the mirror brightness of a knife being held to her throat. I couldn't recall if I was holding the weapon, or if somebody else had accompanied Elizabeth down the embankment. I was able to sequence the flashbacks, but they were incomplete. There was the traffic circle, pulling over to the shoulder, blankness in between and after. Nor could I explain the painful bump I felt for the first time now, rising from the base of my skull. Before I knew for certain who or what had caused my injury, the misshapen visions faded from sight, like a projector incinerating a brightly widening hole into a strip of film just before the reel starts flapping.

I looked off in the direction of the road as the traffic began to pick up. I thought of Sue's car. It would still be parked on the shoulder, plainly visible to nosy parkers, but more importantly, state troopers I feared would be patrolling the roadways on the start of a holiday weekend. If a cop noticed the car and decided to circle back for a second look, he might also walk down the embankment and find me. I stepped in closer to examine the severity of their injuries, dragging them out from under the pines. Sue's ankles were cool but not cold, warm but not feverish. I turned her on her back. Her throat had been opened with puncture wounds saturating the earth under her neck in a sandy muckhole of congealed blood, as if she had fallen asleep in a puddle of dark fruit juice. Her eyes were rheumy and void of any recognition. She gazed dreamily at me. I didn't believe what I was seeing, attributing it to a trick of the mind caused by my drunken sleeplessness. I fought the temptation to stare, fearful that she'd cast an interminable spell over me if she knew I was the last person to see her alive. Heavy, rattling aspirations wheezed from the wounds on her chest. She seemed to want to say something, but the words got caught in the throbs of her emptying arteries. I adjusted her windpipe to assist in her struggle to communicate. Turning my ear to listen closer, I couldn't make out her whispers, and she stopped breathing.

Strands from Elizabeth's long brown hair cultivated marks in the soil where I'd pulled her out, patterning it like a groomed ski run. Her jackknifed knee about touched her chin. My hands trembled as I turned her from her side onto her back, as though my fingers were a conduit for a silently escaping prayer. I scraped the leaves off her legs. She was bruised and gashed on her thighs, and like Sue, most of the blood had poured from her neck area. The fabric of her dress stuck to the holes of her drying wounds, making a gluey sound like wet smacking lips as I peeled up the hem. As she was most likely dead when I found her, I didn't waste any time resuscitating her and left her eyelids closed.

I stowed them under a blanket of twigs and leaves. Although my intention was to camouflage them, a part of me desired to protect their privacy as well, for I figured they deserved to go to heaven decontaminated from the distasteful circumstances of their deaths. I rummaged through their purses for money. All they had were a few crumpled singles that I shoved in my pocket before making my way out of the woods, pinpointing the scent of the salty river.

I made it no farther then a few steps when I heard a decelerating vehicle I sensed in my gut was an approaching police cruiser. My lungs froze as the car slowed, crunching to a stop. The door slammed shut. I saw the yellow stripes of the officer's trousers and his shiny polished jackboots through the leaves as he sauntered past the New Jersey State Police seal painted on the passenger-side door. I hid behind a nearby cedar and squeezed against its bark, wildly afraid I might throw shadows if I twitched. The whistle of the songbirds grew quiet and the locusts' hum fell silent alongside them, as though riveted by the ticking hiss of idling engine pistons. The steady patter of gypsy moth droppings was the only other sound in the forest.

I pulled back my head and pressed tightly against the tree. I didn't have a direct line of sight to the squad car now, watching its red lights oscillate through the foliage. My thighs shook violently as I tried to remain still.

"Have an abandoned vehicle at milepost 31.9 of the northbound lane of the parkway," the patrolman called in, repeating into the mike a series of license plate numbers: "Pennsylvania tag number 847186. Over."

A volley of codes was exchanged, followed by the high, tightly pinched response of a station dispatcher. "Didn't … spot same vehicle earlier…" she sputtered. "Over."

"That's affirmative."

I went over the excuses I would say if I was caught. *Just out on a sunrise walk and thought I'd get in some morning calisthenics, officer. Out checking my muskrat traps, sir.* I knew they would never work, but I was desperate and thought illogically.

"Tow it to Blazer's Garage in Northfield," the dispatcher said.

I breathed a cautious sigh at her orders, conscious of the noises I'd make if I exhaled too abruptly. I remained fearful that the cop's curiosity might tempt him, that he'd scent a mischievousness lurker prowling behind the trees. The door clapped shut again. Stunned to near breathlessness, I heard his handcuffs jingle as he came off the road and onto the grass, drawing closer to me. Tree branches cracked loudly underfoot as he reached the woods. I regulated my breathing to control my pulse, certain the trooper could hear the seismic booms exploding from my chest. I didn't risk glancing in his direction. I was afraid that his eyes would be keen as a deer hunter's for glowing eye movements illuminated by the glare of the pulsating lights. Never in my severest nightmares could I have foreseen being mixed up in something so dreadful, yet here I was, praying that I'd hidden the girls well enough.

He clicked on his flashlight and swept the trees. I followed the beam as it landed on an abandoned chicken coop, then quivered upon a cone-shaped pile of oyster shells on the opposite embankment, exuding a spectral glow like animal bones seen under a desert moon. Maybe the officer was befuddled by the dusky path and feared where it might lead. Perhaps he sensed the presence of ghosts and decided to radio for backup before treading any farther down the trail's entrance. In any event, just at the moment I expected he would turn the flashlight on me, he clicked it off and began walking back to the cruiser. The sounds of retreating footfalls emptied out of the woods. The door closed and the tires spun out, accelerating into the swallow of parkway traffic.

I stood still in the quietness for several minutes after he drove off, tottering with disbelief, thinking if I moved I'd hex myself and draw him back for another look. My prayers had been answered, prayers with such a remote chance of being granted I had to stifle a giggle at the preposterousness of my sudden luck. I didn't wallow in my good fortune, however, for I sensed that my luck would turn bad again if I waited around any longer. Like a platoon leader who finally comes to understand the coordinates of his terrain after studying it only by map and compass, I thought it wise to moderate my enthusiasm and remain focused on getting out of here.

I resumed my southward course at a quicker pace. I figured if I remained inconspicuous and followed the backwoods south while staying near the parkway, eventually I'd reach the Somers Point suburbs, then double back over the bridges into Ocean City, where I'd hop a ride back to Philadelphia, or scrounge up enough money for bus fare and get back that way. From there I would hitchhike to Seattle, reenroll at the University of Washington, and start my life over.

The woods grew denser the farther I went into them, deepening into an untameable underbrush. Snapping off a branch, I hacked my way through the narrowing tangle as if wielding a machete. Thorns nicked my hands, and I fought through a swarm of horseflies. Despite the bugs and the rising temperature, it felt good to work up a sweat, to boil out the poisons burbling under my skin. The notion of a hot shower in a boardwalk bathhouse, of swabbing my abrasions and insect bites with a bottle of disinfectant, grew more enticing with each step.

I came to a marsh inlet at the edge of the woods and took a knee by its edges, allowing a moment's rest from my labors. The crackling mud flats, aerated with fiddler crab tunnels, led out to a number of slender channels flowing beneath a narrow bridge over which the parkway crossed. A hazy river wind glided over the reeds, making a sound like fires smothered with sand. I glanced out across the peaceful downriver current, half-expecting to see an elk quietly slurping a drink, or a convoy of squawking geese fluttering through the tall shafts of emerging sunlight twinkling dimly alongtop the tide's seaward ripple. Overwhelmed by a refreshed purposefulness of direction and a revitalized stamina, I paused to review the fortunate turn of events: The police hadn't found me or the girls yet. All my body parts were intact, and I was blessed with a clear sky to guide me back to Philadelphia. I pulled free a stringy chord of thin blonde hair that caught my eyelash, prickling my neck and forearms with a shuddering, ticklish wave, like bumbling into a sticky web in the black of night. A chill dampness settled into my bones as I turned and looked back toward where I had been. Preparing to leave the surrounding landscape once and for all, I suddenly recalled the clumps of hair and splattered blood laid bare among the saplings and pine needles. In shrouding Susan and Elizabeth, I hadn't paused to consider what evidence I might leave behind. It was a matter of time before a flurry of detectives, upon seeing the car and being notified of the missing girls, arrived at the scene and began microscopically combing the area. In my mind's eye I saw them on their hands and knees, pricking pieces of blood-stained bark with their metal tools, dropping them like lake specimens into their tiny screw-top vials and sealed plastic bags.

I stood, turning once again to look out across the river. Above a stand of cedars on the near bank a circle of turkey vultures plunged one at a time, taking turns jabbing their beaks into the remains of a smashed terrapin. How long, I feared, would it be until the birds scented the remains of human flesh? I searched up and down the channel for thinner cuts of stream to cross, alternate routes of travel that would not require me to slog through these waters. Though not a stranger to these regions, I kept reminding myself I was in New Jersey, not the Florida Everglades or the Amazon jungle, and that I was silly to concern myself with alligators, water moccasins, and other marauding reptiles inhabiting warmer climates. But still, I thought, something treacherous must lurk under these swamp cattails. Uncertain whether this sudden phobia foretold a disastrous future, or arose from a place buried in my adolescence, I tread stealthily across the mud flats to begin my journey home.

EPILOGUE

I stared off into the thickening Florida dusk. The diesel generators, powering both the satellite feed and the shining klieg lights stacked atop the news vans, rumbled in currents beneath my feet. Amid the circus, Dick stood patiently listening.

"And Sue?" he asked.

"Never saw her again. As I said, somebody hit me in the head and I went out."

"What happened after you gained consciousness and discovered the girls beside you, you know, after you made it to the edge of the woods? Where'd you go from there?"

"I swam across the Patcong Creek and stole some clean clothes from a backyard laundry line, then started walking toward Ocean City, following the parkway shoulder. The thatch of reeds growing off the side of the road screened me from the traffic for a while. But then I thought better of it, for by now it was daylight. I knew the cops would be swarming when they saw Sue's car, and I'd be walking right back toward them, handing them my noose, pardon the pun. So I decided to switch directions. I thumbed it, because really I had no other choice. I got a ride from a trucker, a black guy on his way back home to Pittsburgh hauling a load of fresh lobsters. He dropped me off at the 30th Street train station in Philadelphia. When I got there I made a collect call to my mother and told her that somebody mugged me and had stolen my clothes. I begged her to wire me the train fare, and rode the train all the way back to Seattle."

The noise from outside the prison gates grew louder. Flashbulbs popped, cigarettes flickered in the nightfall, like August's fireflies. I knew I'd be ordered back to my cell soon to wait out the long night ahead. As this was the last time I would ever be outside, I milked my waning freedom. Stalling for time, I continued. "At the University of Washington, where I re-enrolled the following autumn, they used to get papers from cities all over the country sent to the library. Every day I'd go there and read the *Philadelphia Inquirer* and the *Philadelphia Bulletin*. I was worried the authorities in New Jersey would track me down, that somebody had seen me. "A week or so after the murders," I said, "I read that Ronnie was arrested for auto theft in Colorado, where they learned he was wanted for questioning by the New Jersey State Police. He went by the alias Chad Shelton, and had done a stint in the Georgia State Mental Hospital. Schizophrenia. Here's where it starts to get weird. Know where in Colorado they held him for questioning?"

"I'd have to think about it," Dick said, "but we really don't have time for guessing games, Ted."

He was right. I looked over at Leverette, who flashed me a hand signal showing I had five minutes left. "Let me save you the suspense," I said. "The Garfield County Jail, in Glenwood Springs."

"Where you escaped from in 1977."

"That's correct, in December 1977-just nine months after Ronnie escaped from the Federal Prison in Littleton, Colorado."

"Small world."

"Just wait. It gets smaller," I said. "In September of '82, authorities from New Jersey and Pennsylvania came down here to interview another suspect in the killings, but for some reason they never talked to me."

"I'm not following," Dick said. "Why were they here on Death Row in 1982 if they weren't here to question you?"

"Someone else had signed a confession," I said.

"Here? Somebody that's here on Death Row, right now, signed a confession to killing Grenier and Haysbert?" Dick asked.

"That's right."

"Who was it?" he asked. His nose quivered like a rodent exploring along a garage wall, deciding whether to lean over and taste the dab of peanut butter spread enticingly on the spring-loaded trap.

"You know him, but I'll give you a hint anyway. He's a serial killer who despises girls who wear the color blue. He piles sticks on the backs of his victims and dumps them in the woods on the side of the road. We'll get back to him in a second. It gets better, I promise."

"Who was it?" he interrupted.

"Who was who?" I asked, playing with him.

"Who here signed the confession?"

"Why are you so curious to know, Dick? I thought the book was about me," I teased, humored by his fervent enthusiasm.

"What did he say, this inmate?"

"He signed and dated it before giving it to the FBI office in Jacksonville. It was dated September 22, 1982. It read something like, 'Going through New Jersey. It was 1972-3. A.C. Expressway. Small sports car, convertible-top Chevrolet. College girls. Custom-gray vinyl top. Signed, Gerald Eugene Stano.'"

Dick chuckled. "You've got be kidding me."

"The one and only," I said. "I know what you're thinking, because I thought the same thing also-the killings took place in 1969, on the Garden State Parkway, not the Atlantic City Expressway, right? Even though Stano was on with the time frame, I could see how he'd be a prime suspect. He killed in pairs, and Elizabeth was wearing a blue dress. Ninety percent of his victims had stab wounds on the chest and neck. He lived on Arch Road in Whitpain Township, which is part of Norristown, while I was staying with my grandparents."

"So let me understand this," he said, befuddled, trying to keep straight all that I was telling him. "You and Stano lived, what, within a few miles of one another that spring, in 1969, when you were staying in Lafayette Hill and going to Temple?"

"And we've lived next to one another on Death Row for the past four years."

"And the FBI, they never bought Stano's confession?"

"Nope. Neither did the police in New Jersey. If they did believe it, they downplayed its importance. Why would they let it get out that they failed to nab one of Florida's most notorious serial killers when he was in their own backyard?"

"What ever became of Ethan?"

"I never did learn his last name. For some strange reason I never understood, the newspapers named practically every suspect except for him. They repeatedly described him as an eighteen-year-old hippy from Norristown who stood six feet-five inches tall. The funny thing is, Ethan could've walked away from everything scot-free if he had just kept his big mouth shut. A few days after the murders he was at a newsstand in Philadelphia and started shooting off about how he knew about the killings because he'd been in Ocean City that weekend. The storeowner overheard him and called the Philadelphia Police Department, who brought him in for questioning. They couldn't pin it on him, and turned him over to the authorities in New Jersey, who grilled him for twenty hours at the Absecon barracks. He apparently flunked a lie detector test. Badly. Again, though, they just couldn't place him at the scene. To this day he's always been their primary suspect.

"Get this," I said. "I read where in 1983, a trucker-to this day I don't know if it was the same one that gave me a ride that morning-surfaced out of nowhere, telling the police he was driving along Zion Road, near the crime scene, at around six on the morning of the killings, when he saw a man duck into the woods as he drove by. They showed him mug shots. He picked Ethan without having ever seen a picture of him before then. He said he felt the need to come forward after he read in the paper that Stano had admitted to the killings. But the detectives still couldn't place Ethan at the murder scene, and he left no trail back to it. He joined the Army in September of '69, went off to Fort Bragg, then went AWOL to Canada in 1970. He didn't do it, Dick, and if after I die they ever decide to try him, you can quote me."

"How did your name finally surface?"

"The New Jersey State Police set up a trailer at the Somers Point traffic circle and kept it there for a year or two after the murders. They had hoped someone not a kook would walk in off the street and say they saw something. One day in 1970, when I was back in classes at U of W, a detective called me out of the blue, said he was calling from this trailer. He wanted to know if I could meet him at the Northfield, New Jersey barracks to answer some questions. Mrs. Syben had given them my name some time earlier, an oversight on their part. I told him I was in Seattle and that it would be inconvenient and too expensive for me to fly out to New Jersey, and could they send somebody out to talk to me, or at least buy me a plane ticket? Calling their bluff worked. The detective, I wish I could remember his name, said not to worry, that he was just asking routine questions to all the young men that Ibby and Sue had had any contact with that weekend. I was one of many, and just got lost in the mix, I suppose. The guy never followed through.

"My theory is that the New Jersey authorities have some record of me on file," I continued. "They never brought me in for questioning, as I said. Evidence dried up, witnesses died, you know? The longer they wait, the more they can lay blame to the passage of time. Imagine the political ramifications, knowing your office had Ted Bundy in their sights and let him go?"

"Did you ever find out what became of Ronnie?"

"I sure did. I couldn't understand how or why he'd been forgotten about over the years, why the police never pursued him as vigorously at they did Ethan. Just out of curiosity, to see if Ronnie and I shared any more of these bizarre coincidences, I did some checking around and made requests through the Freedom of Information Act, and had several of his prison records sent to me here. Like me, he took all the wrong paths in life, and went on to lead a life of crime.

"Where is he now?"

"He's at the McCormick Correctional Institution in South Carolina. He doing a life sentence for the armed robbery and murder of a real estate agent in 1984. Look, Dick, I'm not looking for any reprieve here, I just think, however God judges me, perhaps it will be less harshly if I do one last good deed and clear Ethan's name. And Ronnie's. Jesus, Dick, with all I've told you, you could write another book."

He took a last puff off his fifth cigarette and flicked it onto the grass by his feet, where it smoldered for a second, then went out. "What would you call it?" he asked.

"You tell me. You're the writer."

"But it's your life, about how it started."

"My origins, you mean," I said.

"How about... *The Origins of Infamy?*"

I gazed into the dark woods, mulling over Dick's suggestion. The realization that I wouldn't be here tomorrow hit me for the first time. It was strangely peaceful, like the few seconds of awareness when you are standing outside and it suddenly stops raining. As they had on that morning thirty years ago, the nocturnal critters fell silent. For the first time since then-and over the years I had endlessly replayed in my head that fateful May dawn, trying my best to recreate what I perceived to be a faithful recollection of the events-I witnessed a peculiar phenomenon of the human memory, the truth from that morning long ago now tunneling its way through me, the blankness filling in with vivifying details. I didn't admit to Dick that I'd made up the part about jumping out of Sue's car, then killing her and Ibby. Truth is, I could never recall what exactly happened between the time we pulled over to the side of the road and when I woke up in the woods. Neither did I share with Dick what I was seeing right then, that it was Ronnie Walden, not me, who went berserk that steamy moonlit dawn, who took the knife he had been hiding in his hand and dragged Elizabeth Haysbert down into the woods, stabbing her to death as she screamed for her life. Nor could

I admit how I had stood by like a coward, watching mesmerized from behind a tree as Ronnie fanatically hammered the blade at Sue's throat when she thwarted him. Or how Ethan ran out of the woods, elbowing my head against a tree in his haste to flee.

I looked over at Dick. He stared at me, perplexedly considering my last words as Leverette and Wendell approached to lead us back inside. I smiled, basking in vain contentment, for I had kept the promise I made to myself, of keeping a secret I would take with me to the other side.

Printed in the United States
217704BV00001B/3/P

9 781440 138935